Trapped Between Heaven and Hell

Trapped Between Heaven and Hell

M. Skye

www.urbanbooks.net

Urban Books, LLC
300 Farmingdale Road, NY-Route 109
Farmingdale, NY 11735

ISBN 13: 978-1-945855-30-6
ISBN 10: 1-945855-30-4

First Mass Market Printing September 2018
First Trade Paperback Printing January 2018
Printed in the United States of America

10 9 8 7 6 5 4 3 2 1

This is a work of fiction. Any references or similarities to actual events, real people, living or dead, or to real locales are intended to give the novel a sense of reality. Any similarity in other names, characters, places, and incidents is entirely coincidental.

Distributed by Kensington Publishing Corp.
Submit orders to:
Customer Service
400 Hahn Road
Westminster, MD 21157-4627
Phone: 1-800-733-3000
Fax: 1-800-659-243

Trapped Between Heaven and Hell

by

M. Skye

Chapter One

Tyree sat on the balcony, contemplating the next chapter of his life as he tossed a handful of leaves pulled from a nearby tree. He had been standing there for twenty minutes, slipping off from yet another boring business event. The glamorous party scene was getting old to him, considering he had been doing it since he was seventeen.

Tyree Johnston was hand-picked, "the chosen one," to take over the family business, Johnston Incorporated. After years of grooming, he reluctantly agreed to run it just as his father wished. He had just celebrated his thirtieth birthday and was now about to embark upon his second marriage. The first marriage had taken its toll on him, and all he had to show for it was a beautiful seven-year-old son. After ten years, he only had him as a reminder of the incredible love they once shared.

He met his ex-wife, Mia, when they were children; and he was in love from the moment he heard her laugh and saw her smile. It took him years to gather his courage and finally admit the love he felt for her. They spent most of their childhood together—along with his brother, Miguel, his sister, Asha, her little sister, Janelle, her brother Rick, when he was home, and her cousin, Milan—but it wasn't until they were teenagers that he professed his love. Against the wishes of her father, Richmond, they were married the day after graduation, and they stayed married ten years before splitting. The split was Mia's idea, of course.

Now here he was, sitting on the balcony that held so many memories for him, all of which included Mia. The party he was attending was at the house he had spent so much time in over the years: her house. Well, her brother's house. Mia had relocated two years ago, and he hadn't seen her since the divorce was final. They had been sharing custody of their son, Kyan. Even though she refused to see Tyree, Mia made sure he had his time with Kyan, sending her brother, Rick, and his wife, Cassandra, to handle the pickups and drop-offs between them. The whole thing made him angry, feeling like they were adults and should be able to meet to hand over their son.

As he stood, still leaning over the edge, Tyree realized that as angry as he was with Mia for leaving him without an explanation, he couldn't blame her. The truth was, he was irresponsible, and it cost him his wife. The whole situation they were in now stemmed back to one thing: the kidnapping. His son had gotten taken on his watch, and Mia never got over it, not even after Tyree dropped everything to look for him.

Upon returning home, Tyree quickly found out that his wife and child had moved on without him. As hard as he tried to reaffirm their love and win her trust back, Mia just wasn't having it. She told him she had moved on and, after his repetitive pleas, she ultimately served him with divorce papers. After the divorce, she decided she needed a change of scenery and went off to head the branch of her family's company, Livingston Enterprises, in Paris. Tyree was devastated by her rejection and went back into seclusion, only coming out for work until he met Renee.

Renee came into his life and was a burst of positive energy. She was fun and exciting, everything he needed in his frame of mind. She helped him to get reintegrated into the world. She brought him out of the darkness and helped him find his way back to what was left of his family. He fell for her hard and fast, proposing after a year of dating; and he finally felt like everything was back on track until he learned of the business deal that set this whole night in motion.

Miguel and Asha were both vital parts of Johnston Incorporated; and, despite the failed marriage between Mia and Tyree, their families were still very much intertwined. Not only did they share Kyan, but they also shared an import and export business together, which, up until a few months ago, was small. When Miguel noticed the potential business they could bring in from overseas by expanding, he consulted with Rick, thus making their dealings that much more frequent. This particular party was a celebration of the fact that they had tripled revenue from last year's numbers.

Tyree was ecstatic about the business, but he knew the more time he spent in this house, the more he would drift back into memories of something that no longer belonged to him. He cared for Renee, she was a great woman, but no one would replace Mia. A piece of him would always belong to her.

It had been two years, and he could still smell her perfume. Maybe it was his imagination, but he swore it was getting closer. Sniffing the air,

Tyree knew it wasn't his imagination, it was really there, but he couldn't help the smile that crept across his face. When he jerked around hoping to find her there, he displayed a light, disappointed smile, finding Cassandra walking toward him.

"What's wrong? Already tired of seeing me this summer?" She let her neatly curled hair bounce on her shoulders. Cassandra was stunningly beautiful and, even at the age of forty, she had a youthful presence. As he scanned her appearance, everything about her screamed perfection. From her golden skin to her bright brown eyes, she was amazing.

"No, I could never get tired of you, Cassie." He reached out to hug her, inhaling the scent that drove him crazy. "I just thought . . . well, never mind."

"You thought I was her, didn't you? She sent this perfume to me in Kyan's bag some time ago. I hardly ever wear it, but I just felt like dabbing a little on for tonight. It's a wonderful scent."

"I actually thought you might be Renee coming to join me," he lied.

"Okay, whatever you say. Anyways, what are you doing out here all alone? In case you missed it, there is a party going on in there for you."

"I know. This is more Miguel and Asha's scene than mine. I'll let them soak it up with Rick."

"Always the man behind the scenes. You know you're only thirty, right?"

He grinned and put his arm around her shoulders. "Yes, and I know where this is going. No need to lecture me tonight. I'm happy; I really am. I'm about to marry a beautiful woman, my son is here with me, and the company is flourishing. I'm living the American dream."

"Yeah, you are, except that you really aren't. Let's not forget, I've known you since you were in diapers, and I know when you're lying."

"That only means you're old, Cassie," he joked, trying to throw off the conversation.

"I may be older, but I'm wiser, too. I'm just saying, it's never too late to have it all."

"I have it all."

"Not everything." She turned and left him mumbling to himself.

"I'm happy, dammit." He sighed, slapping his hand to his forehead. Stepping back into the foyer, he looked himself up and down in a full-length mirror. He had frown lines that weren't there before, and he ran his fingers over his semi-wavy fade.

He had always been described as a fairly good-looking man with his chiseled physique, creamy golden skin, and warm brown eyes; but he was feeling like a shell of his old self. He felt like he was way beyond his thirty years and he was desperate to feel some semblance of how he used to. His body was still at its optimum prime, but his face now held wrinkles that made him look a little older.

Tyree sighed, watching Renee walk across the room in her red strapless gown. She hadn't spotted him yet, but he watched her as she scanned the room, undoubtedly looking for him. She had been off with Asha and her husband, Terence, for most of the party, but he knew it would only be a matter of time before she sought him out. Unlike him, she enjoyed these events. She loved the attention.

Renee was a very impressive woman to look at. She was gorgeous, standing five feet six, with creamy caramel skin, bone-straight brown hair, and dark brown eyes. She had the body of a goddess: long legs, thin waist, with a round, supple bottom that he couldn't seem to keep his hands off of. Guys usually fawned over her, but he didn't mind. Really, he didn't. Who wanted someone who couldn't turn heads? Renee was definitely a head turner. She was often the life of the party, and he liked it that way.

Renee continued to scan the room, and when she finally spotted him, she smirked proudly, making her way over. Tyree was leaning against the wall when she approached, reaching out to touch him. Graciously accepting, he pulled her in for a kiss to her temple.

“You about ready to go?” he whispered in her ear.

“Not really. I was hoping you would come and dance with me. I got a few offers along the way, but I was hoping my fiancé would spare the time.”

“Babe,” he exhaled, “you know I don’t dance. It’s not my thing.”

“You don’t dance, huh? Well, what is that?” She pointed to a picture of him and Mia on the wall. Why Rick still had it on display was baffling, but the picture was taken one night at an event like this. Tyree was dipping Mia, and she had the biggest grin on her face. For a second, nostalgia washed over him, and he drifted into that moment only to look up and see the pain all over Renee’s face.

“Renee, come on now. It wasn’t my thing then, and it isn’t now. That was all Mia. She’s the one who loved to dance. I was just her prop.” He was trying to get her to crack a smile.

She didn't. Instead, she propped her arms on her waist, staring him down. "Why?"

"Why what? I'm not sure what you're asking me."

"Why are you with me if all you think about is her? Anything she ever asked, you did without question. I can't even get something as simple as a dance. I think you just like the fact that I'm there anytime you want to get laid. It's convenient for you."

And there it was: round two.

Thcy had been having these arguments over the past week about Mia, but Tyree was sure it had everything to do with the fact that Kyan was with them over the summer. IIe was a great kid, very polite, quiet and, most importantly, respectful. Tyree had always had him for holidays and special breaks but this summer he was keeping him for over a month. Mia had never trusted him enough to allow him so much time, and now here he was with his favorite boy for two months. Because of her generosity, he sensed a thaw in their relationship and so did Renee.

Renee had been great in the time he was with her. He had no complaints and, believe it or not, he was happy. Their relationship was fun and spontaneous, and she made him laugh. It was just what he needed even though others were not convinced. Miguel and their father, John, were pleasant toward her, and his mother was in full support of them until just recently. Asha was somewhat indifferent and Terence, Tyree's best friend, liked her, but he still had his opinion that Tyree was made to be with Mia, despite their many problems. Rick wasn't overly fond of her, but he put on a good face; but he was an angel compared to Cassandra.

Cassandra wasn't one to hide her feelings, and she made it clear that she despised Renee. In Cassandra's eyes, Renee was a social climber who latched on to Tyree to elevate herself in the world. When Tyree first presented Renee to his family and friends, because of their business dealings Miguel and Rick ran a background check on her to be sure she wasn't dangerous. It came back clean but revealed a past of surviving off meager means. She had taken several different jobs to support herself, ultimately becoming a secretary at Johnston Incorporated, where she met Tyree. While most commended her ability to work toward something more, Cassandra labeled her as a gold digger and never looked back. Tyree knew, to her, there was only one woman for him: Mia.

Mia was the little sister Cassandra never had, and she always looked out for her. No matter what it was, she always took Mia's side, trying to shield her from the harsh realities of the world they lived in. It was never a secret that Richmond was known for his shady business deals, and it often affected his family. Mia was usually the one who suffered the most from his ruthless nature. He just never seemed to be able to be the father she needed. Rick, although he was only her brother, tried to fill the void, without much success.

Tyree had been so lost in his thoughts about how this all came to be, he missed that Renee had stomped off, leaving him with a faraway look on his face. Scanning the room, he didn't see her, and he sighed. When he continued to search, he ran into Terence and Asha, pausing to ask if they knew where Renee had run off to. Terence pointed him to the balcony, and Tyree saw when Asha looked at the somber expression he developed. He was going to have to explain to Renee all the reasons he cared for her, in the very same spot he professed his love to Mia many years earlier. When his shoulders slumped and he began to walk over, Asha stopped him, pulling his arm.

"Hey, why don't you let me grab Renee, and you stand here with Terence? I promise I'll only be a minute."

"Sis, I appreciate that, but I should do it myself. I have to clean this mess up before she locks me out of the room again."

"No, really, let me. Sometimes a woman's touch is better in these situations."

Tyree contemplated this for a few seconds before smiling and leaning in to kiss her cheek. "Thank you. I really mean it. Thank you for everything. I know what you're trying to do."

"It's nothing, big brother." She nodded and disappeared, leaving the two men to their conversation.

"So," Terence muttered, and Tyree already knew where this was heading. "What's this argument about?"

"Dancing," he replied sharply.

"Dancing, huh? Dancing aka Mia?"

"Not just Mia. It's about the things she used to talk me into. God, I used to do anything she ever wanted, and now that I'm finally putting my foot down, Renee acts like I'm cheating her in some way."

Terence held his hands up and sighed. "Now, you know I let your sister talk me into just about anything. I know how it is but, in a sense, you are cheating Renee. You've already given out that part of yourself. Don't get me wrong, she makes you laugh and she's a fun time, but what happens when that isn't enough anymore?"

"Man, come on now. Just say what you mean and quit beating around the bush."

"With Mia, you were that man. You were happy, and you laughed all the time. Hell, most of the time it was for no reason at all. You had your son with you, and it was just different. You were a better you."

"Maybe I was, and maybe I was happier with Mia, but I don't remember it being my choice to end all that. She kind of made that decision when she started sleeping with Jake and offered me divorce papers," Tyree growled angrily.

"I know. She was wrong to ditch you, but you have to know ol' boy played a role. Here he was, the one giving everything back that she thought you lost. Women need to be saved sometimes, and he just happened to be the one. That doesn't mean she loves him; it just means he played the game right."

"It shouldn't have been a game. She was mine, my wife, and she shouldn't have left."

Terence shifted and folded his arms over his chest. "You see, if you were really ready to marry this girl, you wouldn't be so upset right now. As your friend, I am asking you to call this wedding off. Call it off and work on getting your woman back."

"I don't want her back."

"You do."

"How do you figure?"

"Just then, you didn't deny that she is still your woman. Now, I don't agree with her just packing up and moving across the damn world, but I think that was to hide from the fact that she still loves you."

"I haven't seen her in two years. There is nothing between us anymore. I am with Renee, and that is how it's going to be. I'm marrying Renee."

"Well, prepare to be miserable in a few years."

"Why can't you people just accept that I'm happy?"

"Because you're not."

Tyree was just about to argue his point when he looked up and saw Asha emerging from the back with Renee at her side. They were laughing, and Tyree felt relief wash over him. He was so happy to have his sister at that moment. She was truly a godsend. When they got close enough, he brushed his hand over Asha's glowing honey-colored skin and let out a deep breath. Asha was the perfect mixture of their parents. She had their mother's charm and features, with their father's strong will and durability.

Asha was the youngest of the three siblings, but she often posed as the fixer between them.

She was always the one playing mediator between Miguel and Tyree when they had their many disputes. They all got along fairly well, but when it came to the family business, Miguel's and Tyree's approaches differed drastically. While Miguel was flashy and loved the recognition, Tyree did most of the legwork, preferring to skip all the glitz and glam.

As well as the import and export business, Johnston Incorporated owned several hotel chains that reached overseas. It was one of the largest luxury hotel chains in the world, making the family a big name locally and internationally. The import and export business was the side they shared with Livingston Enterprises, who also ran a media conglomerate with several big-name magazines that Mia was in charge of. All in all, both families were considered black royalty among their Atlanta circle.

When Tyree focused in on Renee, he noticed the smile she was wearing, and he laid his forehead on hers. Slipping her hand in his, he interlaced their fingers and pulled her closer. He really was trying to make things work with her, and he needed her to feel special. Whatever he had to do, he was willing to be the man she needed.

"You wanna dance, baby?"

Renee blinked rapidly and offered him a gracious smile that spread all over her face. "Really? You would do that?"

"I'm sorry about earlier, and yes, I want to dance with you. It's important to you, and you're important to me." Tyree led Renee over to the floor. They danced to a slow song by Eric Benét, and Asha and Terence joined in behind them. While they all looked to be having a marvelous time, Tyree noticed a pair of eyes in the back of the room, watching him struggle to keep up his happy facade.

Chapter Two

Cassandra had been watching Tyree the entire night and was delighted to see that all wasn't as well as it seemed. He had been keeping up a front for months, but she knew better. She had been waiting for a crack in his exterior, and now that she had seen it, she was going to seize the moment. She knew she had to act fast to make her dream a reality.

Slipping down the hall toward the bedrooms, Cassandra made her way into Kyan's room and closed the door behind her. Kyan had been staying with Tyree for the last week, and he would come over and visit with her and Rick in the mornings. Since they were all going to be in the same place, she convinced Tyree to let them have him for the night. When Kyan saw her, he sat up with bright, innocent eyes.

"Aunt Cassie! I thought you had a party."

"We did, sweetie." She ran a hand over his smiling cheek. "I just wanted to check on you. I can't believe you aren't sleeping."

"I was, but I woke up."

When he looked away suddenly, she knew there was something else bothering him. She nodded subtly, letting him know it was safe to say whatever was on his mind.

"I miss Mama. I wish she could come here and see Daddy with me. Why can't we just stay here like we used to?"

Cassandra just sighed and pulled him into a rough embrace. "You have to understand; your mom and dad are living separate lives now. I know you hate having to leave her, but your dad wants to see you too."

"I know. I like staying with Daddy. I just wish she was here too."

"I do too. Hey, how about we call your mom? I'm sure she would like to hear from her favorite man."

"Yes," he shrieked; and she smiled, walking over and taking the phone from the base. Dialing Mia's number, she sat, waiting for it to ring. Once she heard her voice, she looked over to Kyan and nodded. He knew what this meant, and he squealed, jumping off the bed, nearly tackling her. Snatching the phone, he began to tell Mia all about his trip and all the things he and Tyree had done since he arrived.

After more than ten minutes of conversation, he rubbed his eyes and walked back to Cassandra, holding the phone out. "Mama wants to talk to you."

Taking the phone from his hand, Cassandra bent over, placing a gentle kiss on his cheek. "Okay, sweetie. It's time to get back in bed. I love you, and good night."

"Good night, Aunt Cassie." Before she could exit the room, he called out to her once again. "Can you send my daddy to say good night? Just him."

"Sure, baby. As soon as I hang up, I'll get him."

"Thank you, Aunt Cassie."

Cassandra shut the door and pulled the phone up to her ear, sighing before beginning their conversation.

"What was that all about?" Mia asked sadly. "He sounds . . . off."

"He is off." She paused and exhaled deeply. "Mia, you need to come here, now."

"I can't just drop everything and come. I have a job to do, you know."

"I know you have a job, and I also know that's not the only reason you won't come home."

"I am home."

"Home is where your heart is, and face it, baby girl, your heart is and always will be here. No amount of running will change that."

"I'm with Jake."

"Who are you trying to convince? Me or yourself? Whatever the case may be, your son needs you. He's begging for you. Why do you think I called?"

"What's wrong? Is he not having fun with Tyree? I knew this was a mistake, letting him stay that long. Just get him ready and we will meet up. I'll make the arrangements—"

"No," she cut her off. "If you want him home sooner than August, you will come here and get him. He loves getting to see his dad, but he misses his mom. Now is the time when you prove what's more important: your silly grudge or your son. If you deny him this, you're no better than you claim Tyree is."

Once Cassandra hung up the phone, she left Mia gasping before ultimately hearing the dial tone. Cassandra knew it was a long shot, but it was the only thing she could think of at the moment. After this, one of two things would happen, either of which would work in her favor: Mia would have to either come to Atlanta or call Tyree. Either way, she had the ball rolling now, and the rest would be up to the two lost souls.

Chapter Three

"Tyree, be honest with me." Renee sighed. "Can you really marry me when you know that your son hates me?"

Tyree almost fell off the side of the bed, trying to remove his shoes, when he heard her question. "What do you mean he hates you? Kyan is seven. He loves everybody. He just doesn't know you that well. He's bound to be a little standoffish."

"Yeah, and the fact that I'm not his mother doesn't help. No one can compete with her. She is like a freaking saint."

"Mia is no saint," he snapped. "She is far from perfect, and Kyan knows that better than anyone."

Renee shivered, witnessing his grim expression. He knew she had never seen him so angry. "I'm sorry." She slid herself down onto his lap, straddling him. "I'm sorry," she repeated, kissing her way down his neck, brushing the fabric of his shirt away. "Let me make it up to you. Let me make you feel better."

"Baby, I'm fine. I just don't want you to get down on yourself about her. She is a good mother to him, but she's not perfect. None of us are."

"I know we're not, but I want to please you. Baby, let me please you. We can be as loud as we want tonight. Doesn't that make you happy?"

"Oh yeah," he replied, flipping her back on the bed. She had already removed her dress and was now only clad in a bra and a pair of boy shorts. Tyree ran his hand over her smooth skin, reveling in the goosebumps she displayed feeling his touch. "Very happy."

Dipping his head, he captured her lips while sliding his fingers under the red lace material of her bra. While running his mouth all over her chest and shoulders, he took joy in the sounds floating throughout the room. He had always been a highly sexual person, and with Renee, things were easy. She was always eager to please, and she was really something in bed: not the best he had ever had, but she was willing to try just about anything. That alone made it all worth it.

Renee was good for him; she was safe. There was no way she could inflict the damage Mia had because she would never have the ammunition to. He cared for her, yes, but only one woman had gotten close enough to mean everything. He vowed never to let that happen again.

Shaking away thoughts of anything but the voluptuous body beneath him, Tyree pulled her up, smiling at the giggle she released as he unhooked her bra. When her breasts came spilling out, he placed his head between them, teasing her with his warm breath and then his tongue. Latching her hands onto his head, she flipped them over, sliding her body down his to reach his slacks. When she knocked the button loose and ripped the zipper down, her hand found its way in his boxers, causing a loud groan to tear from his throat. She stroked him slowly at first, increasing in speed as she went on. When she smirked up at him, he gripped her head, knowing what was about to happen next.

In an agonizingly slow manner, she removed her hand, and her mouth descended, taking him in inch by inch. Once he was fully submerged, he wove his fingers through hers, biting down hard on his bottom lip. True, she wasn't the best he ever had, but she damn sure was the best at this. He closed his eyes, allowing a few quiet moans to escape his mouth as she maneuvered her head, taking him in and out.

As much as he enjoyed all of this, something kept playing in his mind: everyone kept trying to push him toward Mia. What the hell were they thinking? How could he possibly still want to be with her when he had a woman like this willing to do whatever it took to make him happy? There was no way he was going to entertain such thoughts.

Renee was still working on him and was unrelenting and, when he felt himself drifting, he closed his eyes and gripped her hair tighter. When he climaxed, he felt the air leave his lungs, and his chest felt heavy. She moved herself up his body and rested herself above his reemerging erection. She smiled down at his flustered expression. "Are you happy?"

"Yeah. How could I not be?" He ran his hands up to grip her thighs. "You always take care of me, baby." He rolled her over, resting between her legs. "Now let me take care of you."

After slipping on a condom, Tyree pushed her legs farther apart, gripping them with his sweaty palms as he pushed inside her. He could feel her breath still in her chest as he pulled back, almost completely withdrawing before plunging back in. Wrapping his arms around her thighs, he continued his deep thrusts, causing whispered notions to fall from her full lips. Tyree was buried in the rhythm he created, and he felt himself pushing deeper and gripping harder. His thoughts were lost to him once he heard her loud exclamations.

Letting the heat, shivers, and chills take him over, Tyree felt his body propelling harder against hers. All day he had been stressed, but her body was his release. The convulsing patterns of her heated flesh had his mind blown. Gripping her tighter, digging his fingers into her supple ass, he pulled her closer, making the breath leave her small frame.

Pounding her, making her scream, filling her body with every last inch of his penetrating member, he stroked her sweet walls with insistence. He was craving the ultimate release and, with her movements egging him on, he was damn close.

Renee was writhing below him, digging her nails into his back as he pulled her down on the bed, placing her legs over his shoulders. He was in heaven as her hands found their new resting place around his waist. For a few seconds, he slowed his pace, pulling her into a false sense of comfort; and then he plunged hard into her, eliciting a loud scream that was music to his ears.

When Renee reached up and placed a hand on his chest, he slowed his erratic pace and looked down at her. She closed her eyes as he continued to stroke her much more calmly than before, but still deep. He could tell when her orgasm approached because she dug her nails into his side and squeezed her eyes shut. He erupted inside her, and she followed shortly afterward.

Rolling to his side, Tyree pulled Renee to him, taking shallow breaths, trying to regulate himself. “You okay?” he asked after, taking in her silence.

"Yeah," she sighed. "I'm just basking in the afterglow."

"Well, you should be because that was damn good."

"Just damn good?"

"Okay, fantastic."

"I like that better." She closed her eyes. "I love you, Tyree."

"Yeah, you too," he mumbled before closing his eyes. When he heard her breathing even out, he knew she had fallen asleep. Quickly, he unwrapped himself from her and went into the bathroom for a shower.

Stepping inside, feeling the hot water cascade down his back, he wondered how long he would be able to get away with not saying it back. She was comfortable saying "I love you" to him every day, but he was having a difficult time with it. Sure, he could love her someday, but feeling it and saying it were two different things. Saying it made it so official, and he had already been down that road before. This thing with Renee was just comfortable and marrying her would ensure the simple life he craved instead of the complicated mess he had with Mia.

Stepping out of the shower and back into the room, Tyree was pleased to see that Renee was still sleeping. He slipped back into bed and reached for his cell. Witnessing the light blinking, he assumed it was probably Miguel calling to tell him about whatever mischief he had gotten himself into.

To be such a smart, business-savvy guy, Miguel sure was promiscuous. He never held on to one woman too long. As Tyree scrolled through the messages and missed calls, sure enough, about three of them were from him. Two were texts, and he had two voicemails. He read the messages and laughed, and pulled the phone up to his ear to check the voicemail. While waiting for the prompts, he looked over at Renee and smiled, thanking God for his simple life with her. Sure, the partying was fun when he was younger but, when all that ended, he wanted someone next to him to share the lonely nights.

Tyree listened to the first voicemail, chuckling at his belligerent brother, and then skipped to the next. The voice he heard on the other end almost made him drop his phone. Two years, two long years, had passed since he heard Mia's voice and just like that here she was steering his thoughts back to her. *Damn her for having that power, and damn me for letting her,* he thought, listening to her message. She wanted him to call her; she even left a number, which she had never done in the past. All of their contact had been messages passed through her brother or sister-in-law. Why was she calling him now?

Hitting the playback button, Tyree memorized the number she left, and he sighed, hanging the phone up. Looking down at Renee and then back at the phone, he hung his head. "So much for the simple life." He sighed, knowing whatever happened next was going to change everything.

He dialed the number. The phone rang twice, and then his heart stopped. Even thousands of miles away, she sounded so close, so familiar, so important.

"Hello?"

"Mia? Can you hear me?" He could hear her breathe. Even without being able to see her, he could tell there was a smile on her face. Against his instincts, he smiled too.

"Yes, Ty. How are you?"

Hello, complications. Standing from the bed, he exhaled into the phone. "I'm fine. How can I help you?"

"We need to talk, Ty. It's about what we're doing to Kyan."

And here it is. I'm completely fucked. Closing his eyes, he sighed, wishing he had just gone to sleep. Now he was going to have to think about this conversation probably for days to come.

Chapter Four

"Hey, big bro, you got a sec?" Miguel poked his head into Tyree's office. When Tyree nodded, Miguel came in and sat down. "I was looking over something I thought you should see." He passed him a stack of papers and waited for him to look over the front page.

Tyree studied it for a few minutes and then looked up in confusion. "What does this mean? I thought all of this mess was cleared up."

"Apparently not. I think you should call Rick. It could be bad for us if it looks like there is still any trace of the dirty money Richmond brought into Livingston. Just think about how Dad would react if he found any of this out."

"He would flip, but I don't have to call. I'll see him in a few hours after me and Kyan pick Mia up from the airport."

Although they shared the import and export business, John mostly tried to steer clear of Richmond's way of doing things. For the most part, John was perceived as an upstanding family man, to all except Tyree, while Richmond crushed whoever got in his way.

For years, Livingston was run under the thumb of Richmond until word of his illegal activities began to get out. At that point, he was voted out as CEO by the board of directors and replaced by Rick. Soon afterward, he appointed Mia as his right-hand man, and Janelle joined the group as well.

For so long, Livingston had been run only by men, and now Rick was breaking that tradition, trying to clean up the mess Richmond made. Bringing Mia in might have just saved the company after all the scandal. Shc was always the most beloved member of their family, besides their mother, of course, and she helped the company shed some of the negative attention.

The illegal and shady activities ranged from hostile takeovers to money laundering. There were even some unfounded rumors of murder for hire, but without any solid proof that Richmond was to blame, he was just removed from the company and didn't have to serve jail time. As a result, Mia, Janelle, and Rick blocked him from their lives and revoked his shares in the company, leaving him with only his personal fortune. It seemed like the turning point for their family was when their mother began to spiral out of control.

Helen Ann Livingston was a remarkable woman marred by the terrible decision to marry Richmond. She was the daughter of a politician, and when she met Richmond, she thought she had found the perfect man. She still thought that through the early years. They had Rick when they were twenty, and had Mia when they were thirty. Janelle came two years after Mia. They lived a happy life for the first few years of marriage, and then the problems began.

Richmond inherited Livingston when he was twenty-seven, and he ran it for years without letting it change him. The first eight years in the business were easy. They had more money than they knew what to do with, but they were still that same loving family who shared dinner and stories every night. They were still lost in perfection until the next year changed everything.

The next year, Richmond was introduced to some contacts in Paris, and more spread all over Europe, who changed life as they knew it. Soon, his times away from home became more and more frequent. The money tripled, but Helen wondered where it all came from. She began to get more and more suspicious until, one day, she found all she needed to know in his briefcase.

There was proof of his plans to cut out several investors and small businesses that helped him get to where he was, practically wiping them out for his own personal gain. She knew it would ruin lives and she couldn't allow him to follow through with it. When she confronted him about it, things escalated from there. The kids were oblivious to it all until Helen developed a dangerous habit. Helen's life truly began to spiral until she found a way to cope.

Cocaine became Helen's go-to drug. Soon, it was like second nature for her to snort it up her nose. It was like she couldn't get through the day without it. By the time her children were adults, Helen was far gone, and had been in and out of rehab so many times they got used to her not being around; and, then, she wasn't. Two days before Kyan's fourth birthday, Helen Ann Livingston died from a cocaine overdose, leaving her children devastated.

Two months after the funeral, Janelle was killed in a hit-and-run accident. There were no witnesses, and the authorities investigated, but no one was ever found. Her body was also never recovered from the scene. The first-response team concluded that Janelle wasn't wearing her seat belt, and she flew out of the car and down the side of the railing into the water below. It was like she disappeared into thin air.

"Hey," Miguel snapped, bringing Tyree's trip down memory lane to an end. "You were somewhere else, I swear. What were you thinking about?"

"Just the past few years. So much has happened, so much that is unexplained."

"You're talking about Janelle, aren't you? I think about that every day."

"I guess back then I just never knew how much she meant to you. I mean, I knew you two were hooking up, but I never thought you had real feelings for her until after she died. I thought she was just one of many for you."

"She wasn't one of many; she was the one. I just hate I never told her. I think about what I should have done differently every day. I just wish I could have that last day with her back. You know me, I've never been in love, so I don't know how to take it when someone says it to me. She told me she loved me, and I just stood there. She smiled, but I could see that it upset her. I should have said it back."

"I know how you feel. Renee says it to me all the time, and I've never said it back. I know it hurts her, but I just can't seem to make myself say it."

"You know I don't get in your business like that, but do you think that maybe you don't say it back because you've tricked yourself into feeling it's real? I see you with her and, I'll admit, you seem happy, but it looks like a forced happy. It doesn't seem genuine."

"We don't lie to each other, right?"

"Right."

"And nothing I say here will leave this room, right?"

"Right."

Tyree sat back in his chair slowly. "The night of the party, just before Mia called, I was having sex with Renee, and I tried to focus on her, but Mia kept popping into my head. Renee was going all out to get me in the mood, and I got there, but it wasn't because I wanted her. It was because I was trying to convince myself I didn't want Mia."

"So did you decide you didn't want her?"

"I was there after we finished. I was ready to commit to Renee, and then I got the voicemail and my mind was back on Mia. It's frustrating because she left me. I should be over her, but she's still in my head. Seeing her today is just going to make it worse, but I have to do this for Kyan. He misses her, and I can't deny him after everything he's gone through."

"Yeah, he has been through so much these past few years, and being packed up and moved away from his whole family couldn't have helped. What the hell was she thinking taking him to Paris?"

"I don't know, man. It was like she couldn't get away from here fast enough. I don't know why she did it. It was like one day she loved me and the next she couldn't stand the sight of me. I know I messed up when I let Kyan get taken but was it enough for her to leave me like that?"

"She blamed you."

"I know." Tyree nodded.

"You were watching Kyan in the park and took your eyes off him for a second. That could have happened to either of you."

"I looked everywhere for him, Miguel, but Mia was so pissed at me, there was nothing I could do to change her mind. I chased every dead end thrown my way for six damn months. I still don't understand it."

"None of us do. So, he just went without making a sound?"

"Not one damn sound; and he doesn't remember much of anything."

"I just don't get why we never got any requests for money. Taking Kyan could have made someone a very rich person. We're worth millions."

"Right." Tyree tilted his head. "We're worth millions, but my wife fell for a man with a regular nine to five. What in the hell does she see in that private investigator anyways?"

"He brought your son back. He's nothing, insignificant even, but he brought her everything she was convinced you lost. I love Mia, and I know she loves you, but she isn't the same woman we used to know. The Mia we grew up with would have never abandoned you or us like she did. You were there for her through all the funerals and when she and Rick got rid of Richmond. There was no way she should have left like that. That's why I just sat back and let you do your thing with Renee. I don't think you should marry her, but she was there when Mia wasn't."

"I'm not stupid enough to believe I love Renee like I loved Mia but, honestly, I shouldn't feel this for her anymore. Mia broke me more than anyone ever has. She broke me down and then took my son. I should hate that woman with everything in me, but I don't. The love I feel is just as strong as it ever was. She's still everything to me even though I don't want her to be."

"That's the thing with love: you can't choose who you fall for. So what are you going to do about Mia? She will be here today, and you have to face the feelings at some point."

"I'm going to pick her up. We will discuss what to do about our son and, after that, I'm staying my distance. I can't get sucked into wanting to be near her again."

"What if you can't help it? I know you want to do what's right, and you want to protect yourself, but what if you can't? What if you're supposed to be with her?"

"I'm not; it's pretty clear. We shared a fantasy. In real life, we're two people who don't work."

"I can't pretend to know what advice to give you, but I will tell you this: if you have a chance, a real chance, don't let it slip by. You both messed up, but you also have time to fix it."

"My chance is with Renee. I have to try to make this work. She deserves someone who is all in, and I want to be that man. Mia is my past."

"If you're sure that's what you want, I'll stand behind you. If not, I'm still behind you."

"Thanks for your support."

"Anytime." He stood to leave. "Well, I have to go, but keep me posted about those papers. It's probably nothing, but I just wanted to be sure."

"I'll let you know what I find out."

Tyree watched as Miguel left the room, and he picked up the papers once again. For some reason, Richmond's name was on documents formulated this year. There was no way Mia or Rick had given him any control over the company, so it had to be a mistake.

There had been so much confusion because of that man. At one point, Tyree was suspicious that Richmond had intentionally put his family in danger just to cover his own ass. He had investigated him for months before he dismissed the notions. It was all around the time Kyan was taken and, when that happened, Kyan became his only focus. All that mattered then was finding his son.

After Kyan had gone missing, Tyree began to receive leads on where to find him, and he went out to follow them. The clues led him all the way to Europe and then they all fell flat. There were several men who seemed willing to help, which made him hopeful, but after the first meeting, he was never able to make contact again. Tyree concluded after days of trying to reach them that they were only sent out as a distraction and he went on to pursue other things, all of which ended up being dead ends.

Tyree sat working for hours until he heard a throat being cleared, and he looked up to find Asha. When he acknowledged her, she smiled and made her way inside, finding refuge in the same chair Miguel had vacated hours earlier. When she smiled nervously, he figured out what her visit was going to entail.

Taking a deep breath, Tyree dropped the paperwork in his hands and focused in on her. “Hey, sis.”

“Hey. How are you?”

“I’m good. I’m actually about to leave here soon to get Kyan and then pick up Mia.”

“Yeah, I know. How are you with all of that? I mean, how are things with Renee and how is she taking it?”

“Renee is cool. She’s putting on a good face, and I’m just doing what’s best for my son. She understands that.”

“Yeah, but how do you feel about seeing her again? Are you really okay?”

“Asha, you don’t have to worry about me. Sometimes it feels like you’re the big sister and I’m the little brother. You worry too much, baby sis. We will all be fine.”

“It’s my job to worry when your heart is on the line. I just want you to be careful.”

“I will, I promise.” He stood and walked to stand in front of her, pulling her from the chair. “Mia can’t hurt me anymore. That part of us is gone. This is just us finally doing what’s right as parents, nothing more.” He released her and ran his hand down her cheek. “Now, I have to go, but remember what I said. I’ll be okay, and she can’t break me.” As he walked out the door, watching

Asha's unconvinced stare, he tried to make himself believe the lies he had just told. Mia held all the power; she probably always would.

Chapter Five

"Daddy, which one is she coming out of?" Kyan asked excitedly. They were sitting in the airport waiting for Mia. Well, Tyree was sitting; Kyan was bouncing off the walls, unable to sit still. He was so excited, and Tyree was dreading it. He had tried so hard to put on a good face and be the mature adult he claimed to be, but every minute that passed brought on a new sense of anxiety and anger. He was anxious because it had been so long, and angry for the exact same reason. Had she not packed up and left, they wouldn't have to do this whole song and dance with their son.

After leaving Asha, Tyree had made his way over to Rick's and picked Kyan up. When Tyree was at work, Kyan always stayed with Cassandra. When Kyan saw him, he flew into his arms with a gift he and Cassandra bought for Mia. Tyree only wished he shared half his excitement.

Tyree fiddled with his fingers as Kyan went on and on about his plans for them once Mia arrived. He was listing so many things that involved them acting like a happy family, and Tyree didn't have the heart to tell him none of it would come true. He and Mia both agreed that once she got there, they would sit Kyan down and explain to him that they would never be what they once were. He needed to understand that they had all moved on. Mia was with Jake, and Tyree was going to marry Renee. He had to know what this all meant.

Tyree was in his own world until he heard Kyan yelp. Tyree watched, frozen, as Kyan ran toward the gorgeous woman making her way to them. She looked just as beautiful as she had the last time he saw her. Her succulent chocolate skin was glowing under the bright lights, and her long, dark hair was cascading down her back in a long, straight flow. She was wearing the most beautiful dress, and she almost looked like she wasn't as stressed as she truly was.

When she looked up at him, she flashed him a light smile and, for a second, he saw a glimmer of happiness in her bright hazel eyes. Looking at him, her dimples, those dimples that made him cave about almost anything, were on full display. He knew he was in trouble when every attempt he made to tear his eyes away failed. She still had a hold on him.

When Kyan threw his arms around her, she dropped down to lift him, holding him close as she closed her eyes and enjoyed the moment. Tyree could tell she had missed their son as much as he missed her. Turning his head, somehow feeling like he wasn't welcome at the moment, Tyree was ready to excuse himself until she walked over and placed a hand on his shoulder. Her touch caused shivers that only she could, and he turned slowly. One glance into her hazel eyes melted the anger he once felt and replaced it with joy he never thought possible again.

Mia smiled subtly, and they stared at each other for the longest time until Kyan broke the silence. "Mama, are you staying with us at Daddy's house?"

Mia and Tyree looked at each other and, before she could answer, he slid a hand on her shoulder and pulled her to him. "Son, we actually have a better idea. Your mom is staying in the old house, and you're going to stay the night with her there. She wants to have you all to herself because she missed you so much."

Kyan's eyes lit up as the idea registered with him; and then his excitement quickly dissipated when he realized Tyree wasn't staying. "What about you, Daddy? Can you stay with us?"

Mia looked at him with panic in her eyes. He knew she wasn't prepared to have that talk with their son in the middle of the airport. She was beginning to shuffle nervously until Tyree spoke up and shocked her beyond measure.

"Sure, I'll stay."

After grabbing Mia's bags, they headed to the car in silence. Once Kyan was strapped into the back seat, Tyree walked Mia to her door, and she halted him, placing her hand on his chest. She inhaled sharply and looked him in the eyes before beginning her statement. "Ty, you don't have to agree to this. I know what I'm here to do, and we don't have to give him false hope. This trip was for us to set everything straight. I don't want to confuse him even more."

"One night, Mia. After two years, I think he deserves one night before we break his heart. I was only going to stay until he fell asleep and then I was going to sneak out. When he wakes up, just tell him I already went to work."

"You promise that's all it is? You're going to leave when he goes to sleep, right?"

"Yes." He shifted back, feeling the anger rebuilding in him. "I'll leave the minute he falls asleep. You don't have to worry about me. I know exactly what this is between us. It's nothing more than an act for our son."

Mia looked a little taken aback by his harsh tone, and she leaned closer to the car. He figured she knew he would be upset, but he never expected to display the anger present in his eyes right now. She had to be wondering how in the hell he had the nerve to be upset because she felt he was the one who messed everything up.

This whole ordeal was all his fault, in her eyes, and she would never forget it. She would always blame him for what happened to their family. Now that he had let her see his real feelings, he knew her trip would go much smoother. There would be no distraction or temptation for him. Just the cold, hard truth. They were over, and there was no changing that.

Tyree drove to the mansion in silence as Mia and Kyan interacted the whole way. When the car stopped, Kyan jumped out and leaped into his mother's arms. She hugged him close and carried him all the way to the porch of their old house.

Mia and Tyree once lived on the grounds in a house Rick had built for them as a wedding gift. The house was a spacious six-bedroom, two-story house that sat on its own portion of land with a white fence separating it from the mansion. Rick had the fence built as a joke because Mia always went on about having a house with a white picket fence.

Tyree watched as Mia sat Kyan down on the porch and inhaled a deep breath. She hadn't been there in so long, it had to be painful for her to experience it all over again. Tyree saw her hesitancy, and he pulled Kyan by the hand, swinging the door open.

Once he walked inside, he saw the place still looked lived in, like they had never left, and it all hit him harder than expected. It was exactly as it was the last time he was there. He hadn't been there since the day she moved away. When all the painful memories came rushing back, he sank down on the couch, trying to catch his breath.

Kyan walked over and placed his small hands on his father's lap. "Daddy, what's wrong?"

Tyree quickly gathered his feelings and looked down at his son's worried expression. "Nothing. Nothing is wrong. I'm just happy to be here right now."

"With me and Mama?"

Tyree looked down at Kyan and then back to Mia, who was still standing on the porch. "Yeah, with you and your mom."

When Tyree looked over to her, he could tell Mia was drowning in the memories and nightmares she had of that place. He thought with the time that had passed she had gotten over it, but the wounds seemed still as fresh as they had ever been. After two years, all the things she had tried to block out appeared to have come flooding back. Watching her expression closer, he moved Kyan aside and walked over to her.

"Ky, go to your room. Give me and your mom some time to talk."

Kyan sprinted upstairs, and Tyree pulled Mia to him, wrapping his arms around her trembling form.

When she felt his arms around her, she relaxed. "Ty, being back here is all too much. I shouldn't have come."

"Mia, he needed you," Tyree whispered into her hair. He oncc again had forgotten the anger he felt for her, and he just held her, running his hand down her back until she realized what was happening, and she backed away. "Mia." He moved toward her, and she bumped into the wall. "Don't—"

"Tyree, stop. We can't do things like that. We can't be that for each other, not anymore."

"Mia, you were clearly upset. Surely you don't hate me that much that you can't accept me comforting you. We have a son together. If you're not okay, then it affects him."

"That's not what's going on here, and you know it. It's what we always do. We become vulnerable and then fall into the arms of the wrong people. It's a pattern that we need to break."

Tyree sighed and stepped away from her until he thought about what she said and looked over at her questioningly. "Are you saying you made a mistake by choosing Jake? Are you finally admitting that you were wrong?"

Mia opened her mouth and then closed it, at a total loss for words. Before she could respond to him, his phone rang, breaking the silence in the room.

Tyree pulled it out, saw that it was Renee, and silenced the ringing before focusing back in on her. "Mia, I'm waiting."

"It's her, isn't it?" When Tyree didn't respond her voice intensified and that beautiful rasp she always exhibited suddenly sounded extremely harsh. "Pick up the phone and answer your fiancée."

"Mia—" he started, wanting to reason with her.

"Tyree, pick up the damn phone."

Tyree laid the phone down and crossed the room, and before she could react, he was standing right in front of her, breathing down her neck. "I'm done with this game, Mia. I've waited two years to hear what you have to say, and you're going to answer my questions. You owe me that much."

Mia shivered and tried to move, but he cornered her, planting his hands beside her head. She looked like she wanted to run, but he offered her no escape. When she tried to sit up from the wall, he leaned closer to her. "Ty, let me go. This is pointless, and I think you should leave."

He smirked angrily and leaned in to whisper in her ear until he heard movement coming from behind them.

"Daddy, are you leaving?"

When Tyree heard Kyan's voice, he backed up, releasing Mia from the wall. As soon as she had room, she fled, putting as much distance between them as she could.

Tyree sighed and plastered on his most convincing smile and turned to face his son. "No, we were just talking about me getting us some dinner for tonight. I'm going to leave for just a second, but I'll bc right back."

"You promise?"

"I promise."

"Just you?"

"Just me."

Making a quick exit, Tyree got out on the porch and took a deep breath. That whole scene was too intense for him, and he had almost lost control. For a split second, he felt intense love and anger all at the same time. He had never had that happen with anyone but her.

Chapter Six

Mia just sat watching the door after Tyree left the house. She shifted about for a while before she and Kyan finally ended up in the living room. For some reason, she had an uneasy feeling about the woman he was involved with. She wanted him to move on, but the way Kyan just reacted made her curious as to what had been going on since he arrived. She knew he might be homesick, but this was something different. Kyan liked pretty much everyone he encountered, but he seemed to have a particular distaste for the new woman in Tyree's life. When Mia took a seat on the couch, Kyan followed her, nuzzling as close as he could, putting his head against her neck.

"Baby, what's wrong? I know you miss me, but is there something you want to tell me?"

Kyan was dead silent for a few seconds as if contemplating what to say, and Mia lifted his chin, forcing him to look into her eyes.

"Come on now, it's me. You tell me everything. What's going on with my favorite boy?"

"I keep hearing the people in the masks."

The people who kidnapped Kyan wore masks most of the time except for one man. He said the man was nice, but he would always have night terrors about them because he was taken away from his family. He was so smart and brave, but even he was entitled to be rattled because of his experiences.

"Those mask people will never hurt you again, baby. Daddy and I are here. We will never let that happen again."

"You promise?" He sighed.

"I promise, baby. Where do you get this feeling? Is it in your dreams?"

He chewed on his bottom lip and looked to be considering his answer before he gave it. "I don't know, Mama." He paused for a second and then switched the subject. "Mama, were you and Daddy fighting?"

"Your dad and I haven't seen each other in a long time and, yeah, we disagreed on something, but we're fine now. We just want you to be okay."

"Why were you fighting? Was it because Dad lives with Renee and you live with Jake?"

"Sweetie, I don't want you to worry about Daddy and me. We are going to be just fine.

We are going to do whatever we need to make sure you know how much we love you."

"So we're staying here?"

"We're going to talk about everything once your dad gets back." Mia wrapped him tighter in her embrace and lay back on the couch. She really didn't have the heart to tell him she had no intention of staying there longer than a few days. She needed to get out of there before her old feelings arose and submerged her back into the sea of confusion and betrayal she fought so hard to escape. The sooner she made Kyan understand, the better. They needed to make a clean break from Atlanta before she lost herself again. Some wounds, even if they were emotional, never healed.

Mia held him, thinking over their situation, until his voice broke her from the thoughts racing through her mind.

"Mama, since you're here now, can we all just stay here? I don't like Daddy's new house."

If she wasn't convinced before, Mia now knew there was something her son wasn't telling. She pulled him up to ask what was going on and she ran her hand down his face. "Kyan, sweetheart, what's wrong with Daddy's house?"

Kyan dropped his head and bit down on his bottom lip before answering. "Daddy isn't happy when we're there. He yells a lot and always looks sad."

"Who does he yell at? Is he yelling at you?"

"No, he is nice to me. He yells at Renee, and she yells back."

Mia knew she was wrong, but she had to know. "What do they yell about?"

"You. I don't think Renee likes you, Mama."

"And what does your dad say when she's yelling about me?"

Before he could answer, Tyree swung the door open, and she put her finger to her lips, letting Kyan know to drop the conversation, and he smiled, agreeing. At that moment, Mia thanked God for having a son who was as intelligent as Kyan. After deflecting his father's inquisitive stare, Kyan bounced over to help with the food, and Mia felt relieved.

When Tyree went out the door to gather more things from the car, she followed, closing the door behind them. "Ty, when we go back in there, can we pretend like that awkward moment didn't happen earlier? I thought it over, and you're right: we should at least act as a family this one time. Kyan deserves to have us in one room, even if it is only for tonight. He doesn't need to see us fighting too."

"Too? What do you mean too?"

"Kyan hears everything. You know that."

"He heard me and Renee fighting? What did he hear?" Tyree asked.

She knew he didn't want her to know all the fights they had were about her. "Just yelling," she lied. "I just don't want him to hear it from us too. We haven't been the best examples of parents, and I want to turn over a new leaf."

"I agree, and I'm sorry for letting him hear us. I know how this must look."

"It's not my business, Ty. Really." She placed a hand on his cheek and smiled. "It's fine. Nobody's perfect." They stood that way for a while until Mia chuckled and reached for a few of the items in Tyree's hand. "Let me help you."

When they walked inside, they both smiled seeing that plates were already set on the dining room table. Kyan had pulled out the dishes they would need for dinner that night. After unloading the rest of the bags, Tyree joined the pair at the table and smiled. They ate, they laughed, and they bonded that night. For a brief moment in time, they weren't a broken family; they were three people who meant everything to each other, even if it was just an act.

Mia could feel Tyree's excitement drain as the night wore on and she couldn't help but feel responsible. She could see in his eyes that he wanted more time before he had to give them up again, but she just couldn't bring herself to allow it. It would never work, and they both knew it. Tonight was a one-time thing that could never happen again, even if it did feel wonderful.

Chapter Seven

Tyree stepped outside as his phone began to ring. He hadn't spoken to Renee all night, and he knew he needed to take her call. He had also conviently missed the meeting he was supposed to have with John, and he knew that was going to lead to an argument. She was bound to be feeling uneasy about his evening with Mia, but he wanted to reassure her that she had nothing to worry about. After tonight, he learned that they could be in the same room without killing each other. It was refreshing and exactly what Kyan needed before they broke the news to him. When he answered the phone, he could hear the sadness in her voice.

"Hey, babe, you okay?"

"I'm okay," she said quietly. "How's it going with Kyan? How did he take the talk you guys had?"

Tyree sucked in a deep breath and then let it go. He really wanted to skip this part. He knew it was going to get ridiculous. "We haven't talked to him about it yet. We wanted to ease him into it. We both felt it was best."

"So what have you been doing over there all day?"

"We had dinner, and I'm about to put him down for bed. He's staying here with her tonight, and we'll figure the rest out later."

"Okay." By her snappy response, he knew she was obviously annoyed. "So when should I expect you home?"

"That's the thing. I will be in late. I promised him I would stay but—"

"Like hell you are! You get your ass home now."

Feeling his anger flaring, Tyree tried to choose his words carefully. "Whoa, I hadn't planned on staying, but you don't talk to me like that. I told you my son needed me, and he comes before anyone, even you."

"You know what? If you want the bitch, then stay over there. I'm tired of this game you play. You keep me at bay, and when she comes to town, you drop everything to be next to her."

"I'm not doing this with you. I'll see you when I get home. Hopefully, you will have your attitude in check by then."

"Don't bother. Stay your ass there." She hung up.

He hissed into the air. He was growing tired of these petty arguments. He was just about ready to say to hell with all the women in his life. He just couldn't seem to make either of them happy. First Mia and now this mess with Renee. He was at his wit's end with all this drama.

When he walked back inside, Tyree found Mia sitting on the couch with Kyan in her lap rubbing his sleepy eyes. He sat in the doorway, smiling at his son and the woman who once owned his heart, and he wished it could all go back to when they were happy. He longed for times like these when it was just them and their son; it was so much simpler. When she saw him, she looked back and flashed him a shy grin. After all this time, he could tell she was still unsure how to be around him; it was apparent on her face.

Kyan broke the stolen glances when he sat up and asked Tyree to tuck him in. He gladly obliged, feeling ecstatic that he still wanted him with Mia being there. He knew his son loved him, but he also knew that he and Mia were as close as any child and mother could be. As hard as he tried, he could never be the parent she was.

Tyree walked him to the room and tucked him in before reading him one of his favorite stories. Kyan fell asleep as soon as he was done, and Tyree leaned over to place a kiss on his forehead.

Smiling over at his greatest creation, Tyree backed out of the room, bumping into Mia, who was listening in the hallway.

"Sorry, I'm clumsy. I was just making sure he didn't need anything."

"It's cool, he's fine. He is sleeping like a baby." Tyree grinned.

"Good. So are you going to wait a little while or are you out of here? I know Renee is probably waiting up for you."

Tyree huffed at the mention of her name. For a second, he had almost forgotten the latest disagreement. Things had gotten so out of hand between them, and he needed some clarity. He also needed her to be the strong and confident woman he first met, not this insecure version he was dealing with now.

"I'm going to get out of your hair and let you have some down time, but I doubt I'll be going home just yet. I need to clear my head. I swear, I can talk to anyone about anything, but when it comes to my little man, I get nervous. I don't want him to see the flaws in his dad. I know he looks up to me, and I just want to keep that admiration. Is that crazy or what?"

"It's not crazy. I mean we've been apart for two years, but I can't bring myself to tell him that we're never moving back here. He misses it so much, and I just feel awful."

"I know you have a life there and you have Jake, but are you okay with being away from everything and everyone? I know you love it there, but I miss him. I wish I could be the dad who's around him every day. I feel like I'm failing him by not being there."

"I'm sorry. I really am, but I can't stay here. Being here now is hard enough." She turned and walked into the living room. "God, why can't this be simple?"

"Mia," he said, putting his hand on her shoulder, "nothing with us will ever be simple. We have been through so much, and I don't think we will ever forget it. Our past isn't pretty, but we can give him more if we just work together."

Before he could form a thought, she turned and flung herself into his arms. Holding on tight, he relaxed against her. He hadn't felt so content in a long time. He stayed in the moment until she pulled away, backing toward the hallway. He once again felt the sting of her rejection, and he straightened up. He was all set to leave when he heard cries coming from Kyan's room. They both ran toward the screams and walked in to find him sitting up in the bed, searching the room frantically.

"Daddy, someone was here! I felt someone touch me!"

Tyree raced over and looked at the window that was closed and then back at Mia. Her eyes were huge, and she was trembling. "Mia, you see something?" When she shook her head, he flew over, pulling Kyan into his embrace. He rocked him, running his hand down his back, and Mia joined them, putting her arms around the both of them.

Mia laid her head against Kyan's back, as he drifted back into a peaceful sleep. Tyree hadn't looked away from the window, and when he felt her hand swipe over his, he squeezed, closing his eyes. "Mia, I'm not leaving him tonight. I'll stay right here and sit up all night if I have to. I'll find some blankets and get settled on the floor. I'll be right here if anything happens."

"No." She jumped up and crossed her arms over her chest.

"Mia, I won't leave my son or you. I—"

"I don't want you to."

Tyree looked at her in confusion and shifted to the side with Kyan still in his arms. "What are you saying?"

She grabbed his hand and pulled him up, leading him to her bedroom, and she opened the door. She sat down and scooted across the bed, signaling for him to join her. Following her lead,

Tyree climbed in, placing Kyan between them, and he lay back on a pillow, trying to relax into the bed he had missed immensely over the years. When she turned to him and placed her hand on his, he gave her a gentle squeeze and closed his eyes, trying to block out all the thoughts racing through his mind. He wanted this all to be a horrible nightmare, and he hoped that's all it was as far as Kyan was concerned.

Tyree, Mia, and Kyan all fell asleep intertwined in the bed. But after a few still moments, Tyree arose, suddenly feeling uneasy about something, and he looked around frantically before looking back down to the two sleeping forms beside him. They looked peaceful, and he soon found his way back, deciding to deal later with the consequences of whatever tonight would bring.

Chapter Eight

Tyree sat up at 3:00 a.m., looking around with sweat beads rolling down his face. He realized he had been sweating for quite a while. Mia was always cold and never ran the AC. It always drove him crazy in the past but, now, he was just happy with the familiarity. It was what he needed in times like these.

As Tyree continued to scan the room, he almost fell over when he saw something moving in the dark. When he swung over and swatted in the direction, he heard a yelp from the other side of the bed. He raced over when he realized he had smacked Mia against the face.

"I'm sorry." He dropped to his knees, running his hand down her face. "Are you okay? I didn't mean to hurt you."

"I'm all right, Ty. I just startled you. I know you would never hit me on purpose."

She tilted her head and, with the angle she held it at and the streaks of light the moon cast through the window, he saw the twinkle her eyes held as she stared at him. It was like she used to look when they were in love. He had convinced himself it had died in her, but now he saw it and inched his lips closer, capturing the moment. But Mia lowered her head, causing his kiss to land on her cheek.

"Tyree, don't. I don't want to make a mistake. We have people in our lives we could destroy with this, and I don't want to do that just for a fling."

"A fling? We will never be just a fling, Mia. We were together for ten years; we have a son. There will always be more between us."

Mia looked up over at him, and a tear fell down her cheek. "None of that matters; it wasn't real. It was just two kids making an impulsive decision. We rushed into marriage and having our son, and we got comfortable. Don't get me wrong, I don't regret anything about him. He's the most important thing in my life, but he was the reason we made it so long, Tyree."

Tyree sank down on the floor and moved his hand from her cheek. Her words stung more than he ever imagined and, before she could utter another word, he got up and took his place on the other side of the bed. He lay there staring at the ceiling until she spoke again.

"It was a dream, right?"

"What?"

"Kyan, his screaming. No one was there, right? I mean, there's security all over, and no one could get in unless they knew this place intimately. They would have to know the grounds, as well as one of us. Right?"

Tyree huffed, tossing it around in his mind; then he threw his hands behind his head. "I guess it's possible. Maybe being here is making him a little on edge. I know he loves this house, but maybc it just made everything come crashing back." The day Kyan was kidnapped had been playing in his head from the moment he stepped through the door, and he knew it had to be affecting her too. "You know I'm sorry, right?"

"About just now? Don't be. We got caught up in a moment. No harm done."

"Yeah, about that, but about everything else, too. I feel like this is my fault. I never got to say these things to you before. I just feel like if I had maybe—"

"I still would have left. Things just started to become evident about us."

"What things?"

"We weren't right anymore. There were so many secrets, so many lies, and that made things hard."

"I never lied to you."

"If you believe that, then you're lying to yourself. There was nothing honest about us. We began sneaking around, and we ended because of those same deceptive tendencies."

"It was never like that, Mia."

"Tyree," she whispered. He could hear the pain in her voice. "Can we not do this? I want to drop it. It's over and done with. Our son is the only thing that matters."

"Okay, but know one thing, Mia."

"What?"

"I loved you. I always did."

She didn't reply. She just put her hand over his and rubbed it. He only wished she could believe him. Everything in him wanted her to, but maybe too much damage had been done. They just had to get past this and possibly be friends as well as parents. With everything floating through his head about what was wrong, he was shocked that she still hadn't let go of his hand.

Tyree didn't know what this meant, but he felt like maybe he was getting through to her. The way she was caressing his hand said that she might be shedding some of the protective layers she had when it came to him. He needed her to if they were going to be what Kyan needed.

***

Tyree woke up, after sleeping better than he had in weeks, to find Mia staring out the bedroom window blankly. She was in her own little trance, and when she heard him moving behind her, she turned, and he saw all those walls he tore down flying back around her. He knew last night was a display of her vulnerability, but today she had it in check and was on the defense. When he walked over and touched her shoulder, she sidestepped him and walked toward the door. He sat there baffled until she spoke.

"I made breakfast, and Ky is in the dining room with your mother. She came over early. Apparently, everyone has been looking for you and Renee was kind enough to direct them here."

"Look, I'm sorry about—"

"About what? She's your fiancée; I would expect her to know where you are. I just hope she doesn't think anything is going on here, because that would be a bad assumption."

"I explained that everything I'm doing is for him. No one means more than he does." He tossed his shirt on and walked in to find Karen sitting with Kyan, telling him a story about her hiking up a mountain with John. He was laughing thinking of her on an adventure. Karen seemed like a prissy type of woman, but the more you got to know her, the more you saw her rugged interior.

"You see, your grandfather never liked the mountains much, but I had been climbing before." Karen grinned.

"Really?" Kyan beamed. "Who took you? Mama and Daddy would never take me. Mama thinks I'm a baby."

"Your great-grandfather Akio took me. And you too little? That's nonsense. You're my oldest and bravest grandson."

"I'm your only grandson. Granny, what was your dad like? Aunt Asha says Dad is like him. Is that true?"

"He was an engineer in Japan." Scratching her chin, she let out a glorious smile. "Yeah, I guess your dad is like him. He was smart, and he helped Grandpa John start up the company."

"Wow. Did he like Grandpa? Dad says he didn't."

Not really wanting to get into the past bad blood between John and Akio, Tyree interjected, bringing their conversation to a halt. "Little man, it's time for you to get dressed."

When Karen looked up from her story with Kyan, she offered Tyree a bright smile, and he greeted her with an equally pleasant grin. Over the years, Tyree had his share of difficulties with his family, but his mother was always one he could count on. They were probably the most alike in the whole family.

"Okay, Dad." Standing, Kyan leaned down to hug Karen's neck. "Will you finish your story?"

"Some other time." She ran a hand over his head.

"Mom, what's up?" Tyree pulled her into a loose embrace.

"Well, your dad and brother were looking for you. They hadn't heard anything back from you regarding the papers Miguel dropped off, and you know how he is."

Tyree ran his hand over his short hair. "I thought I told Miguel not to mention it to him. God, now I'm never going to hear the end of it. I swear sometimes I think that partnering up with them was a terrible idea. Too much history involved."

He knew Karen could tell by his tone that things weren't going well between him and Mia. Only she could get him so rattled that he would question a multimillion-dollar decision. He knew as well as she did that the business was a sound idea then and even better now given the numbers. Even with all the backlash from Richmond's dirty deeds, they were still making a fortune after settling some embarrassing suits filed against the company.

"Son," Karen said, looking at Kyan, "how about you come with me? We can sit and discuss the business elsewhere."

Tyree too looked at his impressionable son, and he shook his head slowly. "Yeah, you're right. Just let me tell Mia I'm leaving."

Tyree walked into the bedroom, found her standing in the same place, and called out to her, but she never turned around. When he told her he was going, she nodded her head subtly without facing him.

After Tyree left, Mia felt like she could finally relax. She had been standing in front of the window telling her heart what her head already knew: they wouldn't work. She just needed to believe it because last night, after he fell asleep, she found herself leaning over placing sweet kisses on his lips. He never stirred, she was sure he never felt it, but she couldn't get it out of her head. She wanted him more than she was willing to admit, and it scared her. After everything they had been through, she couldn't go back there, not with him.

Mia looked at the door wanting to run after Tyree and tell him that she still loved him and everything she said was a mistake, but she knew she needed to be strong. Instead, she grabbed her phone and proceeded to text the only person who could make sense of things for her. After sending the first text, she sighed, waiting for a reply; and she almost fell over when it came. She reread her text and smiled.

I need you. Please come.

I'm so glad to hear from you. I wanted to give you your space. I hoped everything was fine, but I can see that it's not. I have some things to wrap up, and I'll see you in a week. Is that soon enough?

A week is perfect, although I wish it could be sooner. I miss you like crazy.

I miss you too, and I have something for you.

I can't wait. God, I love you.

And I love you. See you soon.

Chapter Nine

"Okay, so do you want to tell me what's going on or do I need to guess?" Karen looked at Tyree, and he knew he looked like a wounded puppy. She had him follow her home to talk about whatever was on his mind. He knew she was ready to let him vent.

"Nothing, Mom. We had a setback with Kyan; he had a bad dream."

"I know all about my grandson. I'm asking about his mother and father. What was going on when I arrived?"

"I was asleep when you arrived." He laughed, trying to bring some humor into the situation.

"Tyree Akio Johnston, lying to your mother is not wise. You know I see through you. Now tell me what happened that has you so irritated."

"It's still early. Do we really have to get into this? Could we just go upstairs and let Dad yell at me about Richmond?" he joked.

"I know it's serious for you to request an argument with your father. Is Mia planning on cutting Kyan's trip short or something?"

"I don't think so, not just yet. We have to talk to him about us, but it's not that."

"Well, don't keep me in suspense. And what is this 'us' business? Did something happen between you two?"

"Of course. We fought. It seems to be our norm. And the best part is she told me we meant nothing. Apparently, if it weren't for Kyan our ten years would have been much shorter."

Karen pulled him to her, rocking him in an embrace. "I'm sorry. I know it must hurt to hear her say that, and I know she doesn't mean it."

"Oh, she meant it. I just don't know what went wrong. She was everything to me at one point, and to say it means nothing is bull . . . it's ridiculous," he cut himself off, remembering who he was talking to.

"Honestly, you could have finished the word." She chuckled. "I know how you feel, and it is bullshit. She loved you more than anything. You weren't here to see how that girl fell apart when both you and Kyan were missing. She really went off the deep end for a while. She would only talk to Asha, Cassie, and Milan. Asha and Milan went over there and sat with her for weeks until that snake showed up."

"Mom, everyone else raves about how great Jake is, but not you. Why do you think he's a bad guy?"

"He stole my boy's family. I don't give a damn how much other people like him. He took what's yours, and I just don't trust anyone who would do that. He could never be as great as you."

"You know you're crazy, right? Nevertheless, I love you for it. I swear you always have my back."

"Of course I do. You're my first born, and I love you. Just so you know, your sister was your biggest cheerleader when you were gone. She tried to stop what was going on, but it was just a dark time. I know you have this whole other life, but sometimes people break away from each other just to find their way back. I think it's the case with you two."

"I think that ship has sailed. How can I even want a woman who would run out on me when things get tough? You know what I went through for her."

"You both went through things, and you will work it out. I'm sure of it."

"How can you be so optimistic? I mean, look at who you're married to."

"Your father is a soul I just happen to understand."

"He almost cost you your family." Grabbing her hand, Tyree hated the look that formed after his statement. "I'm not trying to upset you. I just know how hard it was for you, and he's not exactly husband of the year. I know how close you and Grandfather were."

"We were and, yes, we never quite got it back, but he loved you kids. If I had married the man they wanted, I wouldn't have my beautiful children."

Tyree had heard the story of his parents' meeting so many times growing up. It all sounded so fairytale like when he was a kid but, growing into an adult, he realized what she gave up for his ass of a father. Their grandfather was smart; he knew Karen could have done better than John and, consequently, so did Tyree. His mother was a smart and adventurous woman before she met his father, and Tyree felt her light had been dimmed by him. He didn't even want her working, despite her college degree.

As much as his father claimed the marriage to Karen was a love match, Tyree knew deep down that it was just a smart business decision on his behalf. It was his grandfather, Akio, and his influence that helped John get Johnston Incorporated off the ground. John had the backing from his father's wealth, and Akio's business sense helped them get established as an international powerhouse.

Fifteen years into their business venture, Akio suffered a massive heart attack, leaving his claim to the company to Karen with the stipulation that the kids would someday take over. Tyree knew he was meant to take over, but it wasn't a decision he made lightly. He had other dreams, but his loyalty to his family was something he couldn't ignore and, with Mia gone, it didn't seem to matter anymore. Much to John's delight, once Tyree's divorce was final and he was over the initial shock, he took his birthright and became CEO.

"You think it was all worth it?"

"What? Having you kids?"

"And marrying Dad." He sat back on the couch.

"I don't regret my life, and you shouldn't regret yours either. We make mistakes to grow from them. You and Mia are unfinished."

"We have nothing left to go back to. I did all I could to hold on to her."

"I know, and I think at some point you both were wrong. You can only get back what you put in."

"I put in everything."

"So did she. She just doesn't know that you did the same. Talk to her, again, without all the anger and resentment."

"I wasn't angry."

"Drop the innocent act. I know you like the back of my hand. You let your anger come out, and she shut down. Give me some credit."

"Okay," he conceded, standing from the chair he inhabited.

"Where are you going?"

"Home. Before I get into anything with Mia, I need to take care of my actual house. I need to put out the fire there."

"So you're just going around pissing everyone off today, huh?"

Tyree laughed and hugged her tight. "You know, to be such a lady, you sure have a foul mouth."

"I learned from the best," she smirked, nodding toward the stairs where John was. "He taught me well."

"Good-bye, crazy woman," Tyree yelled on his way out the door, heading to figure out his next step.

Chapter Ten

Tyree walked in to find the sweetest smell greeting him. For a second, he thought he had the wrong house. There was no way that, after the blowup and him staying out all night, she was up cooking for him. When he rounded the corner and found Renee in a lacy negligee stirring pancake batter, he rubbed his eyes and inhaled sharply, taking her all in. She didn't turn around, but he could tell she knew he was there by the way she swayed her hips walking to the stove.

"Rough morning?" she asked sweetly.

"Rough day, night, and morning, but this makes it all worth it."

"What?"

He walked over and placed his hands on the counter in front of her, trapping her body in between. "Coming home to find my delicious woman in the kitchen making me a king's breakfast. I would say all the bull was worth it if I get to come home to you."

"Is that what you still want? I know you've been going down memory lane with your family all intact now."

"I just need my son. All that other stuff is irrelevant. You and Kyan are my family."

Renee smiled and, when she turned around, he saw the worry leaving her face.

"You were upset. Did you think I had left you?" He lifted her chin.

"I didn't think that, but . . . I thought maybe you missed her. I get it: you have history, and it's hard to erase."

"We have history, yes, but I'm only interested in the future right now. Our future."

Renee grinned and leaned in to kiss him, pulling his body into hers. After a few intense moments, she pushed him back, smirking. "Go."

"Go where?"

"Upstairs. You should get a shower, and I laid some clothes out on the bed for you."

Tyree nodded and rushed up the stairs to find his favorite blue shirt and slacks on the bed. He wondered at that moment how he got so lucky. Sure, everyone thought Mia was the one; but he knew they were wrong. Renee was always doing things like this, and he felt shitty for the way he had been treating her. She deserved better.

While Tyree was upstairs, Renee was still in the kitchen, putting the finishing touches on his breakfast when her phone rang. She looked at the caller ID and huffed, clutching the phone tightly in her hand before snatching it to her ear.

"What do you want?"

"Well, hello to you too," a man's voice replied. "I think you already know what I want, so what's your progress?"

"I'm right in the middle of something, and if you will excuse me, I can get started."

"You listen to me," the man snapped. "You have one purpose for being there, and if you fuck me over, you'll be pushing up dirt. Don't think this is a game."

"I know. I've heard it all before. Are there any more threats you would like to relay before I slam this phone in your face?"

"Yeah, one more. If he ever finds out I'm behind this, money will be the least of your worries. I'll make sure to do to you what happened to the others. Don't underestimate me, girl."

"I would never," Renee hissed and tossed the phone on the countertop. She sucked in a deep breath and closed her eyes. She knew when she entered this ridiculous mess that she would regret it and, now, she was cornered. The worst part was, she actually felt something for Tyree now. It was no longer just about the money and power.

Thinking over her dilemma, Renee made a decision and walked up the stairs briskly, wanting to be in Tyree's arms before all hell broke loose. She was overjoyed to see that he was still in the shower and she stripped her clothes off to join him. Pulling the door open and feeling the steam engulf her was wonderful. She needed this as much as she needed him at the moment.

"Hey, you joining me?"

"Yeah, do you mind?"

"Sounds like a plan to me." He snaked his arms out to pull her closer. "Wash my back?"

"Yeah." She smiled, grabbing the sponge from behind him, squeezing the water down his back. "I thought I could do a little more than that since we have the house to ourselves and all."

"I love the way you think."

Lifting Renee into his arms, Tyree's simple shower began to become hazy. Wrapping her legs around his waist, he slipped inside her, turning his back to accept the steady flow from the shower. Pushing her up against the wall, he buried himself deep, holding his hands under her arms to stabilize her body. When she rolled her hips to him, he pushed harder, causing a loud whimper to fall from her lips. After a few minutes, she wrapped her arms around his neck and crushed her breasts into him as he continued to take her higher.

"Uhhh, Tyree," she screamed as he moved in and out of her with such exquisite perfection it made his knees shake a little. The sound he made pulling out and plunging back in was crazy enough without all the screams of pleasure. The screams made everything seem a lot more real in his mind.

Tyree was swimming inside her, and he pushed as hard as he could, trying to block out everything. He wanted Mia out of his head and heart, and Renee was just the person to do it. With every thrust, she met him halfway, causing the best friction they had ever shared. For the first time since he started this relationship with her, he saw only her face. Renee was finally the only one he was thinking about at that moment. The realization pushed him further, and he secured her legs around him and grabbed her hands, sliding them up the slippery shower wall.

Thrusting his hips forward, Tyree pushed her body up and down the wall as he continued to grip her hands tightly. She dug her nails into his hand, causing a sting that only drove him mad. Letting her hands drop, he slid his hands down to grip her hips, spreading her legs farther apart.

Renee then leaned forward, whispering in his ear and kissing his lips gently; and that's when it all came back to him.

Tyree kept pounding into her and, through his haze, memories of last night came to the forefront, and he almost dropped Renee. She gripped her arms tighter around his neck, and he snapped back and looked at her. He kept moving inside her, trying to wash the memories away, but he kept seeing Mia's face and feeling her kisses—her sweet, gentle kisses—on his lips. Honestly, he couldn't be sure if it was real or if he had dreamt it all up. It felt real, or maybe he was just hoping it was.

Tyree was floored by the thoughts and was hating himself for it. He needed to get Mia out of his system. Renee was the future, and he was once again letting the past interfere with what he was supposed to be doing. Focusing on Renee, Tyree ran his hand over her beautiful face and, in an instant, he covered her lips with his. She kissed him back with such hunger, he leaned back into her, pulling her legs tighter around him and he pushed her back into the wall. Renee let out a loud moan, and he covered her breast with his mouth.

"Tyree, oh, God, Tyree. I love you."

He stiffened for a second still not finding the strength to say it back and then he started ramming her so hard her head flew back. He devoured her neck with his kisses, and her legs tightened around him. He knew she was just about to hit her peak and he dove in, hitting a particular spot that caused her to fold in his arms. Her loud screams floated through the shower, and he slid her down the wall to land on her feet. He knew the fact that he hadn't climaxed hadn't escaped her. He just hoped she didn't know the reason why.

When he stepped out of the shower, she grabbed his arm, turning his body back to her. He lifted her in his arms and walked backward into the room, crashing onto the bed with her still on top. Renee slid up to straddle him, and Tyree's head shot back to a pillow, his hands finding her hips. When she raised her body and slammed back down, his head shot up, and he began to caress her breasts. Swinging her head back and forth, Renee leaned down to bite down on his earlobe.

"Tyree, you never tell me you love me. Don't you love me, baby?"

Tyree was in his own euphoria, but when he heard her question, he sobered and looked into her eyes, trying to gather the right answer.

"I feel things for you, Renee, but I'm not a guy who goes around screaming 'I love you' every day. It's just not me. I care, you know that."

Renee continued to rock on top of him, but he could tell she was pissed by his admission. She placed her hands on his chest and pushed herself down as far as she could go and dug her nails into his chest. He knew she did it on purpose and, deep down, he felt like he deserved it. He had been dodging this subject for a while, and he felt like maybe he wasn't being fair to her.

A few minutes passed, and Renee climaxed again and rolled off him leaving him stunned. He knew she was pissed, but she had never left him unfulfilled. This was new to him, and he didn't know what to make of it. When he called out her name, she turned to him with a sinful smirk, tilting her head to the side.

"What is it, Tyree?"

"You okay? I mean, are we okay? You just kinda seemed different just then."

"We're fine, Tyree." She smiled sweetly. "I know what you feel, and I'm the one with the ring, right?"

"Yeah," he murmured, "but—"

"No buts. We're good. I just need to know that, no matter what happens, you remember that I gave everything to this."

"You gave? What are you trying to say, Renee? Are you saying we're done?"

"Of course not. I'm just getting started with you. You and I have a long road ahead of us." She leaned in to kiss him. "You're not getting rid of me that easy." She walked to the door and turned to look at him again. "You should get to work. Miguel and Asha have been calling all morning."

Watching her walk away, Tyree knew he was in for one hell of a day. He just couldn't seem to do anything right. As he got dressed to head into work, he thought about what he would do once he was face-to-face with his father and brother. Miguel was going to be a piece of cake, but he knew whatever John had to say wasn't going to be pleasant.

Tyree finished getting dressed and walked down the stairs to find Renee sitting at the table, eating breakfast. When he just poured himself a cup of coffee and headed to the back door, she tilted her head and put her hand on her cheek. "Aren't you going to eat?"

"I don't have much of an appetite this morning. I think I'm going to head on in, but I was wondering if you want to have dinner later."

"Sounds good." She looked up from her plate. "Let's make it a couples thing. Invite Asha and Terence."

"I'll ask and see what they have planned. I'll call you before we leave the office." He turned to look at her one more time before walking out the door. "Renee, you know I'm sorry I'm not always who you want me to be, right? I just get intimidated by your feelings sometimes. I'm not the most vocal person, but I do love you."

Renee dropped the fork she was holding and looked up at him with tear-filled eyes. She looked overwhelmed by what he had just admitted.

He couldn't believe he had finally said what she had been waiting to hear after all this time. As quickly as he saw the happiness appear, it dropped, and he had no clue why.

"I love you too, and thank you for finally telling me."

"Thank you for being here. I know I haven't been the best or the easiest to get along with, but I appreciate everything you've done for me."

"Please don't," she replied, and he felt a pang of guilt. He knew he was the reason for her disbelief, but he wanted to be better.

"Don't worry, babe. You will get everything you deserve. I promise you that." He smiled and walked out, closing the door behind him.

***

Tyree had been gone for more than ten minutes, and Renee was still in shock. After pulling out her phone and placing a call, she closed her eyes. When a man's voice answered, she sighed into the phone.

"What's the plan to get me out of this? I don't want to end up with nothing."

"You won't, remember? You will have everything we discussed if you just follow my lead."

Renee hung the phone up and laid her head on the table. This was just too complicated for words. She came into this with a clear head and, now, with all the time she spent with Tyree, she was in too deep. Now she just had to play the role until she could get out unscathed. If Tyree ever found out what she was doing, he would blow up, causing a storm that would affect everyone involved.

Chapter Eleven

Mia walked into the mansion, noting all the changes Cassandra had made. It seemed different, and she was pleased. The mansion was where some of her happiest moments happened and also some of the worst. She had walked up with Kyan to bring him for his day with Cassandra. She had spoken with Tyree on his way to work and agreed to keep things normal until they had the situation figured out. She also promised him she would remain in Atlanta for the remainder of the month, which was three weeks in total.

Mia was hesitant about being there so long, but when Kyan overheard her discussing it and jumped for joy, it was hard to say no. As much as she regretted the decision, at least she would have backup in a week. She was counting the days until she could feel comfort in the one person she always confided in, the biggest part of her life besides Kyan. Mia looked around in amazement until her eyes found *the* room. She hadn't been near it since the day she found her mother's body slumped over the desk after the overdose. Letting go of Kyan's hand, she ushered him upstairs until she heard the familiar ramblings of her big brother.

"Yes, tell them it's being handled. There is no way he will get anywhere near any of the businesses . . ." He stopped short when he saw her standing there. "Miguel, I'll have to continue this call later. I think I see a ghost." He laid his headset down on a small end table, making his way to her in record speed. "What are you doing here? I thought I would never see you in Atlanta again."

She wrapped her arms around him and exhaled. "Cassie didn't tell you I was coming? I got in last night. Tyree picked me up."

"Tyree? When did you two start talking? This is all news to me. Sit down and tell me everything."

As Mia went over what had happened, from the phone call from Cassandra to the screaming fit Kyan had last night, Rick sat listening, running his hand through his coal black hair. She saw his handsome face contort and relax more than she wanted to; and, when the story was concluded, she placed a hand on his lap, bringing his eyes to meet hers. "So, what do you think?"

"I think you staying here is an excellent idea. I'll have Felipe take over until you return or permanently; it's up to you. We could definitely use you here."

"I'm going back as soon as the month is up. I just need to be here until we figure out a more permanent custody agreement. I think him only seeing his dad a few weeks here and there is wearing on him."

"Yeah, but what else is there unless you move here? He has school and all the travel will make him crazy."

"That's what we need to figure out, but we have time. We will talk about it."

Rick smiled and nodded. "I'm glad you two are being more civil. I always wondered why you couldn't even speak if it only concerned Kyan. I mean, don't get me wrong, I never minded the trips, but I just thought it was strange."

"It was what I needed to do to get him out of my head. If I had to keep seeing him then, I would have never moved on."

"And did you?"

"Yes," she answered quickly, obviously alerting every suspicion in his mind.

"I know you didn't come here to talk about Tyree, so what brings you up?"

"Oh, I hear Kyan spends his days with Aunt Cassie, and I wanted to keep up the tradition. I want him to have as much time with you guys as he can before we have to go home."

"I really wish you would rethink that. I know you have things going for you there, but do you think Jake would be interested in moving with you? I mean, we could find a place for him at Livingston and make it a family thing."

"He has obligations there. He and his brother are revamping the family business, and he needs to be there to see it through. Apparently, their family used to be a big name there until they hit bankruptcy."

"That's good. What is the business?"

"You know, he's really been keeping it under wraps. He says he doesn't want to jinx it, and he doesn't want us offering to help because of our influence and money. They're very proud."

"A man after my own heart. Well, at least I don't have to worry about him trying to get your money." He laughed. "I'll tell you, Cassie thinks Renee is after Tyree's fortune."

Mia swallowed hard and was met with a pair of worried eyes.

"What's going on? Do you know something I don't?" he asked.

"Not exactly. I just know that Kyan isn't fond of her for some reason. I would have thought it was because he thinks she's the reason we aren't together, but he loves Jake. Have you noticed anything when she's around him?"

"I haven't, but you know I wouldn't allow anyone to mistreat my only nephew. What has he said?"

"That's the thing. He says she's nice to him, but he is just closed off when it comes to her."

"Kids know when people aren't genuine. I don't hate the girl, but I think a lot of the stuff she does is fake. Nobody is that nice. You should meet her. See for yourself."

"Me, meet her? I don't think that's a good idea."

"Why not? She's going to be around your son if they get married. You need to be able to feel content that he is taken care of."

"She will not be taking care of my son. That is his dad's job and mine. I don't let Jake assume that responsibility and neither will she."

When Mia saw his smirk, she knew what he was thinking. Rick had been there from the start to the end of her and Tyree, and he knew how territorial she was. He knew just like she did that she would meet Renee and pick out everything that was wrong about her and it would be on from there. She might not have had any interest in taking Tyree back, but she still wanted him with the right woman, if she even existed.

"Okay, Mia. Whatever you say, but I think you two should meet. If anything, she just needs to know who will be kicking her ass if she messes up with Ky."

"I'll think about it. Anyways, what's this Tyree says about Dad's name being on some papers for the company? Tell me it's a joke. I thought we blocked all his attempts when he came up with those false documents claiming Mom and Janelle left him their shares."

"Actually, his name was, but it's handled now. Those documents were obviously forged. There is no way either of them would have left him anything. He had Janelle's shares, but it wasn't by her doing. It was something that had been in place since we were little."

"Explain it to me: how did he get his greedy hands on anything?"

"Well, when Janelle died, her shares defaulted to him. He had it set up that if anything ever happened to either of us, everything would go back to him. Mom's were passed to us when we first ousted him. She didn't have as many as we did, neither did Janelle, and because we were so busy with other things, Janelle's never got switched back. He isn't active in anything.

I just had to sign the proper paperwork, and voilà, you and I have an even split. This addendum he keeps trying to push states that they both willingly signed over their shares to him. If that were true, he would have more votes than we do. I would never let that happen."

"Okay, just make sure we stay ahead of this. I don't want any surprises when it comes to him. It already feels surreal that Mom and Janelle are not here. I would give anything to be able to give those shares back to them. I miss them every day."

"Me too. I feel like a failure. I was supposed to be her big brother and Mom's protector, and I really botched the job. I was supposed to protect you all, and I let them get killed and your son got taken on my watch."

"What happened to Janelle was an accident, and what happened to Kyan wasn't your fault."

"What about Mom? It was my decision to not send her back to rehab. I really thought she had kicked the habit that time. She was so excited about us all working together and being around Kyan. I just thought she had changed."

"She was better. She was different those last few months, and I thought she was fine too. She loved him, you know. She couldn't call to talk to him enough, and Kyan loved talking to her. I just hate he was here that night. I know he was young, but I think deep down he still remembers."

"Maybe, but he is such a well-rounded child. You would never know the horrors he has been through. I just still can't believe she would resort to drugs while watching him. I just thought she was better than that."

"I still blame myself. I know she was his grandmother, but she had a history of drug abuse. I should never have let her be alone with my son."

"It's crazy. At the time, it really did a number on Kyan. He went into all these stories of imaginary friends. I'm glad he was playing hide-and-seek in the closet and missed her shooting up."

"He was sure there were voices and, God, how I wish it were true. It would at least mean she respected me enough not to do that in front of him."

"It would also mean that someone else did it, Mia. I think we both know Mom did this to herself and, besides, who would want to kill her? Richmond was already gone."

"You can't call him Dad? I don't know why I still do either. This is all his fault. If he weren't such an evil bastard, she would have never picked up that habit. As far as I'm concerned, he can burn in hell. I wish we had what we needed to get him put away. He's lucky."

"Yeah, he is, but I don't want you to think about that. All of it was beyond your control, but what happens next is all up to you."

"Meaning?"

"You know what I'm talking about. It's about time you forgave Tyree."

"I don't blame him anymore for what happened to Kyan. I know it could have happened with either one of us, but it changes nothing. I stand by my decision to leave him. Everything between us was a game. The only part that's real is our son."

"You can't mean that. That boy was crazy about you for years, and when Richmond finally figured out what was going on between the two of you, he threatened to—"

"Rick, stop," she interjected, cutting him off. "None of this matters. We are not together, and we never will be again. Just drop it." She knew he was about to get into it when she looked back with a tearful gaze. "Please don't make me do this with you. I don't want to discuss Tyree anymore, and I wish you wouldn't keep bringing him up. It's done, and I just want us both to move on."

Rick looked to her with a saddened expression and shook his head in agreement, watching as she paced the floor and eyed the door.

Nodding, he silently acknowledged her desire to leave, and he watched as she walked out the door.

Grateful that he had dropped the conversation, Mia got into her car and shed a steady flow of tears that she thought would never end.

Chapter Twelve

"Son, I know what Rick said, but I would like for you to look into it one more time. We have to be sure that Richmond is in no way affiliated with our business."

"Dad," Tyree huffed, "if Rick says it's taken care of, then trust him. God, why did you let us take over the business if you weren't going to trust our judgment? We have things under control. Just go home."

Tyree, Asha, and Miguel had spent the better half of the day contending with John about the business. Asha and Miguel voiced their input but, ultimately, it was Tyree who was the most combative. He always was when it came to John. The two were like oil and water.

"Tyree, you will not speak to me that way. I put my life into this company, and I won't have you run it into the ground by being oblivious to what's really going on."

"What, Dad? You mean oblivious like you were? Wasn't it you who allowed him access to our business in the first place? As far as I'm concerned, it's all your fault we ever had to deal with the slimy son of a bitch."

"You stop right there." John slammed his fist on the desk. "You know nothing about my dealings with him."

"Is that still what you think? I know more than you give me credit for. I know all about you and your sordid past with Richmond."

"Dad, what is he talking about?" Asha asked quietly.

John looked at his daughter apologetically, and Tyree looked on, waiting to see how much of the story he would actually tell. After all, they were adults now, and they deserved the truth even if it showed him in a not-so-good light. Tyree was already privy to the dirty details, and it fueled his resistance to his father.

"Listen," John sighed. "I'm not proud of what I have to say, but I might as well level with you. I don't want any lies among us."

Tyree laughed and crossed his arms over his chest. "Now, this I have to hear."

"Tyree, let him talk," Asha reasoned.

"In the early years of the business, we were doing okay, but we needed more revenue, more acquisitions. I met Richmond when Tyree was one, and we formed a friendship. At that point, neither of us had much, just our dreams. Years later, we partnered up, and he assisted me in acquiring several new properties. The money began to pour in, and I was grateful. I was finally able to pay my father back and take care of you children the way you deserved and, with Akio's help, we took off internationally."

"So, what's the problem here?" Miguel asked. "It sounds like getting his help was a sound decision. If it made you money, then I say it's a win."

"Not all money is good money," John supplied. "I never knew that when we were taking over these companies we were wiping them out. People lost their homes, their livelihood, and some even lost their lives when they wouldn't bend to his will. Once I found out, I took steps to end our involvement."

"So, you never knew? He stole people's companies like he did with Livingston?" Miguel had shock written all over his face.

"He robbed those people. I was ashamed when I found out. I went and confronted him about the deals, and he didn't even bother to lie. He sat there with this smug look and told me everything. I was livid, but there was nothing I could do. He had me cornered; and when Tyree wanted to marry Mia, things got even worse."

"So, you're telling me that you tried to keep me from marrying the woman I love because of the damn business? Does our happiness mean anything to you?" Tyree snapped.

"Your, your brother's, and your sister's happiness means everything to me. I just felt you weren't ready. You know I love Mia, and I am so proud of my grandson, but I thought you needed to live a little before making such a huge decision. I just wanted the best for you."

"You almost destroyed me! Do you know what I went through? The things I had to do, the lies I had to tell to the one person I loved most. It almost tore me apart."

"The fact that you had to lie meant maybe you two weren't ready."

"Don't you dare! She is the love of my life. I needed her; we needed each other. You don't know what a monster Richmond was. I needed to get her away from him before he ruined her like he did Helen."

"Tyree," Miguel whispered quietly, "I need to talk to you. Privately, please." He nodded at Asha and John and waited for the room to be free before he began again. "You want to tell me what that was all about? What was all that 'love of your life' stuff?"

Tyree looked at the door and then back at his brother's concerned face. "It's stuff none of us should have had to endure. I just wish they would let us lead our own lives. I just wanted her. All I ever needed was her."

"What happened? What did he do to you?"

"I don't want you involved. This is between him and me."

"Tyree, trust me. Maybe I can help."

"You can't, and it's no longer important. Mia and I are done. She will never know what I did, and I never plan to tell her. She never needs to know anything, and you promise me you will never bring this conversation up."

"How could I? I don't know anything. You won't tell me what it is that you've done. This whole thing with Dad is crazy, but that's not the most important thing here."

"What is? What are you talking about?"

"In the middle of all your ranting, did you realize that you called Mia the love of your life?"

"She was; you know that. She meant the world to me. Everyone knows that."

"You said 'is,' not 'was.' I told you I would stay out of it, but I can't let you do this. You can't marry Renee if you're still in love with Mia."

"Of course, I love Mia. She is the mother of my son, and it will never die, but it's not the same as being in love."

"I just don't see it with Renee."

"I know, and I really fucked up today."

"What did you do?"

"I told her I loved her, and I'm not sure I do."

Miguel ran his hand down his face. "Man, how do you feel about the girl? You either love her, or you don't. You may have love for her, but you're not in love with her. I can tell you that."

"I'm not even sure I love her at all. I thought I did, but today, looking at her, I realized I feel so conflicted about getting married. I don't even know why I asked her. I think I was still hurt over Mia. Now, I can't even get my head together when I'm around her. I know I should be a better man to Renee, but Mia is still an obstacle."

Miguel put his hands on the desk and closed his eyes, and Tyree knew he was trying to take it all in. "Tyree, what are you doing? Why are you playing these games with that girl? I might not be her biggest fan, but no one deserves to be jerked around. Why don't you just come out and tell her how you feel? Maybe she will help you make a decision. No one likes to be second best."

"She's not. I mean, maybe she is. I just don't know. Me saying anything to her is only going to make things worse. This morning was unreal. I got home after staying out all night, and she was cooking. Who does that? You know how women are, and the fact that I was with my wife—"

"Ex-wife," Miguel corrected him. "Mia's the ex."

"Yeah, whatever, but she was acting like everything was all good. It threw me off. Then, if that weren't crazy enough, she comes into the shower and gives me this crazy sex, and I was into it. I was way into it until I remembered what happened last night. Well, at least I think it happened."

Miguel's expression changed and his eyes bucked. "What happened? Did you and Mia have sex?"

"No. Kyan was in the bed with us, but I think she kissed me."

"You think?" He threw his hands up. "Wait, you slept in the bed with Mia, but you didn't have sex? Man, there was a time you couldn't keep your hands off her, and you had the chance and didn't? You let her kiss you, and you did nothing?"

"Once again, I said I think she kissed me, and it wasn't like that. She had been crying, and Ky was there. A lot was going on."

"Damn, that means she wants you too."

"Too? I'm confused about her, but I never said I wanted her. I'm just . . . I don't know what I am. These women just have me tripping."

"You know what I think?"

"I'm sure you're going to tell me."

"I think you need to take a day off and spend time with your son. He seems to be the only one you're sure about right now. I don't think anyone else can help you."

"Miguel, I know you, Asha, Terence, and Mom are always there. I never doubt you guys. I just need to figure out how to get a handle on it."

"What are you going to do?"

Tyree sat quietly debating, and he knew Miguel was waiting for him to come up with a solution. "Business as usual. I need to focus on how to be the man for Renee." He knew it wasn't the decision Miguel expected, and his expression was less than enthused. "I need you to get Terence down here."

"What can he do?"

"Have him draw up a prenup. I've decided: Renee is who I choose. Mia had her shot and, now, I need to focus on Renee."

"Tyree, can you marry her when you're not sure about Mia?"

"I want a fresh start. With Renee, I have that. It's just too complicated with Mia. Yes, I have feelings for her and I'm sure, with time, it will pass. I know I can find a way to love Renee. I just have to try harder."

"You shouldn't have to try. You should just feel it. So, you can just sit back and let Mia slip through your fingers again?"

"Yes," he replied harshly. "I need to find myself, and I feel like, with Renee, I can do that."

"I can appreciate that, but while you're on a quest to self-discovery, some other man is loving on your woman. You might be mad or hurt right now, but she is still very much yours. Not everyone gets a second chance."

Miguel walked out, leaving Tyree sitting at the table with his arms crossed over his chest. He knew there was some truth to what Miguel was saying, and every time he thought about Mia with Jake, it made his stomach turn. She was supposed to be his. Even with all the confusion, he longed to feel her touch. He knew he needed to stop thinking about her; and, when he finally decided to do so and focus on work, the door opened and there she was.

Mia stood with the door halfway open until he motioned for her to come in and close it. She shuffled nervously and finally came in, shutting the door, and she took a seat in the chair farthest from him. She looked like she had something on her mind, and he studied her, trying to read her expression. She was staring at him blankly until he cleared his throat, breaking her trance.

"What's going on, Mia? What brings you by?"

"I wanted to talk to you about what happened between us."

Tyree began to laugh harshly, and her head snapped to the side, signaling that she was in no mood for his attitude. When she crossed her arms over her chest, he knew he was in for it. "What is it, Mia? You left here without so much as a good-bye, and now I'm supposed to be interested in your explanation?"

"My explanation? You are the one who should be explaining things. You ruined us, not me."

"Here we go again. Dammit, I said I was sorry so many times. I'm a horrible father. I should have been watching him better. I know this, and no one has beaten me up more than myself. I've apologized, but what I won't do is sit here and let you make me feel even worse about it."

Mia's eyes blazed red with fury, and she stood looking ready to walk out the door. "I knew talking to you was a bad idea. This was not about him or that. I needed to talk to the man I once loved about where we went wrong, but I see he isn't here. God, how could I have been so stupid?"

She walked over, put her hand on the door-knob, and froze. "I thought maybe I made a mis-take, but I see I was right about you these past two years. I'm just glad I figured it out before I did something stupid like saying I still love you."

"No, Mia, it wasn't you who was wrong; it was me. I thought we had something real, and when you took my son, I realized we didn't. I loved you with everything I had, and for you to pack up and leave was low."

"And using me wasn't?"

She turned, and he saw the tears falling from her eyes, and he rushed over to comfort her. He pulled her to him, and she let him engulf her in a hug. She had her head on his chest as he caressed her hair and her neck, and then finally he ran his hand down her cheek.

"I would never use you. You infuriate the hell out of me, and I want to hate you for taking my son and leaving, but the truth is I love you. I can't stop loving you. Believe me; I've tried."

"You don't love me. You never did."

"If you believe that, then why did you kiss me?"

Her eyes bucked, and she blushed, and he knew it wasn't a dream. He had been right all along.

"Yeah, I thought it was a dream but, as the day wore on, it all became clearer, and I know it happened. Now, the question is, why? Why would you kiss me if you think all I did was use you, and where did you get a ridiculous idea like that?"

"I . . . Just because you feel nothing doesn't mean I don't feel anything. I have feelings for you against my better judgment. I know that nothing could ever come of it, but I was weak. Last night, you being there for me and Kyan almost felt like old times when we could depend on each other."

"And we can again. I swear I've never wanted anything but to love you, and I do."

"You love me so much, yet you got engaged to the first woman you slept with after me. You know, Jake has asked me to marry him several times, and I just can't say yes. He is great, and I should be jumping at the chance to marry him, but I'm stuck on stupid wanting you. I don't want to want you. I want to be free, but you have a hold on me."

"Baby, it's you who has the hold on me. When I asked her to marry me, I was convinced I would never see you again. I was drowning, and she pulled me up. I mistook my gratitude for love. I don't love her, Mia. I love you."

"Stop with the lies, Tyree. I'm done playing this game with you. When I go back home, I'm going to marry Jake and be happy. I can't keep waiting for you to be something you can't."

"You won't marry him. You love me. I know you do."

"I can't trust you."

"Trust me? You were the one who shacked up with him in my house while we were still married. I came home to find him sleeping in my bed, fucking my woman, and living the life that was supposed to be mine , Mia. Do you know how much that messed me up? I wanted to kill him. I thought about killing you." He chuckled. "I just . . . I lost it for a while."

Mia looked to him with sympathetic eyes. "He was never in our bed. You just don't understand."

"Maybe not while I was here, but I know you slept with him. I don't care what room he was in. I just know you had him in my house. Make me understand. I loved you so much. You could never understand the pain I felt coming home to find him there."

She walked over and brushed her lips across his, and he pulled her in, deepening the kiss. She stiffened, pulling back. Tyree reached for her, and she held her hand out to stop him. "Stop. You drove me to it. I was never more to you than a business deal."

"A business deal? What are you talking about?"

"You know what? Just forget I said anything. Until you can tell me everything, we have nothing to discuss."

"What everything, Mia? I don't know what you mean." She kept her distance, and he grew impatient. "Mia! You're not going to keep doing this to me. Come back here and tell me what I did."

"That's the sad part, Tyree. You've been lying to me for so long even you think it's the truth."

She left him in the room with a stunned expression, and he sat back down at the table. She couldn't possibly know everything, she just couldn't; and, if she did, how did she figure it out? Only two people knew the full truth, he and Richmond, and there was no way in hell Richmond would tell about their deal without damaging himself.

It was all too much, and he knew he needed to make things right. It was time he broke the promise he made to himself and came clean, telling her everything, because witnessing the pain in her eyes and her believing this botched version was painful for him. He would tell her everything, and then he could go back to hating her, or at least trying to.

Chapter Thirteen

Mia found herself on the elevator, trying to no avail to stop the tears that were cascading down her cheeks. When the door of the elevator opened, she wanted to kick herself for how she must have looked the first time she saw *her*. She didn't even need Renee to introduce herself. From all the stories Cassandra had relayed, she knew her at first glance. She was beautiful, which made it even harder to be facing the woman who had the man of her dreams. Mia looked her over for a few more seconds before Renee acknowledged her.

"Oh, I'm sorry, excuse me. Have we met?"

Mia had every intention of trying to be nice when she finally met her, but her fake introduction was making it difficult. She knew damn well who she was and vice versa. Renee stuck her hand out, making sure to flash the huge diamond on her hand. "No, we haven't," Mia supplied, deciding to play the game with her.

"I was just seeing my son's father about our evening. Kyan just loves our time together."

Mia saw something flicker in Renee's eyes then quickly disappear as Renee jumped back into character. "So you're Mia? Oh, goodness, how silly of me. I'm Renee, Tyree's fiancée."

"Well, this is such a coincidence us meeting here like random strangers when we're practically family. I guess it's a small world."

"Yeah, very."

"I've heard so many good things, and everyone speaks so highly of you. I wish you could have joined us last night when Tyree stayed over, but we just dropped like flies after dinner. We really could have gotten to know each other."

"Yeah, it would have been great, but I feel like I know you already. Kyan raves about you and everyone here loves you. They just couldn't believe you and Tyree split. They all thought you two were so perfect together."

Now, Mia was pissed. This smug-faced slut was sitting here rubbing her face in one of the hardest decisions she ever made. Before she could react, Tyree came stepping out of the elevator, halting the conversation. He looked at both women before speaking a word.

"Ladies, what's going on here?"

Renee stepped forward and leaned on his shoulder, placing a light kiss on his cheek. “We were just getting introduced. I’m so glad I finally get to meet the famous Mia. I just know we’re going to be fast friends.”

Tyree looked to Mia, and she could tell he wasn’t convinced. She knew he recognized the fake smile she was sporting. She was about ready to claw Renee’s eyes out and, surprisingly, he looked turned on. She hadn’t meant to let him see the jealous side of her but, she had to admit, it was refreshing to see the look in his eyes.

“Mia?” He cleared his throat. “Is that what happened? Are you two playing nice?”

Mia smirked and reached out to touch his chest. “Don’t worry, Ty, we’re fine. You picked a good girl.” She smiled, but she knew he could feel the heat radiating off her.

As she turned to walk away, he grabbed her arm, stilling her. “I’ll see you soon. Okay?”

“Sure,” she replied without facing him. She couldn’t bring herself to turn around when she heard Renee snickering behind her. It took every bit of restraint for her not to turn and smack the smirk right off her face. “So, should I set you a place for dinner tonight?”

“I have dinner plans, I’m sorry.”

She walked away after nodding.

And then, he called out to her again. "But I'll be there to put him down with you tonight. It's good that he knows we're both here and always will be."

Mia didn't turn, but she was wearing a smile, feeling like she had won that round. She was touched that, as angry as he was with her, he felt the need to make sure she knew they were in it together with their son.

Walking away, Mia watched the reflection in the glass of Renee throwing herself into his arms, practically draping herself over him. She wanted so badly to turn around and make her presence known, but she knew it would be pointless. In her mind, no matter what that little slut did, she would always have an advantage: she was the mother of his child and his one and only love. He had given her an in to fight for him. Now it was up to her to decide if there was anything worth fighting for.

Chapter Fourteen

Asha sat at the table, fidgeting with her bracelet as they waited for Tyree and Renee to arrive. It had been two days since the boardroom fiasco and Tyrcc had postponed their dinner until then. She was feeling out of place, agreeing to dinner when there was obviously something going on among Tyree, Renee, and Mia. It really felt like she was betraying some unwritten rule among them. Sure, she never had a problem with Renee, but Mia was family. She and Tyree may have been divorced, but she would always be like a sister to her. They had shared so much over the years.

Asha was flicking her manicured nails over the table until Terence put his hand on top of hers. "Hey, gorgeous, calm down. It's just your brother and Renee. Don't get so into all this drama surrounding them. It has nothing to do with us." He took his hand and lifted her chin. "You, me, and Meelah are fine."

Asha's thoughts drifted to her beautiful five-year-old daughter, and she smiled. Meelah was always the bright spot of her day.

Terence pulled her into a gentle embrace and kissed the side of her cheek. They were leaning on each other until Tyree showed up with Renee trailing behind him. He was wearing a grand smile that really concerned her. It wasn't his usual genuine smile; something about it was unnerving, as if it foreshadowed what was to come next.

Tyree took a seat after pulling Renee's chair out. He smiled at Asha and reached over to shake Terence's hand. The tension was thick until the waiter came over to get their drink orders. When Tyree ordered champagne, Asha put her hand over her face. Tyree never drank. This had to be a bad sign.

As hard as it was to bring Tyree out of that dark hole before, Asha saw him slipping down a similar path of destruction. She hated seeing this, and she knew only one person could fix it if he stopped being angry long enough to let her in. Mia was going to have to step in and heal him once and for all. Renee was able to pull it off temporarily, but only Mia could fill that empty hole in his heart. After all, she was the reason it was there. She knew Tyree had been promising to see her, but the night after their last argument, he just went home. Asha figured it was an attempt to ignore his problems.

When the champagne hit the table, Terence reached out to grab the bottle, but Tyree cut him off, pulling it out of his hand. Before Terence could protest, Tyree had four glasses filled, and he slid them over to each person. Asha had a big gulp from her glass, and Tyree let out a thunderous laugh. It was definitely going to be a night to remember.

Renee had been extremely quiet, and they all wondered why. She seemed pleasant enough, but something was off. Asha kept studying her, looking for an answer, but when Terence leaned to her and swept his hand over her thigh, she got distracted and averted her gaze. When the waiter came over to take their orders, they all gave him their attention for the two minutes he was there, and then they went back to an awkward silence. It wasn't until Terence broke the ice that they started up again.

"So, I don't mean to be rude, but what's going on here? It's really weird, and we have never had this much tension around us."

Renee looked at Tyree, and then he took the floor. "Nothing is wrong," he said, then pulled her hand to his lips and kissed it. "As a matter of fact, we had a talk and decided to move right ahead with the wedding plans. Which brings us to why we wanted you here tonight. Asha, Renee would like for you to be her matron of honor and, Terence, it's no secret I want you to be my best man. I mean, you'll have to kill Miguel, but it's what we want."

Asha was floored and not particularly impressed with Tyree and his mind games. She wanted to be as far away from this catastrophe as possible. Before she could be restrained, she slammed her hands down and leaned into Terence. "No."

"What?" Tyree looked genuinely surprised.

"I said no. Terence and I, we won't do it."

She could tell both Tyree and Renee were stunned by her loud declaration. She had always been supportive and, now, even she had thrown in the towel. As Tyree stared her down, Asha could see the questions in his eyes. "Asha, could I talk to you? Renee, Terence, could you give us a minute?"

"Yeah." Renee stood. "I need to make a call anyways."

Asha was sporting a mean glare while Tyree wore his sarcastic grin. "Don't sit there with that ridiculous smile while you're shaking everything up," she said.

"Come on, baby sis. You knew I was getting married. Stop acting so surprised."

"Tyree," she yelled a little louder than intended, watching him gulp down his fourth glass of champagne. "Slow down. I haven't seen you drink this much since—"

"Since Mia left me. Go ahead and say it."

"Tyree, what's wrong?" She placed a hand on top of his. "This isn't you. Tell me what's going on. I need to know."

"Baby girl, you really should calm down. I'm fine. I'm just celebrating."

"This isn't celebrating. This is you being destructive, and I can't watch you like this. Plus, you smell like you were at it before you got here."

"Will you calm down? I had a few shots, but I didn't drive. Renee did," he barked, startling her. "I'm not hurting anyone. I'm just having a little drink." He swung his arm out, spilling the remainder of the bottle on the floor. "Damn, now we need a new bottle."

"No. That's enough for you." She crossed the table, taking the seat directly beside him, and she took his hand in hers. "Why do you do this? Don't you know you have so many people in your corner only wishing the best for you?"

"I know that, and I love you all. There is nothing to be all stressed out about."

"Yes, there is."

"Like what? You tell me what I need to do."

"Tyree, what you need to do is, first, end this engagement; and then you need to go to Mia and talk about everything. Tomorrow, you go to her and tell her everything you want, no matter how good or bad. Just get it all off your chest."

"I'm seeing her tonight, right after this, in fact. I need to look at her and tell her what's on my mind."

By the time Renee and Terence were making their way back to the table, Asha had made up her mind that this was for the best. They needed whatever their talk would bring, even if it was closure.

They ate their dinner uncomfortably and sat looking at each other until Asha made a declaration. "You guys, I'm not feeling well, and I need Tyree at the house. Renee, do you think you could just drive his car home? I will make sure he gets back in the morning."

Renee rolled her eyes and crossed her arms in protest. "The morning? Why do you need him all night? You're a little old for a babysitter."

"I need him for a business matter. Not that I have to explain myself to anyone." Asha took offense to Renee's snappy tone. "I will take care of my brother."

"Fine," Renee huffed, snatching the keys and darting out of the restaurant.

Terence just looked on and scratched his head questioningly. "What's going on here?"

"He's going to Mia's. You know as well as I do that he needs this time with her, and I don't want him to go back to being that unimaginable bastard he was before."

"Asha, are you sure about this? She might not want him there like this. And what about Kyan?

He doesn't need to see or hear what's about to go down in that house."

"I'll call Cassie to go and get him. And, as for Mia, she needs to see him this way. Maybe it will knock some sense into their stubborn asses. She needs to know what this is doing to him."

"Hello, I'm still here. I can hear you." Tyree chuckled. "She's not seeing me like anything because I'm fine." Tyree walked out laughing while Asha and Terence stayed back to talk privately.

"Asha, this isn't like you to get involved. What happened?"

"I saw him spiraling and decided to take action before we had to go back to hiding his keys because we were afraid he was going to wrap his car around a tree."

"If one little visit could do this, then imagine what he would be like if she actually left again."

"That's why we need to make sure she doesn't. I am officially involved now. I'm doing whatever it takes to get those two stubborn fools back together."

"It could get messy. There is this little thing called an engagement that he has going on, and she lives with someone back home. Things could get out of hand."

"He doesn't want Renee, and now I'm convinced she's just here for the money. Something about that girl just rubbed me the wrong way tonight."

"I hate to be the bearer of bad news, but I have to tell you: he asked me to draw up a prenuptial agreement for them, and she signed it with no hesitation. That may be the cause of all the drinking tonight. I think he thought she wouldn't, and that would be his sign about her."

"So, what does that mean? Is she really a good girl I'm being a bitch to and overreacting about?"

"No. You should keep your eyes open. I have a feeling that something isn't right with her. Just because she signed the prenup doesn't mean she doesn't have an angle. I know women and any woman would be pissed to be presented with a prenup, but she didn't bat an eye. I think you should watch out for him on this."

"Oh, you can count on it." Asha stomped out of the restaurant. On her way to the valet, she found her big brother on the curb with a goofy grin. Even with all the animosity, she found herself smiling with him. It was amazing how they could have this dramatic scene and then be joking with each other afterward. It really showed how deep their love for each other ran.

Chapter Fifteen

The car ride was uncomfortably silent. Tyree was looking out the window as Terence drove. He felt like a child in the back seat. After minutes of protests to get dropped off at home where his car was, Asha finally prevailed, letting Tyree know that if he drove, she would call the police and report him herself. He knew she loved him and only wanted him safe, and if she had to turn him in to guarantee it, she would. Once she made her mind up, there was no changing it.

When they pulled into the gates and drove the back stretch to end up in Mia's yard, Asha turned and looked at Tyree encouragingly. "This is it; get in there and work this out."

"My only purpose here is to get this woman out of my system for good. I can't believe you shipped me over here like a child."

"You're acting like one, so I'll treat you like one. Get out of my car and make sure you're back by curfew." She giggled.

"You really annoy me." He kissed her cheek.

"I love you too, big brother. Good luck."

"Yeah, I'll need it."

Tyree exited Asha's car and, before he could protest, she drove off, leaving a trail of dust behind her. He waited until she was close to the gate and then he turned to walk up the hill and wait for the cab he was about to call. He loved his sister and, sure, he needed to talk to Mia, but right now wasn't the time. He needed to be completely sober to filter all the thoughts in his head. He started toward the gates only to hear a throat clear behind him, and he cursed to himself.

"What are you doing here, Ty? No dinner plans?"

"I had some, but they're over." He had decided to only disclose what she needed to know. "I'm here to put our boy down. I'm not too late, am I?"

"Yeah, actually you are."

"He sleeping?"

"No, he's gone. He left about twenty minutes ago with Cassie." She scanned the yard and presented him with a weird look. "Where's your car? How did you get here?"

Tyree stalled, searching for the correct answer. "I, um, I needed to walk and clear my head. It's good for me."

"You walked all the way here? The walk up the drive is a mile alone, and you expect me to believe you walked here when I heard a car speed off? Here you go starting in with the lies already."

"Okay, okay. Stop making a big deal out of things. Asha dropped me off. She was being overly cautious and thinks we need to talk."

"Overly cautious about what?"

"I had a few drinks during dinner, and she freaked out."

"You're drinking again? Why?"

"Again? You weren't here for that. How did you know?"

Mia hesitated and he hoped whatever answer she came up with was the truth. He was tired of wondering what was going through her head. He wanted a real moment with her. He thought they owed it to themselves.

"I checked on you a few times when I was gone."

"Checked on me how?"

"I called your mom and sometimes Asha. I needed to know how you were."

"Yeah, you cared so much, you didn't come back."

"How could I when you had already filled my position?"

"You replaced me first."

Mia shifted suddenly, and he could tell she was uncomfortable discussing their past in the yard. He knew they needed to be inside in case their emotions got the best of them. He saw how he had already pulled her out of the calm demeanor she was struggling to display.

"Ty, come inside. Obviously, we need to hash this out once and for all."

"That we do, but it won't mean a thing if you don't tell me everything. I'm so sick of this distance between us."

"Come on." She rolled her eyes, stepping aside to let him in.

Tyree walked in, pacing the floor as she closed the door behind them. Suddenly this was all feeling like a mistake, but it was too late to turn back now; he was standing right in front of her, wanting answers.

"Before you say anything, I just have one question," he said.

She nodded, telling him to go on.

He swallowed hard. "Why did you break up our family?"

"It was going to happen eventually. I just helped it along."

"Why? Wasn't I good enough? Didn't I provide for you? Did I not love you enough?"

"No, you played your role perfectly, but you used me."

"Why are you saying this? Do you want to hurt me? Is that it?"

"You're being dramatic."

"What did I do to make you cheat on me? Why did you have to bring him into my bed?"

"I didn't! I never let him touch me. We didn't sleep together until we moved to Paris. I couldn't do it. Not here, not in the home we shared."

"Mia, I don't know what you think you know, but it's not true."

"You made a side deal with Richmond. I know all about it and the trust fund you received when we got married. So, what was it? You marry me and he gives you shares in Livingston?"

"He didn't want me anywhere near that company. He needed to keep me out to keep his corruption buried. I made a deal with him, but it wasn't what you thought."

"You lied to me for all these years, and you expect me to believe you now?"

"Yes."

"Why?"

"Because I'm telling the truth." Tyree pulled her down on the couch and took her hand in his. She didn't pull away, and he took it as a sign to go on. "Richmond and my dad had bad blood after the business deals went down. When Richmond found out about us, he threatened to turn my dad in if I took the company and married you. His deal was I had to choose one or the other."

"John was involved in that?"

"I don't know to what extent, but I know he is more involved than he's admitting. If I took the company, Richmond would have exposed my dad and ruined everything, leaving Asha and Miguel without a future. It was either marry you or take the company, and I chose you. Yes, I had a trust fund that I could only get if I was married, but that isn't why I did it. I loved you so much and not having you would have driven me insane."

"Why didn't you tell me?"

"I didn't want you to feel like you were the reason Dad and I can't stand each other. I never told him about the deal with Richmond. I just let everyone think I didn't want the company because of my own reasons. When I refused to do what Dad wanted, he cut me off, but you never knew because I refused to let that stand in our way. I used my trust fund to support us. I don't regret what I did, and if I had it to do all over again, I would. I know that I should have had more faith in you and said something, but I didn't want to risk you saying no to my proposal."

"I wouldn't have. I could have never turned you down, but I would have done more to help support us. You should have told me. I would have done whatever we needed to make it work."

"I didn't want you to do that. We didn't need your money, and I'm supposed to take care of you and Kyan. You deserved to be treated like the most precious thing in the world."

"You did all that. I swear I've never felt more loved. I was just stupid. I never should have left you. How can you not hate me?"

"I do. I hate you so much."

She looked at him, stunned by his declaration.

"I hate you because, after everything, after all you've done to hurt me, I still can't get you out of my head. I hate you for still being the one. I hate you because you let him touch you. You let him have what was mine, and I can't stand it. Most importantly, I hate you because I want to kiss you so bad right now. I wish I could erase you, but I can't."

"Ty." She reached out, but he sat back on the couch.

"You gave him something that was only supposed to be mine. You took my joy of knowing no man had ever made you feel the way I did. Your body and your heart were supposed to be all mine. You said you had never been in love before me."

"I hadn't. Ty, you're the only man I've ever loved. You have to believe me. I never let myself fall in love with him. He was just there."

Tyree looked away, trying to restrain himself; and then he focused back in on her. "I came here to say good-bye to you. I need you gone. I need you out of here," he said as he tapped his head. "Let me find my happy ending."

"I can't." She had tears drenching her cheeks. "I love you."

"I loved you, but now," he said, standing and looking in the mirror, "I'm someone I don't even recognize. I could blame it all on you, but I know I'm responsible for some of it."

"I thought you were the one who ruined us, but it was me. I made this happen. I'm so ashamed. I broke the only man who gave me everything."

Tyree wanted to leave right then, but something was pulling him to her. Maybe it was the tears rolling down her cheeks. He could never stand to see her cry. Slowly, he made his way over and pulled her into his arms, leading her to rest against his chest. "I don't know why we hurt each other the way we do, but you were the one. Always know that."

"I'm sorry."

"I know."

Tyree walked over to the couch and slid down with her still in his arms. He kissed the top of her head and closed his eyes. He had been waiting to hold her like this for over two years, and now this felt like it could be the last time. He hadn't known the extent of his anger until he was able to vocalize it. She had caused him to hit rock bottom.

Tyree sat holding her for what seemed like an eternity as the effects of his intoxication wore off. He thought over all the things they said to each other in the heat of the moment, and he regretted the harsh nature of his words. As angry as he was and as much as he tried to accomplish it, he could never hate her. She would always be the one.

"Mia." He ran his hand down her cheek as she slept. "Baby, wake up. I need to talk to you."

"If you're going to yell at me again, please don't. I know I deserve it, but please—"

"I love you." He smiled.

She sat up, leaning her head against his. "I love you too."

"Look, I don't know what this all means. We really screwed up, and I don't want to dance around things pretending like we don't have real issues. You really messed me up, and there's still the whole Jake and Renee situation."

"I understand. So what do we do?"

"I don't know. All I do know is that I won't be getting married, not to her anyways, but I have to handle it the right way."

"Why?"

"I don't think it is something that should be drawn out."

"So what are we going to do?"

Tyree smiled at her using the word "we." He hadn't thought they would ever be a "we" again. It felt good to hear her say it, but he knew her getting involved would be a mistake. "Look, you have to let me deal with this. I can't have you involved. Plus, you have some things of your own to figure out. I'm not saying we're together, not yet, but I need to know that I can trust you to make the right decision."

"About Jake?"

"Yeah, him and other things."

"I guess that's a fair answer. I shouldn't expect things to just fall into place because I want them to."

"Right. Look, I need to get home and wrap my head around some things, but I'll call you." When she didn't voice a response, he lifted her chin, bringing her eyes to his. "Okay?"

"Okay," she sighed, and leaned in and brushed her lips over his.

When they touched, it was like magnets colliding. He deepened the kiss, grabbing a handful of her hair, and pulled her head back to smother her neck in kisses. As his tongue traced a path down her neck, she reached over, running her hands under his shirt and over his toned abs. This was what he missed most: the feel of her against him.

When his kisses seemed to become too much for her, she pushed him back, looking at the lustful gaze in his eyes. "It's been so long since I felt you."

"I really want you, baby," he whispered in her ear. "But are we ready for this?"

"You had sex with her?"

He knew she hated the idea, but she had to understand this was all so sudden between them. "Not in a few days."

"Why?"

"Because I can't think with you around. You're ruining the best part of me." He laughed. "I love sex."

Mia flashed him her adorable grin and took full possession of his mouth, pushing him back on the couch. "You're not going anywhere."

She unbuttoned his shirt and pushed it off his shoulders, and he sat up running his hand under her shirt to caress her skin. He could feel her body reacting to each touch, and he smiled. This was what he had been missing.

Renee always acted like she wanted him, but only Mia showed him that she needed him. With each touch, he felt her twitch. She was kissing her way down his chest when he pulled her up. In a matter of seconds, he had her pajama pants sliding down her legs, and his hands were exploring her, gliding across each sensitive peak with ease.

Mia was wrapped in his arms, moaning as he brought her to rest on the counter. Sitting her down, he dropped to his knees, pushing her legs apart. She had her eyes closed, and when his hands found their way back to her center, she shivered. She let her body rock into his fingers, pushing them deeper until his mouth replaced them. When his tongue flicked over her followed by a gentle sucking motion, her knees began to buckle around his face, and he was growing more excited by the moment.

Raising her thighs to his shoulders, he slid his hands up to caress her breasts as he ran his mouth all over her. This was what he needed, what he wanted. Continuing to pleasure her in a way he had never done for Renee, he let his mouth take on a mind of its own.

She was writhing below him, reaching the brink of her climax and he was anticipating it. He needed it. After all this time apart, he still remembered what it sounded like to make her lose control. The taste of her was seared into his memory, but nothing compared to the screams. Grabbing her thighs tighter, he pushed his tongue farther, caressing the sensitive flesh between her legs harder and faster until he got what he wished for.

"Tyree! Oh, God!

"Yes, baby," he smirked. "I missed that."

Watching her come down from her high, Tyree stripped off his pants and boxers, moving back between her legs. He felt them encircle him, and seconds later she was in his arms. Times like these, he was thankful for her being so small. Pushing her back far enough to reach his hand down, he was already in a state of arousal. Without hesitation, she slid her body over him, causing a guttural groan to escape his lips.

Closing his eyes, trying to get used to the feeling, he was surprised when she threw her arms around his neck, rolling her body against his. Tyree was swimming in ecstasy, feeling her insides pulsate against him. For the first time in a long time, he knew what it meant to truly love the one you're with.

Mia was all over the place, driving him insane. She was lifting her body and sliding back down, moving in a way she never had before. It was so crazy, so unreal, that Tyree had to blink to make sure it wasn't just one of his fantasies. He had dreamed this moment so many times, and here she was, making him feel things he no longer thought were possible. He was holding her in the air, clutching her hips as she moved her body, and he was biting his bottom lip. It felt so damn good.

Tyree let her continue her sensual movements as he found himself walking toward a nearby wall. When he turned and placed her back against it, she stopped, looking into his brown eyes; and he drove into her forcefully. While pushing harder against her, he grabbed her legs, forcing them up to wrap around him and he saw a smile appear on her face.

Soon, they were dancing against the wall together with her giving back as much as she received. Tyree had forgotten it could be like this, having someone who knew you so well they anticipated your every move. Mia always knew what to do to make him explode with passion and, after all this time, nothing had changed.

Feeling her head tilt and her tongue run over his ear, up his neck, and finally across his lips,

Tyree moved his hands to grip hers, and he slid them up the wall. Her legs soon fell to the floor, and he pulled her to him. With a handful of her hair in his hands, he turned her around, lifting her body in his arms and he entered her once more. He knew Mia was stunned by what he was doing, but she quickly caught on, wrapping her arms around his neck. She let her legs meet around his waist. She was wrapped around him like a pretzel, but he couldn't deny it was amazing.

"I'm glad you're so flexible, baby."

"I'm glad you're so horny. This is a new one for us. You been practicing?" She laughed.

"Every day, waiting for you." He kissed the side of her neck and sent her a few more thrusts that had her screaming. Tyree knew he wouldn't be able to keep this up much longer, and he wanted so badly to draw it out. It had been so long, and he never wanted it to end. Every second with her was electrifying. He needed more time.

When Tyree began to walk her back to the couch, he felt the room spinning. His vision was blurred by passion, and his heart was beating out of his chest. Sliding her down, he felt her hesitate, but that was soon dismissed when he slid beneath her to rest on his back. He knew that she would pick up on what he wanted, and she quickly dropped herself on top of him, accepting his full erection in one swoop.

His body once again felt complete, and he let her think she had full control for a second while he readjusted himself for his big moment. When he reached up, weaving his hand through her hair, pulling her lips down to his, he felt a familiar sensation wash over him and, then, her body quivered. Her second orgasm hit, and he saw her eyes closing, until he thrust upward, causing a loud exclamation to roll off her tongue.

When Tyree grabbed her legs, running his hands up her thighs to rest on her hips, he threw another round of exquisite thrusts, and she threw her head to the side. Kissing her neck, he let his tongue linger as he pushed himself deeper into her warm recesses. He hadn't felt this alive in so long, and when her nails raked over his chest, he lost control, allowing himself to give in, releasing between her fluttering walls. Feeling her clamp down around him, he took a deep breath and, a few seconds later, she blessed him with her third orgasm as he finally reached his first.

Holding Mia pressed against his chest, Tyree closed his eyes as they both struggled to regain control of their breathing without disconnecting.

They lay that way for what seemed like days; and, once she was completely back to normal, Mia sat up running her hand down Tyree's face. "You still going home?"

"Home? Aren't I home? This is still my house too, right?"

"Right." She smiled. "It's just that before we had sex, you were saying something about going home."

"I'm not leaving after that." He kissed the side of her head. "And we didn't have sex."

"What was that then? Sure felt like it to me." She giggled. "You were inside me."

"Yes, I was. Still am, as a matter of fact." He pointed to their bottom halves. "But I never have sex with you. Sex is what I did with her. I make love to you."

Mia gave him a gorgeous smile and leaned down to kiss him again. "I don't deserve you."

"You don't," he joked, "but you still got me anyways."

"What about your fiancée?"

"What about your man?"

"My man is here. He just needs to clean house tomorrow afternoon."

"Why so late? I thought you would have wanted me to go over there now and throw her out." He chuckled.

"She can wait. I have so many things to do that involve you, and I just can't spare the time right now."

He looked at her, grabbing her chin, pulling her lips to his. After giving her a gentle kiss, he then leaned back. "I'm going to do this with you again, but you have to promise not to duck out on me if times get hard. Okay?"

"I promise."

"I don't want to discuss the past anymore or think about all the things we messed up on."

"We won't have to."

"Well, I lied. I have one more thing to ask you, and then I'll drop it."

"What is it?"

"How did you find out? I mean, I'm glad it's in the open now, but how?"

Mia glanced off, but he tilted her head back to face him. "Jake. He found it while looking for you. He looked into a lot of things about all of us."

"What else does he know?" When she hesitated, he locked eyes with her. "Mia, what else?"

"He knows about you looking into Mom's and Janelle's deaths."

"How long have you known?"

"Since before I left. Why didn't you tell me?"

"Because, well, because I thought Richmond was involved. I know it's ridiculous, but I was suspicious of him."

Mia laughed nervously and laid her head on his chest. "That's crazy. They were accidents. There is no other way to explain it."

"Yeah," Tyree sighed. "No other way." He held her tight and listened to her breathe until she fell asleep. He was too distracted to join her; their conversation had awakened suspicions he thought he had buried long ago. Everything he thought he discovered back then led to a trail of dead ends. There was no way it could be possible. Or could it?

As the pieces of the puzzle began to replay in his head, Tyree turned and slipped out of Mia, placing her on the couch, and he threw on his boxers. When things began to go south after Kyan was kidnapped, he hid some things in the corner of his closet to keep them out of Mia's hands, and he hoped they were still there. Moving a few things and sliding behind Kyan's clothes, he found the envelopes and pulled out a few papers while taking a seat on the bed.

As Tyree read over the papers, his thoughts were taken back to a conversation he had with Janelle. Her words were cryptic that night and, although she had been drinking, she had given him something to think about. They were talking about Janelle's mother, and she was emotional and guilt-ridden. They all knew of Helen's drug abuse, but they wanted to give her the benefit of the doubt, and they failed her horribly. Janelle's issue was what they didn't know about her. They never knew she had started shooting up. In all the years of drug abuse, she had always snorted. Something just didn't seem right to Tyree.

He was still looking over the papers when Mia crept up to the doorway quietly watching him. "What you got there?"

Tyree looked up slowly, not really surprised that she came to find him. Anytime they made love and she was out of his arms for longer than a few minutes, she couldn't sleep. It was the reason he always made a habit of holding her the entire night. "Just some things I stuffed away. I guess there's no point in hiding it from you now." He held the documents out, and she looked at the papers, bucking her eyes in shock.

"Where did you get these?"

"Janelle, before she died."

"She was helping you?"

"Yeah." When she dropped the papers suddenly, he walked over, picking them up and lifting her eyes to his. "What is it?"

"This report. This is not how the scene looked."

"What do you mean?"

"It says she was found with her arm tied. It wasn't. There was just the needle lying beside her."

"Maybe it was just a mistake."

"She wasn't like that. I saw her myself. The needle was lying beside her. Oh, God." She paused for a second, gripping the papers tightly. "How did I not notice?"

"Notice what?"

"It was lying beside her right hand."

"And?"

"Mom was left-handed, Tyree. She couldn't do anything with her right hand."

Tyree knew it was something, but instead of worrying and stressing her out he decided to keep his suspicions to himself until he had more proof. "We're just paranoid. It's late, and our minds are running wild. Let's get into bed. We need our rest to deal with everything and everyone tomorrow."

"Yeah." She smiled weakly. "This has been a crazy day."

"Hey, don't be like that." He kissed her hand.

"It's not every day a man tells me he hates me and then makes love to me."

"I still hate you," he said, smiling, "but you're lucky I love you more."

"Such a romantic."

"I have my moments."

Chapter Sixteen

"Mom, where are you?" Asha called out as she made her way through her parents' house. Something about the previous night just felt strange for her, and when she thought back on how her mother had flipped the script on Renee, she knew there was something to it. The more she thought about it, the weirder she felt about everything.

As she walked through, looking in every room, she heard Karen's voice calling out to her. When she finally arrived in the den, she found Karen sitting alone with coffee and a breakfast tray. "Since when do you eat breakfast in the den?" She took a seat.

"Since Dad had a boys' trip I wasn't invited to, and I have to dine alone."

"Where did he go?"

"Some golfing expedition on a course they just had to see. I told him to have at it." She chuckled.

Asha let out a smile that didn't quite reach her eyes, and Karen picked up on it instantly. "What's going on? I know you didn't come over this early to discuss Dad's trip. Is something wrong?"

Asha didn't know how to come out and ask about Renee without getting Karen angry, so she decided to just lead with something else. "How are you?"

"Me? Well, you never ask me that, but I'm fine; just a little upset with your dad, but it'll pass as long as he does what I say."

Asha's ears perked up, and she was feeling more at ease. If Karen was already upset, then maybe she already knew something.

Karen looked at her expression and ran a hand through her hair. "I feel as if you might already know why I'm angry. Don't you?"

Asha exhaled and nodded slowly. "I mean, I think I know, but I need you to fill in the blanks. What is the deal with Renee? I have a bad feeling about her, and you seem to share that opinion."

"What's going on is your dad is an idiot. I told him if he doesn't fix it, I'll kill him. I mean it, too. Your brother has been through enough with women to let this tramp come in and benefit."

"So, you're suspicious of her too? I wasn't at first but, after last night, I feel that we don't know the real her."

"You're never going to know the real her. She's always in character. That's what actresses do."

"Actresses?" With that question, Asha saw that Karen had said something she didn't mean to reveal; but there was no way to cover it up now. Asha just stared her down, waiting for a response.

"Yes. Renee is or was acting at first. John met her before Tyree and thought she would be good to pull Tyree out of his depression. She was only supposed to do just that and then disappear, but she had other ideas. She got into Tyree's head and convinced him she was something she wasn't and, before we knew it, he proposed. I didn't know until it was too late, or I would have put an end to this long ago."

"You two set him up?"

"I had nothing to do with the setup. I only found out about it recently. I'm trying to end that silly engagement and get my son away from that horrid girl."

Asha felt like the air had been knocked out of her and she sat back on the couch. She had no idea the lengths her father would go to control their lives. She knew he wanted Tyree in the business, and she also knew he only came to join them after Renee. She must have influenced him on John's orders. "That bitch!"

"What? What are you talking about?"

"No wonder she signed the prenup so easily. She was already getting paid by Dad."

"Your father isn't paying her; at least, not with any of our accounts. I watch them daily, and if anything goes out, I know all about it."

Asha was replaying all the awkward moments in her head, and now they all made sense: the hushed conversations when she walked into a room they had been in; the guilty looks when certain things were brought up; and the obvious distance between Renee and Tyree. She was growing more and more agitated, until she thought about what she did the night before. When a smile crept over her face, Karen looked at her in confusion.

"You know, what Dad did was wrong, but I don't think we will have to worry about it much longer."

"Why, did you kill her last night?" Karen snickered.

"No, but I think we have another contender."

"Mia? Did something happen? Did they make up? Tell me everything!"

"I dropped him off at Mia's last night. I didn't get a call back, and I didn't see him leave. He doesn't know this, but I waited at the main gate for an hour before going home, and he was still there. I'm assuming things went well, but we will have to talk to him and confirm it."

"This is exactly what we needed to rid our family of that infestation."

"Don't get your hopes up just yet. He was pretty loaded when I dropped him off. I just hope he didn't pass out on the couch or make a fool of himself."

"Oh, goodness, I hope not."

"Well, I have to get going. I need to make an appearance at the office."

"Will you talk to Tyree?" Karen asked.

"Of course."

"Great! Well, call me and tell me everything."

Asha hugged Karen and kissed her forehead before turning to leave. She had renewed belief that things would be okay, but she had to talk to her brother first. She hoped he had gone over and put everything on the table, leading to a new relationship with Mia, but she knew never to get her hopes up too much.

Things always had a way of crumbling before their very eyes. She just hoped for it so she wouldn't have to out her dad. What he was thinking by introducing Renee to Tyree, she would never know. It had to be on the list of the dumbest things he had ever done, and he was lucky to be on a trip, or he would be getting an earful from her. Maybe he still would. That's what cell phones were made for.

Chapter Seventeen

Tyree found himself on top of the world, sitting on the edge of the bed getting dressed to head into work. He had reluctantly left Mia in the bed sleeping and came home to face the music and break things off with Renee. As much as he wanted to be a good guy, he also wanted to keep the promises he made to Mia. They had been through so much together, and they needed each other. He hadn't said anything more about Helen, but he was no longer convinced he was wrong before. He knew there was more, and he made up his mind he would find out what it was.

Arriving home, Tyree had noticed Renee's car missing; and, walking into the kitchen, he had found a note on the fridge. Apparently, Renee had taken a trip to her mother's and wouldn't be back for a few days. This definitely put a wrench in his plans. He wanted to get this over with so they could all move on, but you don't end an engagement over the phone. He wouldn't be that cruel. He wanted to be face-to-face when he severed things just to be sure she knew how serious he was about her not starting any shit with Mia. He knew Renee well enough to know she would want to cause a scene, and he wanted to head it off before it began.

He could just see the looks on his family's faces once he told them that Renee was out, and Mia was back in. He knew they would all be ecstatic. Hell, he was ecstatic. Things were finally going his way, and once he cleared up his suspicions about Helen, he would be at ease. He thought Mia and Rick deserved peace. After Helen died, they both blamed themselves, and with what happened to Janelle, it just made things unbearable. If he could give Mia answers, he would feel like the man she deserved. He needed to be that man.

After getting dressed, he grabbed his phone, looking for some sort of proof that Mia was thinking of him, and she didn't disappoint. He loved how she used to always surprise him with some text or voicemail, showering her love all over him. It was the little things that made being with her so much more special. As he read the text, he felt like a teenage boy all over again, drowning in her mystery.

Mia: Last night was wonderful. I never knew I could feel this way again. Handle your business and get home to me and our son. I love you.

Tyree kissed the phone and leaned against the dresser, replying without hesitation.

Tyree: Last night was spectacular and you, my little sex kitten, kept me up all night and then slept like a log when I had to make the walk of shame. I love you, but you owe me big.

Tyree walked downstairs, holding his phone and briefcase, waiting for her response. He was making a pot of coffee when he heard his phone vibrate. He almost dropped the coffee pot when he saw what she wrote.

Mia: I love owing you, and speaking of big, um, I could really use something big inside me right now. My legs are shaking, my breathing is shallow, and my mouth is watering. I need you, I want you, I ache for you.

Tyree heard the coffee percolating and felt himself breaking into a light sweat. He loosened his tie and ran his hand over his head. Now, he wished he could skip work. He had so much time to make up for with her, and with Kyan being home tonight, they couldn't get as crazy as they had last night. Picking the phone up, his palms were sweating as he typed his response.

Tyree: Slow down, kitten. Our son will be in the house, and you know I have work. I don't want to be thinking about touching you while I'm sitting behind a desk, and I have news I don't think you will like.

Mia: What news?

Tyree: Renee is out of town, so I haven't been able to break things off.

Tyree placed the phone on the countertop and poured a cup of steaming coffee into his favorite mug. He knew the next portion of the conversation wouldn't be the most pleasant. He actually hated having to tell her. He knew she was going to flip.

Mia: So, I'm still the side chick? Wow, I'm sharing my man with some money-grubbing, slick-faced whore? Kinda turns me on. I kinda like the sneaking around.

Tyree: If you like it, then we could make it an everyday thing.

Mia: Not on your life. The first chance you get, you better ditch that ho.

Tyree laughed at her response. Now, this was the Mia he knew and loved: jealous and fiercely possessive. Her intensity always led to insane nights. He knew she was right, but he had to be sure she knew what his demands were, too.

Tyree: I'll do just that when she's back, but you know I'm not the only one with something to handle. You still have that little Jake problem, and you better handle it because if I have to see him, I'll bash his head in.

Mia: Babe, I'm sorry. I know I hurt you, but I'll handle it. You won't have to see him, and I'll make it up to you. You're my everything.

Tyree: You're my everything as well, kitten. Now let me get to work. I'll see you tonight.

Mia: Unless . . .

Tyree: Unless what?

Mia: You want lunch?

Tyree: I would love lunch. You cooking?

Mia: Sure.

Tyree gulped down the rest of his coffee and darted out the door. He was really looking forward to whatever Mia brought over. For a woman who grew up privileged with maids and cooks, she still knew how to throw down in the kitchen. She was always on top of things as far as taking care of him and Kyan. She always worked but, amazingly, she was always home before him with a hot meal on the table. She was really something. He couldn't break his thoughts away from her the whole drive over to work. His every moment was filled with memories of her.

Tyree arrived at work. His feet seemed to glide off the elevator. His mind was clouded with emotions he thought were unattainable. Images of her beauty danced through his mind; the smell of her hair burned through his nostrils. He was intoxicated with joy, drunk off love, lost in a fantasy, until he walked into two pairs of distracted eyes, greeting him in his office.

The vibe was undeniable, and Tyree tried hard to spread his exuberance, but neither Asha nor Miguel shared his mood. They both looked extremely stressed and, when he sat down at the table, Miguel handed him a couple of papers. Glancing over the documents, Tyree sighed and slammed them on the table. "What is this? What's going on here?"

"There is a problem with Janelle's and Helen's shares. Their estates are being challenged by Richmond." Miguel seethed with anger. His tone was flat and snappy. "Rick did his best to squash it, but it's now a very real problem."

Tyree could tell it was eating away at him that Richmond would use his dead daughter's will to inch his way back into the company. "So, what does this mean?"

"It means that the shared business is suspended until we can figure everything out. Mixing the money could get dicey, and we don't want any added stress."

"This is bullshit! I thought Rick assured us he had this handled. Was that just a lie? We can't deal with a cutoff like this. We could lose contracts."

"I know," Miguel snapped. "Rick did have it under control, but it's out of his hands. He and Mia are both blocked from all business acquisitions until this is resolved. They are just as screwed as we are, if not more. At least we still have the hotel chains. We will be fine, but it could really hurt them. Their whole business is in disarray until they can reach an agreement."

"Mia is going to go off. She doesn't need this, not with all the drama concerning Helen on her mind. I swear she woke up like ten times last night." Tyree was rattling so quickly he completely missed the smiles appearing on his siblings' faces.

"So, you and Mia, is this a thing? You back home?" Miguel smirked, and so did Tyree, completely forgetting their dilemma momentarily. "What'd you do?"

Tyree lowered his head, hiding the blush spreading over his cheeks. For a brief period in time, nothing else mattered except the fact that he had the woman of his dreams back. "Look, you guys. I was so stupid to think I could ever want anyone else. I love that girl, and I can't be anywhere but with her and my son."

“Thank goodness!” Asha chimed in. “So how did Renee take the news when you sent her packing?”

Tyree chuckled at her excitement, and he laid a hand on the table. “I wish I could tell you about it, but she wasn’t around when I got home.”

Asha’s eyes bucked just as her palm slapped the table. “What are you waiting on? Get rid of the ho.”

“You have been spending too much time with Mia.” Tyree snickered. “She just said the same thing; but not to worry, sis. I’ll take care of it as soon as she comes back from out of town.”

Staring at Tyree blankly, Asha became really quiet, and Tyree could tell she had something heavy on her mind. Never voicing her thoughts, she just sat with both her brothers looking on curiously. Neither Miguel nor Tyree knew what was going on, and they were completely thrown off.

Tyree and Miguel both looked on as they saw something click with Asha. She looked deep in her feelings when she stood and exited the room without speaking. Asha’s strange behavior did nothing but raise the suspicion of both brothers.

After a few moments, Miguel sat up, looking uncomfortable in the silence. “What’s up with baby sis? She’s usually more—”

"Reserved?" Tyree butted in. "Man, I don't know, but ever since dinner last night she has been a little out of it. I always thought she liked Renee, but last night she dumped my drunk ass in Mia's yard. She has been strictly anti-Renee ever since."

"You know Asha. She's the one who pretty much always keeps it together. We're the screwups, and she fixes things. She probably saw you going down the wrong road again, and now she's fixing it."

"She is always fixing me, huh?" His voice dropped low. "She's awesome. The best little sister we could have ever asked for. It's because of her I have Mia back."

Miguel's sneaky smirk reappeared, and Tyree knew what was coming next. "So, what exactly did you do last night? When you walked in here, you looked like a man who had a good night. A really good night."

"I had a great night."

"So, what now? Now that you've gotten the awkward sex thing out of the way, where do you go from there? I mean, because she still has a life elsewhere, and so do you."

"I know all that and, yeah, I've thought about what's next. I know things aren't easy between us. They probably never will be, but I love her.

We can get through anything as long as we trust in each other this time. I have faith in her, and she said she is here for the long haul, but I have a concern."

"A concern?"

"Yeah. You remember all those suspicions I had about Richmond after Helen's and Janelle's deaths? Well, I might just be on to something as far as it all not being on the up and up."

"What brought this on? I thought you decided they were all accidents."

"I thought so, but something was wearing on me last night, and I went and found all the old papers. While I was looking them over, Mia walked in and added more pieces to the puzzle. I didn't want to tell her, but I no longer think any of it was an accident. I want you to look into it, but keep it quiet. I don't want Mia knowing until I have something more."

"Are you sure? You just got back with the woman, and you know all those secrets ended things the first time."

"Mia understands, and I won't keep anything from her if it gets too crazy. I just don't want her to worry for no reason. My suspicions could be unfounded, and she has enough to deal with."

"As long as you know what you're doing." He shrugged. "I'm happy for you and hope you can iron out all the details, and you know I got you on the info tip. If there is anything to find, I'll find it."

"Thanks, little brother."

"It'll be fun having little man around all the time. You know, for me, it's almost as good as having my own."

With crossed arms and a huge smirk, Tyree looked at his little brother, now seeing the softer side. "You thinking about a family someday?"

"Nawh. I'll just have to settle for spending time with my nephew. You know he's my little mini me."

Tyree chuckled, thinking about how much Kyan really did favor Miguel. They had the same shade of brown eyes, he looked just like Miguel did when he was younger, and Kyan acted like Miguel in the sense of being extremely goofy. It was like seeing Miguel as a kid all over again.

"You know me and Mia had a thing, right? You sure he's yours?" Miguel insinuated that he was Kyan's father, causing Tyree to almost fall out his chair, laughing hysterically.

"You wish, little brother. You wish you had the swag it takes to pull a woman like Mia."

"So I take it Jake has swag, huh? You know he hit that, right?" Miguel was hitting a touchy subject, but he always liked to see how far he could go teasing his sickeningly happy brother; Tyree knew this.

Tyree's smile never faltered. "He caught her in a weak moment, but only a real man can hold down a woman like that. He couldn't even get a yes to his repeated proposals. She's home to stay now. I'm never giving her up again."

"That's the attitude. Never let anyone take anything from you. Mia is yours." The room was quiet for a second. "Now that I'm done." Miguel snickered, seemingly pleased with himself until he heard the door open.

Tyree stood quickly. He knew by witnessing the look on his face that Miguel could tell who it was without turning.

"Hey, Mia."

"Hey, Miguel." Her voice was light and pleasant. Tyree could smell the breakfast she brought, and he felt his senses taking over.

"I see you haven't lost your touch, Mama Mia. I hope you brought enough for your favorite brother-in-law." Miguel was already licking his lips as he eyed the basket of food she entered with.

"Yes, I did. I have enough here for everyone: me, you, Ty, Kyan, and Asha. Where is she, by the way?"

"She had some business to attend to," Tyree stepped in, deflecting the question. He pulled Mia's lips to his. Kissing her this way reminded him of how they were in the beginning. Tyree could tell Miguel was really happy for them, watching how they interacted, until he heard a booming little voice.

"Daddy, why are you kissing Mama? I thought you had a girlfriend and Mama has Jake."

Miguel swooped Kyan into his arms and shook him up a little. "Which do you like better, little man? Your daddy kissing your mom or Jake?"

Sighing and squinting his eyes, Kyan gave Miguel a look. "I like Daddy better. Jake is nice, but he's not my daddy."

The look on Miguel's face said he was loving this. Kyan was so much like him: always straight to the point. "What about Renee?"

"She's not like Mama, so that's why Daddy doesn't like her that much."

"What do you mean, little man?"

"She doesn't do anything. She sits in the house all day, and Aunt Cassie says all she does is spend Daddy's money. Mama has her own money."

Miguel shook his head and gave Kyan a high-five. "That's right. Your mama is one hell of a woman."

“All right, boys,” Mia interjected. “Let’s just eat. Enough about Renee.” Tyree could tell she was so over the whole subject.

Tyree watched as Mia pulled out plates and handed them around. She was great. No, pretty much amazing. Yeah, amazing was the word. Leaning over, he kissed her cheek. “Kitten, how you doing?”

“I’m great, babe.”

“With the whole Richmond thing, I mean? I know it has to be hard.”

“We’ll talk later.” Her grin was contagious. He couldn’t hide his either. She was making him forget his problems.

“Okay. Thank you for coming here and bringing Kyan. I needed to see you two.”

Her fingers found their way to his hair, stroking his scalp, sending tingles through his body. “I couldn’t wait until lunch. With everything going on, I needed to see your face. You always make everything better.”

“That’s why I’m your man.”

“My man. I like that.”

“I love it.”

Chapter Eighteen

Terence watched as Asha paced the living room and she knew he was confused. She had called him a few hours back, saying she needed to talk, but he got held up at work. His assistant had delivered all of her messages. She wasn't trying to get him worked up, but what she had to say was major to her.

"Baby, what's up? I got your messages."

"What did you find out about Renee? I know you were digging into her past. What did you find?"

"Not much. Nothing more than what the background check provided; but what is this all about?"

Raking her hand through her hair, Asha turned to him with tears glistening in her eyes. "I think she and Dad are up to something. I need to know anything that can connect the two of them before she met Tyree."

"Anything like what? This is your dad we're talking about. He's like the father of the year to you. What is it that you think they're doing?"

Trembling, her hands went back to her hair. It was a nervous habit she had. "I don't know. I just . . . I just know he's lying to us. I didn't want to believe it, but how else do you explain all this? I . . . I need to know."

Hot tears streaked her cheeks, and Terence reached out to cup her chin. A tender kiss followed, and she felt her body relaxing against him. "Calm down, sweet girl. Everything will be fine. I'll fix it. I'll get you whatever it is you need."

Stuttering, she laid her head against his shoulder. "What if you can't? What if I can't? I don't know what to do. Telling Tyree could cause some serious problems and not telling him means I have to let them get away with whatever they're doing."

"How about we figure out exactly what that is and go from there? You don't have to worry. I got you." Kissing her head, he pressed her against him exhaling into the air. "I know it's rough, but how about we do something that's very obvious?"

Asha's head lifted, and she felt a glimmer of hope resonate in her. "What?"

"You should call him. John may be a lot of things, but can you really think he would deliberately hurt Tyree? I know they have their differences, but I believe he loves his children. There has to be an explanation."

Taking Terence's advice, Asha fished her cell out of her purse and dialed the number, while he placed his hand over her chest. Her heart was racing against his palm with each ring; and when she got the voicemail, she turned to Terence, who was looking on anxiously with a shrug. He smiled at her reassuringly, and she ended the call feeling as defeated as she had when he first walked in.

"Plan B?" she huffed.

He nodded. "Plan B."

After the ringing had silenced, John slammed his phone down on the bed, hissing quietly. He had seen Asha calling, but he had more pressing matters in front of him. He had to get a handle on his life. He was quickly losing control of everything around him. He needed stability.

"What's wrong, Johnny boy? Things not going your way?" a woman's voice called out from the bathroom.

In the manner of a caveman, he marched to the bathroom and pulled her out, tossing her on the bed.

Renee was stunned, blinking her eyes rapidly.

"If you would have done what I asked I wouldn't be having these asinine problems. You had one purpose, and you're blowing it. All my hard work is going down the drain."

"Your hard work? Just what in the hell have you done? I think I'm the one who has done everything!"

"Yeah, about that 'everything': that needs to end. You were supposed to take him on a few dates, get him to come to the company, and disappear. You were not supposed to be fucking my son!" He grabbed her chin and held it firmly. "When we get home, you're done with him. I want you out."

Sliding a finger across her chin, Renee let out a wicked laugh and lay back down on the bed. "That might be a little hard to do, seeing that we're engaged and all. I can't think of a single reason to give up such a sweet deal."

"With the money I've paid you, you should have been gone long ago. What he has is chump change compared to me."

"Actually, he has more than he thinks. He just doesn't know what we do."

With a deep, heavy sigh, John ran his hands over his face. "I'm working on things. It should have been done by now, but I just got Tyree on board with the company. I needed to be sure it was for the long haul before I switched everything up."

"Whatever you say," she hissed. "You've been making promises for over two years, and I'm tired of waiting. Tyree is ready to take me places while you're still playing house with the shrew."

"You're the one fucking my son. It was never supposed to go that far between you. You were only supposed to do some light flirting and get him to take the business."

Sitting up, running her hands down his chest, she caressed it through the open shirt. "You promised you would leave Karen, and I'm still waiting." She nibbled his ear. "I wanted you. You were the one, but he can give me what I need right now."

"You will stop this. I mean it, Renee. This thing between the two of you needs to be over. I won't have you with him when I serve Karen with divorce papers."

A smile appeared on her face, and she slid into his arms. "Are you really going to do it this time? What about all the other times you promised?"

"I have all I need now. Tyree is committed to the company, and Richmond has their company in so much turmoil they won't even see my next move coming. I know everyone has high hopes since Mia came home but, that girl, she won't be a problem. She hates him, we saw to that. She won't be able to convince him to turn his back on the family again."

"You're sure this is going to work?"

"It's going to work. I have faith in this. Everything we've done so far has gone perfectly well. Everything besides you shacking up with Tyree."

"That could have all been avoided if you would have told me what I meant to you. It's all I wanted, and you couldn't deliver."

He ran his fingers down her cheek and laid his head against hers. "I love you, baby. I always have, ever since I saw you standing in the rain that day. Thank goodness for your car breaking down, or I never would have laid eyes on you. I just wish things would have gone differently."

"Things just got so messed up. I don't know how we fell so far."

"I had to do something when Karen got suspicious. The timing was off, and Tyree wasn't ready."

"What's so important about Tyree taking the company? I mean, you already had Asha and Miguel."

"He has to for this all to work. It was always my dream to have all of them alongside me at Johnston Incorporated. And with my new queen bee, we can run Atlanta."

"And don't you think Tyree will have a problem with all this? The guy did propose to me."

"Don't flatter yourself, doll. He doesn't love you. He's just passing the time with you. He loves Mia. He will always love Mia but, as long as she thinks he screwed her over, she will never forgive him. He was never going to marry you."

"You think so, huh?"

"Yes. Now, go get dressed. We have dinner plans."

Watching her retreat, John pulled out his cell phone and dialed Asha back. When she answered, he felt a smile creep across his face. No matter what lie he was telling, the voice of his daughter made him feel like he was doing the right thing; she helped him drown out his demons.

Chapter Nineteen

Rick sat in his study, looking over the documents, and then sighing as he tossed them across the room. For days, he had been trying to figure out how Richmond was able to outsmart him and Mia. He had challenged their positions at the company and managed to get them both suspended until the issue was resolved. He used that addendum to Janelle's and Helen's share appropriations, voided the agreement they signed when they voted him out, and exploited it, leaving him with more votes than Mia and Rick combined. They blocked him from the company, but the 2 percent they left him with was their downfall. He combined everything he had to oust them. He had also managed to sway the board in his favor. Now, both he and Mia were out of Livingston until terms were reached.

While Rick was livid, Mia seemed to be relieved. This meant she didn't have to return to Paris and face the problems there. She had all but moved Tyree back into the house, but she hadn't told Jake they were over. He knew she didn't want to be with him, but she didn't have the heart to break up with him over the phone. She thought he deserved more. He was there for her in a very challenging time, but he just wasn't the one. Deep down, he always knew it.

As elated as he was for Mia, Rick only wished he could share in her relief. They both had been working so hard to fix the reputation of Livingston, and he was fulfilled. He loved running the company, and although Mia was in Paris, they talked all the time, somewhat bridging the gap between them. The company had helped bring them closer together, and he didn't want to lose that.

Rick and Mia didn't always have the best relationship. When they were younger, and Janelle was still living, they were practically inseparable. Outside of being with Tyree, Mia was glued to her big brother and so was Janelle. They both looked up to him. He was more of a father than Richmond was. Rick had assumed so many of the responsibilities with the family Richmond had skipped out on. Rick was their rock until things started to take a turn for the worse with Helen.

When Helen began to falter, so did Rick. In a time when he usually would have been the biggest support for his little sisters, he closed himself off, only letting Cassandra in, driving a wedge between the siblings. While Mia found comfort in Tyree, Janelle found comfort in men and alcohol.

Janelle had never been a drinker before, but it was like once she started, it was a habit that took over her mind. She struggled with the addiction and, ultimately, it was Tyree and Miguel who made her see what it was doing and how it made her someone else. After six months of fighting the urges, she found herself coping without it. She was moving in the right direction and was starting a romance with Miguel.

Miguel and Janelle had always flirted around with each other as children, but as adults, they had something more than their families ever imagined. Janelle had taken the reluctant bachelor and given him love he never thought himself capable of. She etched her name in his heart without even trying.

While Rick drifted down memory lane, Cassandra stood in the doorway, watching him. He smiled at the thoughts of his beautiful sisters and then scowled at the memories of the hardships they had endured all because they were the children of Richmond Livingston. People often envied them because of all the money and material things, but he would have traded it all in to give them a normal family. They could have been so happy.

Seeing the turmoil Richmond's decisions plunged his sisters into, Rick vowed never to let his daughter suffer the consequences of any of his actions. Picking up her picture, he grinned, thinking of the beautiful girl he raised. Whitney, his daughter, was away at Oxford, and although he missed her, he was glad she was far from the madness. He needed to protect her the way he felt he didn't do for Mia and Janelle.

"She misses you." Casandra walked into the room, running her hands along the picture of her daughter. "She called this morning, but you were out. She sends her love, and she wanted to tell you about her grades this term. She made the dean's list."

A smile spread across his face as she found a place in his lap. "Our girl is something, isn't she? So young, and already making us proud. She's damn near perfect."

"She's great, but I hate that she is so far away. I miss my little girl. She was my Barbie doll. Now, I have no one to dress up."

"Cassie, she's our daughter, not a toy." Laughing, he kissed her hand.

"I know. I just like shopping with my doll. Now I have no one but Kyan. He's so cute and adorable, but he hates to shop. He argues with me until I cave and take him to a game shop. I'm such a pushover for him."

Her head found a resting place against his neck, and he stroked her hair. "He is like Mia. He can get us to do anything, but you have that persuasion yourself."

"Meaning?"

"You got Mia here, didn't you? You're such a sneak, but I'm glad you went for it. They're so much better now."

"Yeah, but it's not over. They might be over there in the honeymoon phase right now, but they haven't faced reality. They still have to dump the leeches."

"I thought you liked Jake."

"Correction: I tolerate Jake. I never liked him. I have something against a man who would link himself to a woman in a state as fragile as Mia was. She was barely over what happened to Janelle and Helen, and she was confused about Tyree. He should have stayed his distance."

"Look, maybe he was wrong for stepping in and making it anything more than friendship, but Mia is a grown woman. She had a choice in the matter."

"She wasn't thinking clearly. What if you were Tyree? Wouldn't you want to kill Jake? He was only trying to protect her, and this is what he got."

"Are you done?" he smirked.

"Hell no. I'm just getting warmed up, smart ass. I should knock you out for letting it happen."

"Whoa, hold up now. You know I don't get into Mia's sex life. You may not like Jake, but he was there when Tyree wasn't. I like Tyree, but they were going through something. She thought he was something he wasn't, and it was up to her to figure out what she wanted. I feel it will only make them stronger."

"Yeah, well, you're lucky my plan worked. The next option was going to be to kill Renee. I already had my funeral dress picked out."

"Cassie, you're absolutely psychotic. I swear you get more extreme every day."

"You just better never get on my bad side, sweet cheeks." She leaned in and kissed his cheek, running her hand through his hair. "Anyways, I have to go. I'm taking Kyan to the zoo today to give mommy and daddy some adult time. They have been playing the happy little family, but I know they need some alone time."

"Didn't want to hear that, but that's nice of you. Have fun."

"I will. He's my favorite little guy, even though he won't go shopping with me."

"Maybe someone will have a girl you can steal next time." He laughed.

"Yeah, maybe," she huffed, spinning out of the room.

Rick shook his head, thinking about how ridiculous his wife was. She was very passionate about her family, and he was secretly envious of her ability to always say exactly what was on her mind. He only wished he could be as vocal as she. Maybe if he had been, his family wouldn't be in shambles.

Trying to dismiss the thoughts racing through his head, Rick picked up his phone, deciding to make a call he swore never to make again. He had to know what the motivation was for this sudden interest in the company after three years of absence. He needed answers only one person could give.

The phone rang twice, and then he heard the voice that made his blood boil. "Rick."

"Richmond."

"You may not like me, boy, but you will show me respect and address me as your father. To what do I owe the pleasure of your call?"

"I just want to know what in the hell you're doing interfering with the company. Why would you do this after everything you've cost us?

Wasn't Mom enough? We're just trying to fix a mess you created."

"You have no idea what it is to lose someone you love with all your heart, but you will if you try to stop me. Stay out of this, boy. Stay out of Livingston. You and your sister."

"I try to have a civil conversation with you, and you threaten Mia and me? You are one twisted old bastard who is going to get everything he deserves. I hope you know that." Rick slammed the phone down so hard his screen cracked. He didn't know why after all this time he still let Richmond get to him. All of his threats were empty, and he was going to do whatever it took to make sure he paid for all the pain they suffered. Richmond was going down.

Chapter Twenty

"Bye, baby. Be a good boy for Aunt Cassie." Mia kissed Kyan on the cheek, and he gave her a goofy grin, wiping it off.

"Mama, I'm not a baby. I'm seven."

"You're my only child, so you're still my baby." Her smirk was unchallengeable, or so she thought.

"Well, maybe you should have another baby. Just not a girl. We already have Meelah, and all she does is play with dolls." He turned to face Cassandra. "Aunt Cassie, maybe you can take Meelah shopping."

Mia could tell the idea hadn't registered, but Cassandra was definitely on board. "Maybe tomorrow. Today, I have a zoo date with the most handsome nephew alive."

"You and Mama are silly." He laughed, hugging Mia's neck, and then whispered in her ear, "Be nice to Daddy while I'm gone. I don't want him to forget he lives here now."

Mia felt her heart getting heavy. She never knew how much this meant to him. Thinking of how unhappy he must have been when they were living in Paris almost brought tears to her eyes. "You like it here, don't you?"

"Yes." He nodded. "I like us being here with Daddy. We both have fun with him."

"Well, you don't have to worry anymore. I think we are staying right here with Daddy. You don't have to miss him anymore. Okay?"

"Really?" His tone was bubbling with excitement. "We don't have to go back?"

"No."

"Thank you, Mama."

"You don't have to thank me. Just be a good boy for Aunt Cassie."

He hugged her again and ran toward the door. "I will. I love you, Mama."

"I love you too."

Mia watched as Kyan bounced out of the house talking Cassandra's ear off, and then she turned to head to the bedroom. Tyree was in bed asleep, and she climbed in, pushing the covers aside. They had been staying together every night and, with Renee still out of town, they were able to block out everything. Even if it was just for a short period of time, things were perfect.

She ran her hand down his chest. He still didn't stir, and she wanted him awake if they were going to enjoy the time alone. It was the middle of the day, and he was still asleep. They had gotten up earlier and had breakfast, and he retreated to the bedroom, saying he was still tired out from the night before. They had taken Kyan swimming and sat out by the pool for hours before heading back to the house for dinner. Cassandra and Rick joined them, and Cassandra presented the zoo trip.

Kissing her way down Tyree's chest, Mia giggled when she saw his lips curving into a smile. Either he was having a good dream, or he knew what she was doing because she would have had to be blind to miss his obvious excitement. Running her hands down to grip him, she felt him shift his hips to give her better access. Raking her nails up and down his shaft, she felt him shiver, but his eyes remained closed.

"I see I'm going to have to pull out the big guns," she said as she brought her head closer to him.

Stroking him gently and then adding her tongue to the mix, Mia felt herself getting excited. After a few strokes, she removed her hands completely, letting her tongue do all the work. Sliding her hands up his chest, she found a stopping point up near his shoulders and continued to swirl her tongue around him, surprising herself with how much she was enjoying her little idea.

Tyree thought he was in a glorious dream and decided to keep his eyes closed. He didn't want to wake up and end this sensation that felt so real. Surely Mia couldn't be doing this to him. She had never explored those waters before, and for her to be this great at it would be too good to be true. He knew it had to be his imagination and, against his own instincts, he decided to open his eyes.

Tyree slowly peeled his eyes apart only to realize the sensation was still there. Even in a dream, she left a lasting impression. His legs were weighed down, and feeling his hips bucking involuntarily, he pulled the covers back to reveal the reason why. She was excellent, every bit as amazing as he described earlier.

Mia had every bit of his arousal working for her. Her tongue was swirling around him, and every time she took more of him in, she toyed with his testicles tickling and licking all at the same time. Tyree couldn't help the moan that escaped his lips, and he found his way to the back of her head, sliding his fingers down to rest on her scalp. She took that as a request to go harder and increased her sucking technique.

Tyree felt the room spinning as he gripped her hair, closing his eyes once again, trying to regain some stability. He needed to gather himself before he lost all control. Running his hands through her hair, he was just about at his breaking point and let out a deep moan.

"Mia, uh, when, uh, did you start enjoying this? God, it feels so good."

"You like?" she asked, even though it was more of a statement.

"I love. You just keep surprising me, kitten. I've missed you."

"I missed you too, baby," she breathed in between strokes. "I missed you like crazy, and I made a decision today. One I think you'll like."

Tyree couldn't think straight, and he knew this was her objective. She always knew how to distract him before dropping big news in his lap. She had to be gearing up for something major.

"What is it, kitten? You know I can't say no to you when you're doing things like this. You're too damn persuasive."

Mia tilted her head to the side and ran her tongue up and down his shaft, causing him to shake beneath her. His grip tightened on her hair, and she pushed him all the way into her mouth. He could feel himself hitting the back of her throat, but she didn't gag; she just dug her nails into his chest.

Tyree's legs jerked from the bed, and he whispered into the air, "Mia, whatever you want, it's yours. Yes, to everything. Tell me what you want."

Mia gave him a sweet grin, stopping her actions briefly. "I just want you to know that Kyan and I won't be going back to Paris. I was thinking we could stay here, in this house with you. Move in with us, baby."

Tyree sat up slowly, pulling her into his lap. Moving his hands to her hips, sliding her panties down, he leaned into her neck kissing, sucking, licking until she whimpered against his ear. He could feel her wetness pressing against him, and he dug his fingers deep inside, watching as she arched her back, pressing her breasts against his mouth.

Stroking her, Tyree lost himself in the wild panting and clawing at his back. He loved it. He loved her. She was his in every way, and he couldn't wait to hear her scream his name. As he licked, sucked, and caressed her nipples into a rock-hard state that was driving her into oblivion, he slid her back, positioning himself to enter her and thrust inside, causing his own heart to race.

Tyree moved her hair and kissed his way from her ear to her neck, and then to her breasts. Mia had her arms locked around his neck, and she pulled his mouth up for a decadent kiss. He was inebriated as he took her body to an all-new high. Tyree grabbed her hips and moved her against him, rubbing her into her first orgasm.

"Baby." She dropped her head to his neck that was glistening from the sweat beads. "You didn't say anything about my offer."

Tyree pushed himself farther inside her and reached back to lock her legs behind his waist. He grabbed her face and brought her lips to his, kissing her senselessly before voicing a response.

"Just like you, I know how to use my body to make you cave. I'm sorry, but I can't live here with you. There are too many memories in this house."

Mia looked as if the air left her lungs. Her eyes fluttered, but not in the good way they did before. He saw the tears beginning to form in her eyes, but he knew she refused to let them fall. Seeing all this, Tyree stopped pounding into her and cupped his hands around her face.

"Kitten, just because I don't want to live here doesn't mean I don't want to be with you. I just want a fresh start for us, and for that to happen, we need to leave the past behind. We need a new place, one neither of us has any past demons to go along with."

"You want to give up our homes? Where will we stay?"

"Anywhere, everywhere. We can pack the kid up and travel until our new house is ready. We will pick one out and have movers take care of the rest."

"Tyree." She put her hands on the bed behind her and leaned back. He didn't need her to say anything else. When her eyes rolled back in her head, he knew she was on board.

Tyree pulled her legs until they hit the headboard and he put his hands back around her waist. Buried deep inside her, he rolled her body into his, completely drowning in the pleasure that surrounded them. Mia was wheezing and short of breath after several minutes of his sweet attack. Once he was sure she was on the brink, he flipped her over, finding a place between her thighs.

Placing her feet around his calves, Mia positioned her hands on his waist, pushing him deeper. Tyree felt like he was approaching his climax with all the intensity clouding the room. When Mia's moans grew louder, he became more intense, and her moans were transformed into full-out screams.

The bed was rattling against the wall as Tyree pushed her to the limit. She was digging her nails into his skin, leaving marks wherever they landed. Mia's screams floated throughout the house as the door to the bedroom creaked open. Mia was the first to see it, and she pushed her hands against Tyree, who misunderstood and pushed himself deeper, hitting all the right spots, causing both of them to orgasm. Looking down at her, he saw she was desperately trying to hold back the scream and push him back all at the same time.

"Kitten, what are you doing? I was hitting it so good just then. We could have gone for another round."

"We have visitors," she whispered, trying to cover herself. Standing frozen in the doorway was the one person Mia had been anxious to see: her beautiful cousin, Milan. After a few awkward moments, she backed out of the room, retreating to the den.

Laughing, Tyree tossed Mia's clothes over and began to throw his on. He loved the mortified look on her face and couldn't hide his amusement. He knew Mia wasn't taking it as easy as he was.

"I'm glad you're amused with the fact that my cousin walked in on you screwing my brains out."

"We were celebrating, babe; and if she hadn't come in, I would still be putting it down."

Grabbing her hips, he pulled her to him. "If you don't hurry and get dressed, I'm going to put you up against this wall and finish the job."

"I would love it if my favorite cousin weren't downstairs waiting for me to do the walk of shame. You complained about doing it the other day with no audience; now my cousin, her new husband, and her little girl are here to see me."

"She didn't see much of you, babe." He snickered. "It was my ass in the air."

"You're so crazy." She ran a hand down his neck and rested it at the base. "Let's not keep them waiting. I'm ready to talk to Milan and meet the new man. I've heard great things."

"Me too."

After getting dressed, Mia stepped away, walking toward the door, and she looked back at Tyree. She was stunned by how much she loved the man in front of her. When she turned to him with a brilliant smile, he walked over and linked their hands. Pulling her down the hallway, he wrapped his arms around her waist, steering her into the den.

"Well, hello, you." Milan looked up from talking to her daughter to look at Tyree. "You're the last person I expected to find here."

Mia walked around the corner and ran to the woman sitting at her bar. "Milan, I wasn't expecting you until tomorrow. I missed you so much."

"Well, when I got your text it sounded urgent. I juggled some things around, and here I am. Come here and meet some people." Milan pulled the man from behind her and revealed a smiling baby girl in his arms. "My husband, Jackson, and my pretty girl, Sydney."

Milan was Mia's cousin on her mother's side. She had been living in Los Angeles for the past year or so and hadn't been home for almost the same reasons as Mia, trying to escape the past. Milan's mother was Helen's sister, and the girls were raised practically as sisters along with Janelle. Milan was one of the few people who understood what it was like to grow up with parents like hers. Milan's mother, Evelyn, was just as horrible as Richmond, if not more.

"I'm so happy you're here!" Mia squealed like a teenager. "We were just getting up from a late nap."

"Yeah, I heard a little sample of that nap." Milan blushed. "I thought you were having a bad dream or something so I came in. I saw more than I meant to."

Mia laughed, reaching back to grab Tyree's hand. Tyree sat there with a mindless smile and squeezed her hand tighter. He kissed the side of her head before looking over to Milan. "Little Millie, it's been a long time, girl. I see you're doing well, and this baby is adorable. She looks like you."

"She's my little twin." She smiled lovingly. "I have to admit, I'm surprised to see you here, but I'm glad." She chuckled.

Mia looked around to the handsome man standing beside her cousin, and she extended a hand for him to shake. "I've heard so much about you, Jackson, and I want to personally thank you for all you've done for my cousin. She is lucky to have a man like you."

"It's nice to meet you," he supplied, shaking her hand.

"Jackson, this is Tyree, my—"

"Her boyfriend, ex-husband, baby daddy, whatever you want to call him," Milan offered, obviously trying to bring some humor into the situation.

"Thanks, Mills." Tyree looked half amused and half embarrassed. "Thanks for airing our sordid past."

Jackson just laughed and reached his hand out for Tyree to shake. "Hey, I don't judge, but Milan tells me you guys all grew up together. I bet you have some pretty good stories about her."

Milan threw her hand out to Jackson's chest, stopping him in his tracks. "Babe, we have things to unpack. How about you take Ty and bring them in?"

"You trying to get rid of me, love?"

"Yes." She flashed him a sweet smile. "I need to catch up with Mia. Give me my pretty girl."

"Here you go." He handed Sydney over. "Don't get into any trouble while I'm outside."

"Go." She pushed him toward the door. "Get to know Tyree. I have a feeling you guys will be good friends."

Tyree walked out the door. Jackson followed him, giving Milan a brief look, and then he disappeared out the door.

Hearing the door close, Mia turned to see Milan beaming. "Millie, you look so good." She ran a hand over Milan's. "Not like the last time. I am so proud of you for getting rid of Adrian. He was toxic."

Milan's ex-boyfriend Adrian was someone they met in high school. He was very controlling and abusive toward Milan, forcing her to give up everything and everyone she knew. He had cut her off from everyone until she met Jackson. He came in and rescued her, giving her a beautiful life and real love. He proved his devotion to her repeatedly, and when Adrian cornered them with a gun, Jackson took a bullet meant for her.

"I feel good. We are so happy, but enough about me. What is going on here?"

Mia felt her heart fluttering. "Oh, God, Millie, things are great. We got everything out in the open, and now I feel better than ever."

"It really looked like you reconnected; I got an eyeful. I thought someone was killing you." She laughed. "You hadn't updated me, and I thought you were here all alone."

"I had no intention of doing this, but I'm so glad I did. We're so in love."

"So, you know I hate to ask an awkward question, but how did Jake take the news? Weren't you two practically engaged?"

Huffing quietly, Mia's eyes widened. "No. He asked, but I never said yes. It just didn't feel right. It never did."

The girls talked and caught up for a few more minutes while the guys brought the rest of the bags in. Mia took Sydney from Milan's arms, lifting her in the air, complimenting the curly-haired beauty. She was the mirror image of Milan as a baby and was an incredibly happy child. Her bubbly three-month-old daughter inherited Milan's bright gray eyes and dark curly hair. Although she took most of Milan's features, her beautiful caramel complexion was that of her father's. Jackson was an incredibly handsome man with chiseled features and dazzling hazel eyes, and he treated Milan like a queen.

"So, what did he say when you broke the news?"

Mia turned away from Milan's watchful stare and inhaled deeply.

"Mia?" When she still didn't respond, Milan gasped loudly. "Oh, Mia, you haven't told him, have you?"

"I want to, but I can't do it over the phone."

"I understand that, but you have to do it sooner rather than later. These things have a way of coming back to bite you. I can't believe Tyree is letting this ride."

"He understands, and since he is still engaged, he can't say much."

Milan shrugged, nodding her head awkwardly. Mia knew this situation was more complicated than she first believed. "So, what are you two going to do about all this? It could get messy, and I don't want you mixed up in some crazy drama. This isn't like you to be sneaking around with your own man."

"I'm not afraid, Millie. Being with Tyree is what I have wanted since we were kids. I love him."

"Well, then that's all there is. I'm going to be here for a week, and I'll help you sort through this mess."

"I'm so glad to have you here."

The girls hugged, and Mia closed her eyes, feeling secure in her cousin's loving embrace until they heard what sounded like raised voices outside. When Jackson walked inside with a sorrowful look on his face, Milan stood, securing Sydney in her arms. She walked toward the door. "Babe, what's wrong?"

Before he could respond, Tyree came storming inside with Jake right behind him. Both guys looked like they wanted to strangle the other, and Mia felt herself walking backward. The room was dead silent, and everyone was waiting for her to respond. When Jake stepped forward to touch her, Tyree almost charged at him until Jackson stepped in, grabbing him from behind.

"Dimples, I missed you." Jake smiled, giving Mia a gaze that made Tyree almost snap.

"Dimples? Aw, hell." Jackson sighed. "Come on, man. Let's let her talk to him. We should get some air."

After being pulled from the house, a reluctant Tyree followed Jackson outside, trying to regain his composure. Making sure he had his feelings in check, Tyree pulled himself together momentarily, and both guys headed to a nice cool spot to talk privately. Once outside, Tyree leaned against the house, trying to calm himself down.

"Look, I'm sorry I just lost it there. That dude pisses me off. He used something I did to steal my wife. I just got her back and seeing him walking in here like some saint made me snap."

Jackson sighed crossing his arms over his chest. "I get it. If some man ever tried to get next to Millie, I would kick his ass. I don't know, dude, but it's not cool."

They walked around the house with Jackson trying to calm Tyree down. He was telling him all about their life in Los Angeles when they walked up on the side of the house that Kyan's room was on. Tyree was listening, but something caught his eye. He had gotten to the point where he only heard every other word. When he looked further, he saw the footprints leading up to his son's window.

Jackson stopped talking and looked at the footprints as well. "These yours?"

Tyree shook his head now realizing that Kyan's screaming may have been warranted. Someone could have really been in his room that night. He now feared for the safety of his son and the woman he loved. Tyree saw the confused expression on Jackson's face and looked back, trying to mask his fears. "Look, you guys should let me help you take your things up to the main house. I think you will be more comfortable there."

Tyree could tell Jackson was suspicious, but he didn't push. He just nodded, accepting the excuse. "Yeah, I'll tell Millie; but what are you going to do about your girl?"

"I need to get in there and check on things, but I'm talking her into not being here tonight either. She is going to argue with me, but it is for the best. That way they can stay up all night catching up."

"Your girl sounds a lot like Milan."

"They are so much alike it's scary."

Jackson laughed and patted him on the back. "You good?"

"I'm good."

Tyree and Jackson walked inside to find Mia sitting uncomfortably on one of the barstools and Jake on the couch. Tyree tapped Jackson's shoulder, pointing him to the stairs Milan was standing on, and he walked away, pulling his wife with him.

Jake was sitting, salivating over Mia, and Tyree fought down the urge to punch him in his face. Being in the room with both guys seemed to be a bit much for Mia and Tyree watched as she inched toward the kitchen. When Jake got up to follow her, Tyree walked closer, making his presence known.

"Jake, you'll get your turn with Mia. I need to talk to her before I get out of here."

Jake nodded in agreement, and Tyree took off after Mia. He found her pacing in the kitchen and walked up behind her, putting his hand on her back. He was wondering if she had second thoughts, but the way she leaned into him said otherwise.

"You okay, kitten? I just wanted to check on you."

Turning, with her arms finding a resting place around his neck, she smiled weakly. "I just hate having to tell him like this with an audience. You might not care about him, but he was sweet to me. I don't want to embarrass him."

"He's going to be embarrassed either way. He came all the way here for a woman who belongs to someone else."

"Yeah, but he thinks we're together."

"He better not for long. He's not sleeping next to you tonight."

"I know. I just need some time alone, just me and him to break things off."

"I'll give you time. I want to take Milan, Jackson, and Sydney to the main house. I think you guys should stay up there tonight."'

"Why?"

"More space and you have the maids up there. Don't you want to impress your new family member?" he smirked.

Mia eyed him skeptically. “I thought you agreed not to lie to me. There’s more.”

“There is, but I’m not ready to share. Please just do this for me. You have to trust me.”

Watching her roll her eyes, he knew she never liked being left in the dark. “Sure, whatever. Just take Kyan’s clothes up when you go. Are you staying with me?”

“If you still want me after seeing old dreamy-ass Jake,” he teased.

“Of course I will. I told you we’re starting over.”

“All right, so if I leave you here, do you promise I won’t walk in and find you mounting him when I get back?”

Mia chuckled and kissed his lips softly. “I promise.”

Taking a deep breath, Tyree walked out of the kitchen. Mia followed him after taking a moment to collect herself. The situation was stressful, and she was glad Tyree had allowed her some time alone to have a mini meltdown. Watching Tyree walk up the stairs, she saw how Jake’s eyes followed him and then snapped back to her. She knew he was thrown by her stoic expression, and when he advanced, she stepped backward.

“Hang on. Let everyone leave, and then we can catch up.”

"That sounds great." Jake grinned only to receive a timid smile from Mia.

Tyree and Jackson moved everything to drive it up to the house; and, before closing the door for the last time, Tyree looked at Mia, giving her an encouraging nod before disappearing. At that point, Jake slid off the couch and walked to stand directly in front of her. He ran his hand through her hair, and she shook him away.

"Jake, stop. We need to talk."

"I'm listening," he smirked. "Talk first, and then I want to take my woman upstairs."

"That's just it. I'm not going upstairs with you and, I've told you before, I will never have sex in this house with anyone other than Tyree. It's disrespectful."

"Yes, I forgot." He sighed. "Well, now that he's gone, we can go off just the two of us. It feels like it's been forever."

Jake was rattling plans off to her, and all she could hear was the beating of her heart in her ears. The feeling was getting extremely intense until she just blurted it out: "I'm back with Tyree."

Jake looked like he couldn't believe his ears. He looked as if he had heard her wrong. "What?"

"I can't be with you. We don't work, and it never would have because I love him."

Mia saw the anger flicker in Jake's dark brown eyes. His jaw clenched, and she saw his slender body tense while his creamy almond skin took on a red tint. He backed away from her, dropping his hands before looking back in her direction. "I won't accept this. He lied to you, he used you, and you want him back?"

"I know what I said, but I was wrong. He loves me, and I was stupid. I'm so sorry I used you."

Jake dropped the angry scowl and replaced it with a look of defeat. "I don't want to lose you. I don't think this is the end of us. Come on, dimples, I just really missed you, but I'm sorry for coming here when you clearly needed some time to yourself. Don't let this get between us. Okay?"

"I'm sorry, Jake, but I can't tell you I will be coming back to you. You are a great guy, and I should have explained that I wasn't finished here. As much as I wanted to, I never let go of Tyree."

"I'm sorry, Mia, but I'm not going to make it easy for you to leave me. We love each other."

"I wanted to love you; it would have made things so much easier."

When Mia backed away slowly, Jake almost broke down. He walked toward the door, pausing to look at her before opening it. "I won't let you just walk away. You deserve me, and I deserve you."

"Don't do this to yourself. You should find a woman who can give you the love you deserve."

"I just don't see it. He may be doing and saying all the perfect things right now, but I feel like he will only let you down in the end and, when that happens, I'll be there like always."

"You should go home and focus on yourself. I wouldn't be happy knowing you're wasting your time waiting for me."

"I'd wait forever for a woman like you."

Offering Mia one last glance, he walked out. He stood on the porch for a few minutes and then walked back to his rental. He drove down the entrance slowly, and she just watched tearfully, hating that she had to hurt him. He was great, but he just wasn't the one. Deep down, she felt he always knew this, even before she did.

Chapter Twenty-one

Karen sat quietly, and Asha knew she was trying to figure out what her visit was really about. She had been carrying on very strangely over the past few days, and she knew Karen wanted to know why. Asha had really taken this thing with John and Renee to heart.

While Asha sipped her tea silently, Karen cleared her throat, causing her to look up. "Why are you here? You know I love seeing you, but I know you're dealing with something you need to let out."

"I'm just checking on you. I know you must feel lonely with Dad out of town. Someone should keep you company."

"Is that all, dear child? Your dad is upstairs. He got in late last night, swearing he has some big announcement to make."

Asha's tea glass found a position on the small table beside her, and she turned to stare her mother down. "What kind of announcement? What does he want now?"

Asha could tell her snappy tone had thrown her mother off, and she tried to scale it back, plastering a fake smile on her face. Despite her best attempts, Karen looked unconvinced.

"Asha, why are you really here? I know what you said, but you must know I'm not buying it."

Looking at her mother, contemplating whether she should tell her all the suspicions she had about John and Renee, Asha sighed. She didn't know if she should tell her that the resort John swore he was visiting was just a front. She and Terence had taken a quick trip down there, and John was nowhere to be found.

John was sneaky. At first, they thought everything he told Asha when he finally called back was on the up and up. He somehow had the direct calls from his room transferred to his cell, but Asha was no fool. She knew something was off and decided to pay a visit to this so-called golfing trip.

It wasn't hard to obtain a key to his suite, considering he had booked the room under the company's expense account. All she had to do was flash her badge to the building, and the key was turned over quickly. The maid informed them that John had only been at the room one day and he didn't even stay the night. He had only stopped in for a few hours and disappeared.

The only contact they had with him after that was when he called in to settle the bill.

Asha just couldn't believe her father could be so manipulative. She knew he thought he was in the clear, but she was hot on his trail. She had Terence digging into every possible avenue he could to find out what the extent of John and Renee's relationship was. She didn't want to believe they were still trying to deceive Tyree, but all the signs pointed to it.

Asha had picked up her tea glass and was sipping from it slowly when Karen made a hissing sound, snapping her out of her thoughts. When they locked eyes, Asha saw the worried expression on her mother's face, and she felt horrible. She could tell she was wondering why she was so displeased, but she couldn't tell her anything without solid proof. She couldn't ruin over thirty years of marriage without being completely sure.

Just as Asha was about to make up an excuse explaining what she was so riled up about, John came speeding down the stairs. When he raced over and pulled Karen from the couch, lifting her in his arms, Asha stood and set her glass down suddenly. Both John and Karen looked at her in confusion. John slid Karen's feet back to the floor and walked over to stand in front of Asha.

"What's wrong, sweetie? You look as if you've seen a ghost. Come and tell me what is going on with you. I feel like I've been so far out of the loop with you kids this past week."

Asha huffed, thinking how right he was. If only he knew how out of the loop he was. "Things have been interesting. We have had so much to put into perspective."

"Like what, doll face? What has been going on around here?"

"I should be asking you the same thing," she sniped.

John leaned back and placed his hand on his chin. "What has gotten into you? What is going on with my sweet girl? Tell me what's wrong."

Asha opened her mouth as if to say something but closed it suddenly, thinking that this wasn't the proper time to get into their issues. "Nothing, Dad. I'm just a little out of place with the changes happening at Livingston. We don't know to what extent it will affect us yet. It could be bad, and I feel horrible for Mia and Rick. I can't believe you didn't know anything about this."

"You know I can't be everywhere at once. I'm sorry I needed a break, and this happened. I'm not God; I can't fix everything."

His statement disgusted Asha and, before she could think, she blurted out her frustrations: "You sure like to act like it."

"Asha, just what are you talking about?"

Standing and recovering her senses, Asha crossed her arms over her chest. "Dad, how could you let this happen? You knew if Richmond got his hands on any part of that company what he would do. How could you allow this? You said you handled him."

"I thought I had. I don't know what happened, but I can assure you I will get to the bottom of it, doll face. I can't have you thinking less of your old man behind this. I know what the company means to you."

"It means everything, Dad," she hissed. "It's just as important as our family; it's our legacy."

"Exactly, which is why I will fix this. You have nothing to worry about, my sweet. I never want you to worry your pretty little head about this. In fact, how about you take a few weeks off and take my granddaughter and Terence on vacation? We will have this all resolved by the time you get back. I'll just need your signature placing me in charge of your affairs for a while."

Asha and Karen both looked at each other, trying to figure out what John was up to. When she shook her head slowly, he huffed in aggravation.

"Dad, I'm not going anywhere. I am a part of the business, and I will roll with the punches. I am not a quitter, and I think you know that."

John didn't notice the hidden meaning in her words, but Asha knew Karen had instantly. Asha was on to something big, and it was undoubtedly going to wreak havoc on whatever John had up his sleeve. The determination she had was the same determination she saw in her mother over the years; it was where she had gotten it from.

While John was oblivious to all the signs, Asha noticed Karen studying her carefully. She seemed completely engulfed in her thoughts, trying to figure out what was really going on, until she heard John's ecstatic request. "Asha, darling, you and Terence must join us tonight for dinner. I want the whole family there for this announcement."

"What announcement?" Karen voiced, letting them know she was involved in the conversation.

"Darling, it's a surprise, and it will have to wait. No one gets a clue until dinner tonight."

"Is this dinner kid friendly or should we leave Kyan and Meelah with a sitter?"

"Why on earth would they need a sitter? Kyan's mom is in town now. Why can't she watch him while Tyree attends to some family business?"

"I doubt Tyree will want to come to dinner without his woman by his side."

"What does that have to do with Kyan? Renee doesn't have to watch him with his mother here."

When Asha looked at Karen's face, she looked almost ready to burst at the seams. Asha smiled at her and drew in a deep breath. "Well, you guys, I guess there's no time like the present to inform you both that Mia and Tyree are back together. She has decided to stay here, and they are going to be a family with Kyan."

"This is delightful news!" Karen jumped off the couch and rushed over to her daughter. "This is what I've been praying for."

While Asha loved the joy on her mother's face, she studied John, noticing the shock on his. At that moment, she knew all she needed to know. John was definitely conspiring with Renee. Now, all she needed to do was find out exactly how deep. As pissed as she was, she knew she needed to keep her cool.

"Well, you guys, I need to go. I'm supposed to meet the boys at the office for a little while. Miguel said he needed both Tyree and me there."

"I should join you." John stood. "We should get a handle on things before they get more out of hand."

"No, Dad." Asha put her hand up in protest. "Let us handle this. That is why you put us in charge. We are more than capable."

"Nonsense. I can help."

"John." Karen placed a hand on his shoulder. "Let them do this on their own. You are retired, and they have it under control."

"Karen, I—"

"No, John," she snapped. "Stay out of this."

Asha was waiting for his rebuttal but, instead, she got nothing. John just nodded and intertwined his fingers with Karen's. "I will let them handle this for now, but if they get in over their heads, I'm stepping in without a second thought."

"Fine," Karen responded and winked at Asha. "Get out of here, darling girl. We will see you tonight."

"Yes, Mother." She smiled and raked her hand over Karen's dark curls. "I will see you tonight."

Asha vacated the room, leaving her parents to converse among themselves. When she jumped into her car, she looked down to see that she missed a call from Terence. She rushed to check her voicemail hoping he had more information. She would like nothing more than to bring out all of John's secrets during this dinner he had planned.

Watching Tyree walk into his office, Miguel dropped the papers he was holding and let them fall to the floor. His nerves seemed shot. They hadn't seen each other since they began digging into the past once again. Watching Miguel sit up, Tyree looked at his brother, dreading the news he was about to break.

When Tyree sat down and placed his hands on the desk in front of them, Miguel cleared his throat. "What's going on? Why'd you walk in here like that?"

Tyree sighed and ran his hand over his face, knowing he looked like hell as he sauntered into the office. "Man, you're going to think I'm crazy."

"What happened?"

"I think someone was in Kyan's room that night. I've been trying to wrap my mind around it for the past hour, and I just can't shake the feeling that something is wrong."

"Did you find out something? 'Cause, I gotta tell you, what I'm seeing is making me think twice about things too."

"What'd you find? Why'd you call me down here?"

"Look at these." Miguel leaned down and retrieved the papers he dropped and handed them to Tyree. "I started looking into things like you asked me to, and there are some strange occurrences."

"Like what?" Tyree lifted his eyes to the papers and glanced over them. "What is this I'm looking at?"

"Phone records. I know you thought Helen's death wasn't an accident, so I thought maybe there would be a clue in her phone logs. Look at the number that called her five times the night she died."

"Richmond," he hissed and laid the papers down. "I thought they had no contact after the divorce." He picked the papers back up, looked over the last six months of Helen's logs, and inhaled deeply. "It looks like they were in contact quite often. The calls range from five minutes to thirty. I thought they hated each other."

"Yeah, so you can see why I called you here. I think you might be on to something about Richmond. If he talked to her, he would have known she would be there alone that night."

"If that's the case then he should have known that Kyan would be there, too. Was he heartless enough to set her up with my son in the house? He was a terrible father and husband, but he loves Ky. I can't believe he would do that with him in the house."

"He would if he didn't know. Maybe Helen never told him she was watching Kyan. I don't know, Ty. Maybe we're just jumping the gun, but I just wanted you to see this."

"Yeah, maybe you're right. Good looking out, though. I think I might just be reacting to the crazy day I had."

"I thought things were all smiles and rainbows since you got back with Mama Mia." He laughed.

"Yeah, that's straight. Me and Mia are better than ever, and you know I love her. I just have this feeling that it won't be as easy as we want it to be. I still have to break things off with Renee, and we both know how that's gonna go."

"She's not going to be happy." He snickered. "I don't envy you one bit. You're going to have to referee your girls. Renee is a little hood, but my money is on Mia. That girl gets crazy protective when it comes to you. She would beat Renee senseless."

"It won't come to that. I would never let Mia fight over me. What I'm talking about is that things just have never seemed to happen easily for us."

"I know you're not having doubts. I was skeptical, but after seeing you two together with little man the other day, I know you're in it for the long haul."

"I trust in my baby, but I know the temptation to walk away she will face when everything comes out. I'm not saying she will, but it would be easier for her if she did. With that raggedy-ass Jake here, it only makes things worse. She feels awful about having to dump him, but he is not the one. She knows it, I know it, and deep down he does too."

Miguel jumped out of his seat, and it toppled over. “He had the nerve to show his face around here again? After all the drama he caused, he brought his ass back to the States?”

“I’ll do you one better: he is at my house.”

Miguel grabbed his keys and crossed the room suddenly. “Let’s go. Let’s get over there and whoop his ass. What are you waiting for?”

Tyree laughed and crossed his arms over his chest. “You know I would love nothing more than to tear him apart, but I’m not gonna bust in there like some barbarian. I told her I would let her have time to end things.”

“Are you crazy? He stole your woman once, and you left him alone with her again?”

Tyree smiled and nodded slightly. “I have to trust that she will do the right thing. If I can’t trust her now, then we won’t work. I can’t hold on to her if she doesn’t want to be mine.”

“That’s true, but letting him have a chance to weasel his way back in isn’t smart. We don’t lose if you get over there and fight for your woman, now.”

“I’m not worried. I made sure she knew where home was before I left her. He’d have to scrub every inch of her body to erase me. I was all in it.”

Miguel hissed at his statement and reclaimed his seat. “I still think it’s a mistake to leave him alone with her. I’m sure she knows better now, but I don't trust him. After what he did to you, I hate I was ever cordial to dude."

"It's okay," Tyree sighed. "No one knew what he said to get next to her. She wasn't talking. Hell, I had to get in her face drunk to get the truth."

"Yeah, speaking of that, you never did tell me what you said to her that night."

"I said a lot of stuff. I told her I hated her and then I took her on the kitchen counter."

"How do you tell a woman you hate her and she still gives it up? No wonder I've been striking out. I need to adjust my tactics."

"No, what you need is a woman you feel good enough about to settle down with. When you find that and give her what she needs, she will do things that would blow your mind."

"I like watching you with your family, but I don't think that life is for me. It's too complicated. I saw what losing her did to you before, and I don't want to take that chance."

"Love is beautiful, and having my son and his mother is like nothing I've ever felt. I can't describe it, but you would be lucky to feel half of what I feel."

"I get that, but I just don't see myself feeling that way for any woman. You and Mia have known each other since we were kids. You worked a long time on that connection."

"Yeah, well, I'm not going to keep grilling you about a family. I think one day you will change your mind and give me a little niece or nephew."

"Fat chance. But, anyways, you never told me why you thought someone was in Kyan's room."

"Well, earlier today, after Jake showed up, I lost my head, and Jackson had to drag me outside and—"

"Jackson? Who is Jackson?" Miguel interrupted.

"You heard about Jackson, Milan's husband."

"Mills is here? When did this happen?"

"They just got here today. Dude is cool, and their little girl is as cute as can be. Man, you're getting me off track. Anyway, after he pulled me outside, I saw footprints near Kyan's window."

"You have guards there. Maybe it was them. You should ask around before you freak out."

"I just don't see this as a coincidence, but I'll try it your way. Until I figure everything out, I want them staying in the main house. I can't take any chances."

Miguel nodded and sat up in his seat. "Yeah, better safe than sorry; but what about you? Where are you staying?"

"Wherever Mia is."

"You are so whipped. I can't wait to see what happens when Renee gets home and finds you shacking up with Mia."

"It's going to be interesting, but I don't care. I will just have to man up and break it off."

"Well, good luck."

Tyree knew Miguel was watching to see if his expression would waver, but it remained positive. In a way, he knew Miguel envied him for having that kind of love for a woman. What Tyree and Mia shared could outlast all the problems that were sure to come their way once Renee figured out she was no longer in the picture. As big of a problem as Renee would be, he knew they should also expect some type of disturbance from Richmond. For some reason, he was dead against the union of those two. The strange part was he seemed to genuinely like Tyree, but when it came to him being with Mia, he strongly disapproved.

In the time before Richmond figured out Mia and Tyree were an item, they seemed to have a father-son relationship. Their relationship seemed to be better than the one he had with John. Richmond had taken him under his wing and groomed him in the ways of business, which ultimately helped him in his endeavors with Mia years later. Although Richmond was a ruthless, unfeeling, godless man when it came to his own family, he cared for Tyree until he figured out what had been going on under his nose. Once the truth about Mia and Tyree got out, Richmond withdrew his support and became as hardened about Tyree as he was about everything else.

As Miguel continued to watch his big brother, Tyree tried to let his confidence shine through and was only broken from his thoughts when the door to the office swung open. Both brothers looked up to see their little sister looking distracted, and Tyree stood to receive her. When he placed his hands around her shoulders, she shivered, and his eyes widened. They had never seen her so off-balance.

While Tyree saw to Asha, Miguel broke his stare from them to look down at his phone. He had received a text in the midst of all the confusion, and he was reading it with a crazy look on his face. Miguel was glued to his cell phone when Tyree finally voiced his concerns about Asha.

"Baby sis, what gives? Why are you looking like you just saw a ghost?"

Asha was still in a daze, and it took her a minute to respond to what she was being asked. When she looked at Tyree, she opened her mouth but was halted by Miguel's ghastly exclamation.

"Miguel?" Tyree questioned as his attention shifted from his sister to his stunned little brother. "What's wrong with you two?"

Tyree was lost, and when Miguel's and Asha's eyes connected, he knew both were keeping something from him. As if conceding to go first,

Miguel stood, and Tyree saw Asha shake her head suddenly. Catching this, Tyree looked at them, demanding answers.

"Okay, one of you is going to tell me what's going on here right now."

"Ty," Miguel said quietly, "sit down."

"I don't want to sit. What is going on, Miguel? What did you find?"

"Ty, sit down." Miguel slammed his hand on the desk. "I need you to trust me right now."

Tyree knew Miguel saw his nervous stance as he paced the floor before flopping down in the chair in front of the desk. Instead of talking to Tyree, Miguel turned his laptop around and brought the monitor to where he could see everything. When Tyree saw the outside of his and Mia's place, he froze. It only took him a second to realize what Miguel was freaking out about. Tyree and Asha both leaned in to take a closer look, and both saw the dark, hooded figure who crept off the porch that night.

Tyree sucked in a deep breath. "Someone was in my house?"

Before Miguel could react, Tyree was out of his seat and charging toward the door.

"Where are you going?"

"I'm taking them away from there. I can't let them be in danger a second time. I won't allow it."

"Ty, there's more."

"What?" Tyree yelled. "It had better be important because, right now, all I can think about is getting them out of there."

"Richmond, Ty. He, well . . . I think you're right about him."

"Why? Just a few minutes ago, you thought I was overreacting."

"That was until I saw this." Miguel handed him his cell and silently awaited a response.

Tyree read over the information and closed his eyes after seeing all he needed to, and he passed the phone back to Miguel. "So he got a huge payoff when both Janelle and Helen died, huh?"

"Yeah, millions on the insurance policies and their stock in Livingston. It's how he was able to take the company from Mia and Rick. This addendum was just proved as valid. Mia and Rick have been fighting it for years." Miguel looked at Tyree and shook his head. "I guess she didn't tell you. Probably wanted to keep you out of it. It's a motive, and also very legit. His claim to Livingston is valid, which means the company is all his. With both Janelle and Helen dead, he has their shares, which gives him the majority vote. This makes him untouchable."

"Untouchable? He can't think he is going to get away with this, right? There are too many loose ends, too many people who could figure this out."

"Maybe his plan was to wrap up those loose ends. I don't know."

"I have to get to them now. I have to make sure they leave here. They were safe as long as they weren't here. I talked her into this; I put them at risk."

"Tyree, the safest she will be is with you," Asha voiced after coming down from the shock. "You can't let them out of your sight. It would be disastrous."

"Asha, I let him get taken once before. I have to ensure their safety this time."

"Then stay with them."

Tyree looked to his brother, who nodded in approval, and then he looked back to Asha and clutched her hand. "I have to do what's best for them. I promise you both I will make the right decision." They sat quietly as they let all the information sink in.

Tyree let his sister's and brother's hands drop after several minutes, and he stood to leave the room. Just as he was reaching for the door, he turned and looked back to them. "I'll see you two at dinner."

"You're still coming to that?" Miguel looked completely surprised.

"Yeah. The old man obviously has something on his mind and I, for one, think he knows more than he is telling about Richmond. I'm going to get to the bottom of it."

"With Mia beside you?" Asha asked.

"With Mia beside me." He nodded. "I thought about it, and you're right. Besides, without her here, I would be stressed and worried to no end."

"Good." Asha offered a timid smile. "Go to them now."

Tyree was long gone, and Miguel found himself asking questions in his head. He was wondering what was going on with his sister and why she seemed so distraught. Huffing, she placed her hands on the desk, and Miguel sat up in his chair and leaned in to question her.

"Tell me."

"Tell you what?"

"Asha, don't play with me. Tell me what you figured out."

"Later, Miguel. This will all make more sense later."

Asha stood to leave, and Miguel called out to her. "Where are you going?"

"To get ready for dinner, of course. It should be interesting."

"Ash, you okay?"

"Yeah, big brother. I'll be fine."

"All right. I guess I'll see you tonight."

"Bye." She walked out of the office.

Miguel shook his head as he absorbed all the secrets exposed today. He found himself looking at the computer again, trying to figure out why he just couldn't shake the familiar feeling he had when watching the video. It was completely baffling, considering Mia and Tyree both assured him they didn't have cameras installed around the house.

Something besides the obvious was going on. He had no idea where the video had come from, but he wasn't sure how to tell Tyree that. If he knew the video came from a mysterious source and the text had come from a blocked number, he would freak out even more.

Miguel was confused about how everything seemed to fall into his lap, but one thing puzzled him the most: why was it that the person in the video seemed so familiar? The closer he looked, he realized what he thought was a man before was actually a woman. The slender frame was cloaked in dark clothing, but he could tell, without a doubt, it was a woman.

As he allowed his mind to run freely and explore every possibility, one name popped into his head: Renee. It had to be her. She had to be the one messing with Kyan that night. It was the only possible explanation.

As Miguel thought it over even more, he laughed to himself about how silly he was being. It had to be her. Renee knew the grounds of the house as well as Tyree and Mia. She also would have the most to gain if Tyree and Mia split again, and she knew what triggered it the first time.

Now, Miguel felt silly for setting off all those alarms in Tyree's head about Kyan being unsafe. Their only problem was a scheming soon-to-be ex. He sighed in relief, taking pleasure in the fact that Tyree would soon be rid of her; and he packed his things up to get ready for dinner.

Miguel left the office and closed the door behind him. When he got to the elevator, he realized he left his desktop on, and he doubled back. After swinging the door open, he heard voices that sounded like they were in his office and raced around to see what the source was. After he saw that it was just his desktop playing, his laptop fell from his hand. He was clubbed over the head, and he fell to the floor. And then everything went black.

Chapter Twenty-two

Sitting at the dinner table, Tyree found himself shuffling around in anticipation of seeing his brother again. Asha was already there with Terence, and they looked like they had something to prove. Things were rapidly getting out of hand and, the more he thought about it, he knew he didn't want Mia present for whatever drama this night would bring. He had to do a special song and dance to keep her staying at the house with Rick and Cassandra, and Jackson had assisted in getting Milan on board with his wishes. Now all he had to do was wrap things up between him and Renee, and they could move on.

The threat to his family, he convinced himself, was very real. He knew he needed to get them away from Atlanta until he had a handle on things but, now, he was sure he should be with them. He could take some time away from the company and spend it jet setting with his family.

The reality was if they were always moving, then no one could touch them. That was his plan: to never get touched.

Tyree kept watching the door in anticipation of Miguel's arrival, and he sighed when he only saw John and Karen entering. As much as he loved his mother, his father was not a person he wanted to be around when things were so tense in his life. He always seemed to amplify any bad feelings. Karen was always amazing in providing her warmth and comfort but, at the present time, he wasn't ready to share what he was feeling, even with her.

Sitting with his eyes closed, quietly contemplating where to go first, Tyree felt a body slide down in the chair next to him and place her hands in his lap. His gorgeous smile appeared thinking that Mia had gone against his wishes and joined him anyway. As much as he wanted to keep her away from the drama, he had to admit he needed her close. He was feeling displaced and needed to feel the love only she could offer. Raising her hand to his lips with his eyes closed, he placed a gentle kiss on her hand.

Tyree knew Mia's touch anywhere, and something was definitely off. When he opened his eyes, he dropped the hand suddenly, realizing it was Renee. He saw the hurt expression on her face, and he slid his chair over slightly. When Tyree glanced around the table, he saw the confused expression held by his sister and mother, and he shrugged. He had no idea she was back in town, let alone attending the dinner that was meant for family only.

Looking over and catching his sister's hateful gaze, Tyree stood to walk over to her side of the table to explain what was going on. He had promised to end things the minute he saw Renee, and he was caught off guard and knew Asha was about to blow a fuse. Before he could effectively make his way over, John halted his progression. With his hand in the air, John cleared his throat, and Tyree huffed.

"Family, I would like to begin."

"Miguel isn't here," Tyree hissed quietly.

"I'm sure your brother will be joining us soon, but we need to go ahead and get started with my announcement. It's too wonderful to keep hidden any longer."

"What is it? You know I don't understand why we had to come to dinner to discuss something that could have been handled over the damn phone."

"Tyree Akio Johnston," Karen interjected, "you will show some respect. I know your feelings about your father, but you will at least give me the respect I deserve. I would very much like for you to take your seat and hear what he has to say."

Tyree looked to his mother and nodded slowly, pulling his chair out and flopping down. As much as he wanted to flip the table and grab John, shaking him, making him come clean about Richmond, his loyalty to his mother made him stop in his tracks. No matter what he was going through she always had his back, so he would do anything she ever asked, even listen to his ass of a father.

Tyree watched as John smiled brightly when he reclaimed his seat and leaned down to kiss Karen's cheek before beginning again. He had to fight back the urge to fly over the table watching that man touch his mother. He always thought she was too good for him, and now he was sure of it.

Tyree fiddled with his napkin while waiting for John to begin and he shivered when he felt Renee's hand graze over his legs and then rest in between them. In the past, this act would have made him crazy but, now, it was just unwelcome. He began to get uncomfortable when her hand began to circle his zipper, and he drew in a deep breath. Reaching down, grabbing her hand, he placed it back in her own lap and tried not to notice the look that formed on her face. He was ready to leave this place and all the madness it came with.

Knowing Renee's advances were the result of her not knowing the truth about where they stood was the only thing that kept Tyree from snapping her neck when her hand found its way back to his zipper. This time, she pulled it down and let her fingers venture inside. Letting out an uncomfortable growl, Tyree jumped up, grabbing Renee by the wrist. Pulling her into the lobby of the restaurant, he sat her down in one of the open seats.

Running his hand over his head, he sighed and turned to her. "You can't do shit like that."

"You looked stressed, and you know my talents of making you forget it." She stood, advancing on him.

He held his hands out, stopping her before she got too close. "Stop. We are in a restaurant with my mother here. Have some decency."

Renee looked stunned. He had never denied any of her crazy propositions, ever. "What's going on, Tyree? Why are you acting like this? I would think you would be happy to see me. I've been gone over a week, and you should be ripping my clothes off, unless—"

"Unless what?" he asked knowingly. "Go ahead and ask."

He noted the shock on her face, and he inhaled deeply. Here it was: the moment he could finally move on. Or so he thought. Tyree waited for her to voice her suspicions and he could confirm and be done with this whole mess, but she stood silent and then let out a casual giggle.

"You know what? I'm just tired. My mind is playing tricks on me. Of course, you don't want me groping you under the table with your mother there. Sorry, it won't happen again."

Tyree was stunned. He couldn't wrap his mind around how it wasn't obvious to her. He sat there, looking blankly as she darted back to the table. Following her after a brief moment, he sat down, pulling her ear level with his mouth. "We need to talk."

"I know, but not now." She smiled, turning to look at John, who was still waiting to make his announcement.

"Now is the perfect time. I need to tell you something important."

"That's funny," she smirked, "so do I."

Tyree swallowed the lump in his throat and placed his hand on the table in front of them. "Let's get out of here. We need to talk in private. There is a lot we have to discuss."

With a smug grin, Renee turned to him and ran her hand down his face. "In due time, baby. Right now, let's see what John has to say."

"Fine," he huffed, "but the minute he is done, we're out of here."

"Anxious to get me home, huh?"

"Oh, you have no idea."

Standing, dinging his glass, John looked around the table beaming. "To my beautiful family, as you know, there have been some troubles with one of our partners and, as a result of that, I have made a huge decision." The whole table grew silent and gave him their undivided attention. "I've decided that, as of tomorrow, I will be returning to Johnston Incorporated full time."

Tyree glanced to Asha and rolled his eyes before jumping up, causing his fork and knife to fall to the floor. "Great, just great, because I have an announcement of my own." Everyone looked his way, and Asha gave him a nod of encouragement. "I'm taking some time off to travel with my family."

Renee held her remarkable smile and placed a hand on his lap. "I'm glad you feel that way, because our baby needs the attention."

"Our baby?" Tyree choked out breathlessly.

"It's my news." Renee beamed. "As of three days ago, I'm two months pregnant."

The table was completely silent as Tyree slid back into his seat. John and Renee shared a brief look that didn't go unnoticed by Terence and Asha.

They were studying everyone's reactions carefully until the ringing of Tyree's cell phone brought things back into focus.

"Yes," Tyree barked into the phone. He paused when he heard what was being said, and he let out a deep sigh. "I can do that, but do you need us now? We are kinda in the middle of something." He was gripping his phone tightly as he spoke. "Okay, fine, I'm on my way." Shaking his head, he exhaled. "No need to call anyone. We're all together."

Hanging up the phone and placing his head in his hands, Tyree allowed himself a brief moment to break down as a few loose tears fell.

Karen was instantly at his side when he raised his head. "Son, what's wrong? Is it Miguel? Where is my baby?"

Tyree took her hand and pulled it to his lips for a gentle kiss, and he put his hand to her hair. "Mom, don't freak out. It's nothing like that. It's just something we were working on that fell through. Asha and I are going to need to leave with Terence and meet up with Miguel to get it handled."

Karen drew in a deep breath and placed her trembling hands in Tyree's lap. "Well, do you have to go right now? We haven't had dinner. We were in the middle of a celebration, and your brother hasn't arrived."

"Unfortunately, yes, but I assure you there will be time to celebrate everything in the near future." He pulled her up and wrapped his arms around her. Tyree walked out and turned to find Asha and Terence behind him with confused expressions. But before he could get inside his car, Renee walked over, placing a hand on his shoulder. He turned to her and tried to put on his calmest face. "Renee, now is not the time. I have to fix something."

"I understand that. I just wanted you to know that I'm going to head to the house. I think I should get some rest; the baby makes me tired."

"Yeah, get some rest," he huffed. "We'll talk later."

Tyree got into his car and buckled himself in before reaching over to grab his cell. He wanted to remain calm but, inside, he was terrified. The call he received had nothing to do with the business. They were really going to see Miguel in the hospital. Melvin, the security guard, found him passed out in his office and was instructed to call Tyree, Asha, Terence, and no one else because Rock, the head of the family's security, arrived shortly after he discovered Miguel. He wasn't sure what all the secrecy was about, but he was sure it had everything to do with either Richmond or John, if not both.

He knew whatever was going on had to do with the fact that he and Miguel were looking into Richmond, but he was discovering John had just as much to hide, if not more. Even though he was sure they were behind it all, he found himself wondering how he could have been stupid enough to put his family in danger like this once again. He knew he was definitely to blame and he took the weight of his decision and Miguel's condition on his shoulders. Now, all he could do was damage control.

Chapter Twenty-three

Walking into the quiet house after leaving the hospital, Tyree found himself exhaling into the air. He had no idea how he was going to do what was necessary, no idea how to begin to wrap his mind around what needed to be done. Walking down the hallway, he stumbled into Jackson rocking Sydney in his arms and singing a light tune. Chuckling, Tyree reached over to touch her cheek.

"Late night?" Jackson laughed.

"Yeah, you?"

"Just putting the princess to sleep. Millie is out cold, and I didn't have it in me to wake her up when she looks so peaceful. Syd was crying, and I wanted to keep the noise down. Singing always gets her to sleep."

"Yeah, looks like it. She's sleeping pretty soundly now."

"Yeah. So, what's going on? You look like you have something on your mind."

Tyree leaned against the wall and shoved his hands in his pockets, trying not to make eye contact. "You ever know you need to do something, but know if you do you will never be happy again? Have you ever known the thing that would hurt the most was the only plausible thing to do to protect the people you love?"

Jackson shifted Sydney to his other shoulder and focused in on Tyree. "It's those footprints we saw, right? You found more to them?"

"There's a lot I can't explain right now. I just need you to do me a favor. I need you to take Milan and Sydney away from here. Take them home. Do whatever you need to do to convince her to leave as soon as possible."

"I can do that, but what about your girl and son? Are they safe?"

"For now. I'm working on that, too. I don't want to freak you out; I just want to make sure your family isn't involved in any of our mess."

"I can appreciate that, but you know my wife and your girl. They're going to want answers before we can get them to do anything."

"I'll handle Mia; don't worry."

"Tell me this: are we at least safe here for the night? If not, I'll wake Millie up."

"I have security surrounding the place and no one will get in here. I called Rick and let him know what was going on. No one will get into the main house undetected; that's why I needed you here."

"How serious is this?"

"Very," Tyree admitted before reaching out to shake his hand. "Don't worry about tonight; I got it covered. But get away from here tomorrow. You think I can ask you one more favor?"

Jackson nodded, stepping back into the next room while Tyree followed him. They were in the room with the door closed for a few minutes, and then Tyree emerged, walking down the halls in search of Mia. He needed to find her and see her beautiful face to help him deal with all the turmoil in his life. She was always the one who helped him hold things together. She would help him for the night; but in the morning, he would have to do the hardest thing he had ever done, and he wasn't sure he was ready. He loved children, his son was the greatest gift he could ever ask for, but this news of Renee's wasn't what he needed. He had always wanted another child, but he wanted it with Mia.

Searching the obvious rooms, Tyree saw no sign of Mia. He did, however, find Kyan sleeping peacefully in the normal room he took when visiting. It had all of his favorite things, and it was where he was the most comfortable in the house. Sitting down on the bed next to him, Tyree rubbed his back, speaking to what he thought was a sleeping child.

"I've always wanted what's best for you, little man. I always wanted to make you proud to be my son, but somewhere along the line, I feel like I failed you. If it weren't for me, your life would have been so much easier, happier. I just need to protect you. You and your mom. You're so important to me."

Wiggling under Tyree's palm, Kyan flipped over and reached up to hug him. "Daddy, are you leaving me and Mama again?"

"I don't want to leave you or your mother. I just need you to be safe."

"Why are you scared, Daddy? Are you scared I'm going to go away again? I didn't mean to run away. The man just said Grandpa sent him to get me, and I really wanted to see him. I missed him."

"Son, people will tell you whatever you want to hear to get you to do what they want. I want you to know it wasn't your fault. None of it was. I should have been watching you better."

"I was okay, Daddy, I promise. They took care of me; they were nice to me."

Tyree had never gotten this much out of Kyan regarding his kidnapping. They always assumed he was too young to remember, but now it seemed like he knew more than they thought. "Ky, do you remember how you got back home? Do you know who had you?"

He shook his head no, but the look on his face said otherwise.

"If you know something, you can tell me. I promise I won't be mad, and you won't get in trouble."

"Renee scares me, Daddy. She doesn't do anything mean, but I know she doesn't like Mama, and she just reminds me of when I was gone. I had a dream about the mask people, and they sounded like her voice. I don't like it when you leave me alone with her. The mask people said they would kill Mama if their plan didn't work."

"Is that why you told your mom you don't like my house?" Tyree held his breath, anticipating the answer. He had no idea what he would do if his son were to admit the woman he was living with had something to do with taking away the most important parts of his life.

"Yes, but if you want me to, I can try to like your house if you stay with me and Mama."

Sighing, he offered his son a subtle smile, trying not to alert him to the thoughts racing through his head. "No one is going to hurt your mama," he said and touched Kyan's nose.

"I'll make sure she is always fine. Listen, even if I'm not with you all the time, just know that I love you. Nothing I do is ever your fault."

"I know. Are you going to be here when I wake up?"

Tyree grinned and ran his hand down Kyan's cheek. "I'll try, but if I'm not, just know I'll see you soon. Is that okay with you?"

"Yes, Daddy."

Kyan turned over, closing his eyes as Tyree snuck out of the room and pulled the door shut. He continued to search the rooms for Mia, and then instantly he knew where she would be. Walking down the long hallway all the way over to the west wing of the house, he stopped right outside the door to his favorite room in the house: Mia's old room. They had spent so much time there when they were younger. It was the room they first made love in. It was special.

Twisting the knob and pushing the door open, he found her lying down with a fleece draped over her legs. She was dressed in a short silver negligee that left nothing to the imagination. She was clearly waiting for him. He ran his hand over her smooth skin, and her eyes popped open, locking with his, holding them both in the moment.

"Hey, handsome. How was dinner?"

"Hello, kitten. I really don't want to discuss dinner when you're lying here in my favorite room wearing this sexy little thing."

"You like it?" She sat up, and he ran his hand down her side.

"You know I do." He leaned in to kiss her, and she lay back on the bed. He ran his hands through her hair and smiled against her lips.

"Anything I can do to make you forget your troubles?"

"You're here. You're already doing it. Just being you makes me forget the world, babe. God, I just need you. Let's make tonight perfect."

Still kissing his lips gently, she wrapped her arms around his neck. "What's so special about tonight? We have so many more to look forward to. I know it must have been hard sitting across from John, but I know you did your best."

Feeling guilt washing through him, Tyree pulled back, stopping the indulgent kisses that were drawing him in.

Looking at him with confusion in her eyes, Mia huffed. "Why are you being weird? Did something happen?"

Not wanting to lie to her, Tyree ran his hands over her face and sighed. "Kitten, I didn't want to tell you this way, but Miguel is in the hospital. Someone broke into the office and laid him out on the floor. I was with him earlier, and it doesn't look good. He was hit pretty hard, and he hasn't come to."

"Aw, baby, why didn't you call me? I would have been there with you. I would have stayed right by your side."

Feeling the pressure build in him, Tyree forced himself to smile at her. "I know. I just needed this time with him, and I needed for you to enjoy your cousin. I know how you've missed her, and I wanted you to have that. You deserve it. You deserve the best."

"Tyree," she said, scooting closer to him, "why do I feel like you're keeping something else from me? We promised to be honest; now, level with me. Tell me what's wrong."

"Mia." He kissed her hand. "Right now, tonight, just let me enjoy being with you, loving you. I swear as long as I live I will never forget this night if you just grant me this one thing."

Looking at his flustered expression, she nodded and pulled his head to hers. "If what you need is me, then it's what you will have."

Pulling her head to rest in the hollow of his neck and holding it there, he let the tears he had been holding back wash down his cheek. Tonight would be the beginning of so many things, the beginning of the end of life as he knew it. Running his hands up and down her back, he held her as tight as he could until she leaned back to look at him. Without saying a word, she leaned in, kissing the tears from his cheeks.

Tyree allowed himself to enjoy her lips on him and he reached down to tug at the silver material. Once he had it firmly in his grasp, he pulled it off and tossed it across the room. Revealing her body to his hungry eyes sent him into overdrive. Pushing her back and snatching at his shirt, he tore the material trying to get to her by any means necessary. Moving his hands down to pop the button on his pants and slide his zipper down, Tyree threw his pants and boxers, sending them to the same fate as her nightgown.

Feeling the need to give her everything, Tyree ran his hand down her stomach with his mouth starting at her neck. Trailing his tongue down her chest and flicking around her breasts, he dug his fingers inside her vibrating flesh, and she eased herself farther down the bed, pushing him deeper. He moved his lips back to her neck and kissed the spot he knew drove her crazy, and he flicked his tongue over her sweet-smelling skin. She intoxicated him to the point where he blocked out everything but the smell of her skin, the feel of her warm flesh and, when he looked at her, the love in her eyes. He loved the understanding he got from them, and the trust he didn't deserve.

Tyree found himself with a burst of energy he didn't think he was capable of and he bit down on the pulse point on her neck throbbing beneath his lips. Becoming overwhelmed with emotion, he added another finger, causing her breath to still in her chest. Sinking farther inside her, he felt her body trembling. Placing himself between her legs and removing his fingers, he took her mouth leaving her breathless. Gazing into her eyes, he loved the look she was giving him. Although she was in control of her senses, he knew that she needed him.

Drawing back, reaching for a condom, Tyree grinned, admiring her beauty. He returned once he had what he needed and he ran his hand over her. She had her legs spread out around him while he fiddled with the wrapper in his hand. Before he could gather his thoughts on the situation, Mia rolled him over, knocking the condom from his grasp. He wanted to reach for it. He wanted to so bad, but he was frozen looking at her. The woman was everything he always wanted, everything he needed. Sitting up and wrapping his arms around her, he pulled her down, submerging himself within her warm center.

Smiling as she crossed her arms around his neck, Tyree grabbed her hips, rocking her into him. He didn't have to do much because she was set in a rhythm that was driving him crazy. She still had her hands latched around his neck and was lifting herself and dropping back down on him with such precision his eyes began to roll backward. She continued this, watching him and feeling his nails dig into her sides. Tyree was lost in her and needed to regain his restraint before he snapped.

As if sensing his need, Mia released his neck and lay back on the bed throwing her legs over his shoulders in the process. Still in his seated position, Tyree clutched her thighs and began to roll himself into her. Pulling her farther to him, he felt her legs tensing. He knew what this meant, but he was still unrelenting in his attack on her body. Instead of letting up, he drove into her harder and faster, allowing himself to enjoy the tiny tremors her body exhibited.

Stilling his movements inside her, Tyree moved her legs down, disconnecting them momentarily. Resuming his position between her legs, he once again took her mouth into a steamy kiss. Just before releasing her, he slipped back inside, causing a shock to her sensitive flesh. Feeling him enter her again, Mia tensed and dug her nails into his back causing a light chuckle to break from his mouth. Although it stung, he loved the reaction he could get from her when she was all in. It made the experience so much more worth it.

Taking her legs and wrapping them around his waist, he began to move inside her. This time, it wasn't the hungry, erratic strokes he was accustomed to. This time, he took his time planting kisses everywhere as he moved in and out. Running his hands down her sides, he found a stopping spot on her hips and drove himself in as deep as possible and stopped. Her eyes that were previously closed flew open, and they shared a moment.

"Tyree," she whispered. "Why—"

"Kitten, I love you. I love you so much, and to think that this . . . I just love you. Always know that."

"I know you love me, but why—"

She was cut off when he grabbed her hands, sliding them above her head as he pushed himself against her. Her soft cries filled the room as he worked to rid her of all the questions he knew were clouding her brain. Kissing her neck, running his tongue all over her, he blocked them out of his mind too. He couldn't tell her the truth: that he wanted her to leave because he was afraid. She would never go for it, so he knew to save her, he would have to break her heart. If he only had one night, he was going to spend it making love to the woman he needed more than life. He would spend the rest of his life in misery if he could save hers.

After what seemed like an eternity together, Tyree ran his hands under Mia, taking her soft flesh under his fingertips, and he pushed himself as deep as he could, spilling himself inside her. He felt her flutter and witnessed her beautiful orgasm as she clung to him breathlessly. Tyree was so connected he didn't want to move. He wanted to stay like this with her forever even though he knew it was an impossibility. He never wanted to leave her side even though he knew he had to.

Rolling off her, he lay back on the soft pillow, and her head found his chest. No words were spoken. He just ran his hand up and down her back, relaxing her into a deep slumber he knew she needed. Listening to her even breathing was how he fell asleep, but not before setting his plan in motion. Tonight really would be one to remember. It would be one that shaped the rest of his memories.

Chapter Twenty-four

"Asha," Terence sighed. "Maybe you should consider leaving this room. I'm sure he will be fine the rest of the night. The guards are standing outside the door and won't let anyone in."

They both had been stationed at Miguel's bedside, with Asha refusing to move an inch. Tyree had left hours earlier to check on Mia and Kyan, leaving the two of them alone with him. Terence had been pleading with her for over thirty minutes with no luck.

"Terence, someone tried to kill my brother," she hissed. "I'm not leaving him here alone. Whoever did this may come back."

"They can't get by Rock, you know that."

Rock was the head of security for their family. He was only brought in when there was a severe situation. Rock had been with them for over twenty years on and off and had just recently come to work for them full time. He was a no-nonsense ex-marine who got the name

Rock because he was solid muscle standing at six feet five. Rock had an intimidating demeanor that frightened most in his path, but all three of the Johnston kids knew he was as genuine as they came. He was always a big part of their lives, much to John's disdain. All three of them seemed to be closer to Rock than they were to John.

"I know, but I don't want him to be alone. If it were one of us, you know he would be sitting right where we are. Since Tyree has something to take care of, I'm all he has."

"*We're* all he has. If you're staying, then so am I. I had the babysitter take Meelah to your parents' house. I'm sure she will be fine."

"No, Terence. You have to go and get her," she snapped. "I don't want my daughter in the house with that man."

"Your mom is there too, honey."

"I don't care. I don't trust him. Go and get her now!"

"Fine, I'll go, but I'm coming back here tonight."

Asha sighed and held her hand up to object. "I don't want to argue with you. Just take Meelah home and let her sleep in her own bed. She doesn't need to see her uncle Miguel this way, and I would just feel better if she was home with you."

Nodding, Terence stood and leaned over to place a kiss on her lips. Holding her forehead to his, he looked into her eyes. She knew he hated not seeing the confidence he usually saw. There was a mixture of things replacing it, fear being one of them. "Baby, you get some sleep. I know it's hard to believe right now, but things will be fine. I promise you that."

"I'm scared."

"Don't be." He pulled her closer and squeezed her tight. "Just trust us. We have this under control."

"You might, but what about Tyree? I don't agree with what he wants to do."

Shaking his head slowly, Terence knelt before her. "He has to deal with everything his own way. He has to do what's best for him. We can't interfere."

"It's a mistake."

He stood, walked over to the door, placed his hand on the doorknob, and turned back to her. "Well, it's his mistake to make. Stay out of it, baby."

"Sure," she voiced unconvincingly. She knew he saw through her fake answer but was too drained to keep up this back and forth with her.

"Fine." He smiled, pulling the door open and walking out.

Looking back down at Miguel, Asha grabbed his hand and gave it a gentle squeeze. After a few moments of silence, she resumed a conversation with him. "In just a little while, I promise you, we will be fine. Just trust me, little brother. I'm watching out for you. No one will ever hurt you again. Not Richmond, and not Dad. You know, I feel stupid. I used to look to Dad with such admiration only to find out he is as rotten as Richmond, if not worse." She continued to rub his hand and lifted it to her lips.

Dropping Miguel's hand, Asha got up and walked over to the door, and it creaked as she opened it. She found Rock standing with two other guards, and she waved him closer. "Rock, I need it to be just you here right now. No one gets in here," she stated firmly.

"Sure thing, Miss Asha." Waving his hand, he cleared the hallway and nodded back to her. "Anything else I can do for you?"

"Just make sure you have some trusted men at my house. Terence will be arriving with Meelah shortly."

"Already covered, Miss Asha." He got closer to her ear and whispered, "And that other thing you asked for, I'm working on it."

"Thank you." She nodded and turned to walk back in the room.

"Miss Asha," he called out before the door closed.

"Yeah?"

"Things are not always as they seem. They are also not always as bad as you think. You all will be fine, I can assure you."

"Thank you, Rock. You always know what to say."

"No problem." He nodded and turned to his cell phone.

Watching him as she entered the room, Asha saw the text he fired off. She could see the words clearly, but she was a little thrown off by what it meant.

Things are going just as we planned. Make sure you have it handled on your end. No more loose ends.

Seeing the sun break through the dark panels, Mia felt when Tyree sat up, pulling himself out of her embrace. As soon as he was on his feet getting dressed, she was up looking at him. Wiping the sleep from her eyes, she yawned, getting his attention.

"Good morning." He grinned.

"Good morning. Where are you going? I thought we could spend the day with Milan and Jackson."

"I wish I could, but I really have somewhere I need to be. Maybe next time," he replied quickly.

Not knowing why he was in such a snippy mood, Mia got up and went to the dresser, slipping on a shirt and sweats. They both left the room without speaking a word again until they made it to the other end of the house. She watched as he went inside Kyan's room, closing the door behind him. She was lost as to what was going on until she heard Cassandra's and Milan's raised voices downstairs. Kicking into overdrive, she raced down to find Renee standing in the foyer, contending with both Milan and Cassandra.

"Just who in the hell are you?" Renee snapped.

"I'll be the one kicking your ass if you don't get out of here." Milan moved toward her only to be cut off by Jackson. "Get off me." She threw her hands out, trying to make contact. "Tyree is upstairs with my cousin. He doesn't want you. Get over it."

"You need to go, ragamuffin, it's true. Tyree is with Mia now," Cassandra hissed.

"Like hell he is." She reached and pulled her phone out, shoving it in Cassandra's face. "He asked me to meet him here. He said we needed to talk."

Making her way to the forefront, Mia pushed past a fuming Milan and Cassandra, standing before Renee with a look of determination on her face. “I think you should leave my house before I have to get physical.”

“Not a chance, princess,” Renee snapped. “I’m willing to ignore the fact that you’ve been fucking my man while I was away and keep myself from ripping you limb from limb. You better get out of my face before that changes.”

With a surge of built-up frustration, Mia drew back and slapped Renee so hard it sounded through the entire foyer.

Renee stood holding her face, looking at her blankly before responding, “You bitch, you’re going to regret that.”

Renee stepped forward, swinging at Mia and connected one hit before Mia tackled her to the floor, pinning her body down. Once on top of her, Mia swung ferociously, attacking Renee with everything she had. Mia was just about to throw another round of hits when she felt herself being lifted from Renee’s prone body.

“Get off me!” She swung at the person restraining her. It only took her a second to realize it was Tyree and, without a thought, she reached back, slapping him so hard her hand began to throb. After the initial shock had worn off, Tyree slid her feet to the floor, holding his jaw.

"What is going on down here?" He sounded angry and annoyed.

"You let her come in here insulting my family and me. You were supposed to handle this," Mia yelled.

With a devious smirk, Tyree held his hands up and stepped back. "Look, you got this all wrong, Mia. I never promised you anything. We had what we had. It was damn good but, now, it's a wrap. Consider yourself played, sweetheart."

"What?" Milan sounded shocked. "You're really gonna play her like that, Tyree?"

Completely ignoring Milan's inquiries, Tyree walked to Mia, running his hand down her cheek. "You know, I had fun this past week, but we don't work. Renee, she's my ride or die. When you packed up and hauled ass, she was here giving me what I needed, and now it's time I did the same for her. What kind of man would I be to just leave her and my baby alone?"

"Baby?" Mia uttered softly. "When were you going to tell me about this? And what about our son? What are you going to tell him?"

Tyree chuckled and looked over to Jackson, who was just watching quietly. "I'll tell my son to stay away from women like you." In a mockingly sarcastic tone, he stated, "These hoes ain't loyal," and Mia tried to go upside his head.

"Hoe? Have you lost your mind?" Mia had anger lacing every word.

"I said what I meant, and now it's time for me to go." He walked over, lacing his fingers through Renee's. The whole room watched in amazement as he walked her over to the door. Before stepping out, he turned to Mia. "Feel free to pack up and leave again. It's what you do best. The only thing is, this time, I won't be missing you. This time, I'm in control."

Mia raced to pick up one of the vases on display, and she flung it at his head, missing by a few inches. "You stupid son of a bitch, you're going to regret this. You'll never see our son again."

"Somehow, I doubt that matters." He shrugged. "I'll have another one. I'm sure of it." He ran his hand over Renee's stomach. "Let's get you checked out, baby, because if she hurt you in any way, she'll regret it."

"I'm fine," Renee smirked, running her hand down to rest at the base of his neck.

"Even so, I would feel much better if you did."

"Okay, fine. You're already beginning with the spoiling."

"You know it." He pulled her out of the house.

Undoubtedly witnessing the devastation in Mia's eyes, Milan pulled her close, swallowing her in a strong embrace.

Mia had yet to let a tear fall, but when she felt Milan's arms, she broke down. "What is going on? He came back to me; he wanted us to be a family. He made love to me last night."

"He's an ass, Mia. You deserve better, and you'll find that."

"He is," Jackson chimed in, walking over to wrap his arms around his wife. "I hate to be the bearer of bad news, but we have to leave, today. There is an emergency with Envision, love. We have to be there to handle it."

"Can't you go without me?" Milan huffed. "I need to be here for Mia. I don't want to leave her like this."

Mia looked over and saw the hesitation on Jackson's face and spoke up. "Mills, just go. I'll be fine. This time, I won't let him take me there. I have to hold it together for my son. He needs at least one of his parents acting like an adult."

"Mia, I don't like this. I don't want to . . . Hey." She looked to Jackson, and he nodded in agreement, crossing his arms over his chest. "Mia, don't shoot me down, but I thought since you don't have work anymore, why don't you come with us? It could be a nice getaway, and we could still hang out. Whenever we settle whatever crisis is going on at work, I'll be free again."

Mia looked at both Milan and Jackson, trying to come up with a response, when Cassandra stepped up, voicing her opinion. “Go ahead, Mia. You and Kyan could go out and soak up some of that California sun. It will be fun.”

“Actually, it’s on one of the shoots. They’re on location.” Jackson grabbed Milan’s attention. When she turned to look at him with confusion dancing in her gray eyes, he shook his head subtly, and Mia knew something was up.

“So, what do you say, Mia? Somewhere exotic may be exactly what you need to escape this mess.”

“Why do I feel like you are all trying to get me out of here?” Mia scanned the room.

“Because we are,” Milan answered confidently. “You need space.”

After a brief deliberation, Mia reached her hand to Milan and nodded. “Okay, you twisted my arm. I’ll go.”

Before anyone could say anything else, Cassandra offered up their family jet, and Milan accepted, running her hand through Mia’s hair. “Come with me, Mia. Let’s get packed. I promise you, a little fresh air and you’ll be saying, ‘Tyree who?’”

Mia smiled, but it didn’t quite reach her eyes. She was just trying to put on a brave face when

Milan pulled her toward the stairs. She knew Milan hated seeing her like this. Only one man could sink her to such depths. Only Tyree could take her dreams and smash them in the matter of one morning. Now, as much as she needed it, she was dreading this trip. She was going to have to spend the majority of it putting up a front for her cousin.

Chapter Twenty-five

Hours had passed since the big blowup at the house, and Tyree was sitting in the bedroom, watching *SportsCenter* when Renee entered, flopping down next to him. Smiling at her, he wrapped his arms around her, pulling her closer. She relaxed into his embrace and sat quietly gazing at the TV for a few minutes. She ran her hand down his face, and he rolled her over, looking down into her eyes.

"What are you doing, crazy man?" She let out a small giggle.

"Playing with my babies. How are you feeling?"

"Like I told you at the hospital and in the car, I'm fine. Our baby is great, and the heartbeat is strong. You heard it for yourself."

"Yes, our little man has a strong heartbeat." He grinned.

"Yes, our *daughter* does, but that's not why I came in here. I just wanted to talk. You said you wanted to talk earlier, but I kinda just feel like you brought me there to stick it to Mia. Not that

I mind because she was sleeping with my man, but why?"

"Look," he sighed. "I'm sorry you had to go through that, but I needed her to feel like she made me feel. The only way I could do that was to give her false hope and snatch it away."

"The things you said, though." She paused. "It was like you were a completely different person, not my sweet and loving Tyree."

"Having someone take your kid and abandon you the way she did to me would make you do crazy things, but I never meant for you to get hurt."

"I'm not hurt. Well, I'll admit, coming home to find out that you've been sleeping with her wasn't fun, but as long as you promise to never let it happen again, I'm okay."

"Just like that, you forgive me?"

"Just like that." She grinned. "With me, you don't have to jump through hoops. You just have to be you."

"Good, because that's all I can be. But I wanted to ask you something."

"Yeah?" She gave him her undivided attention. "What do you want to know? I'm an open book."

"When you were gone, where were you, really?"

Stuttering, she sat up slowly. "I was at my mom's, you know that."

Running his hand up and down her back, he held his gorgeous smile. "Yeah, well, I wanted to surprise you, so I called down there to talk to your mom about popping in, but she said you hadn't been there in over a year. So where were you?"

Obviously not knowing what to say, Renee stared at him blankly until the ringing of his cell phone broke the silence.

"Hang on, I need to get this."

He sat up as Renee watched until he ended the call. Turning back to her, he placed his hands on either side of her neck. "I have to go. Miguel is awake and asking for Asha and me. We'll finish this later."

Springing up and leaving the room, Tyree left Renee, and he knew her head was spinning. Things were not going as she planned, he knew, and now that he knew she was lying, she was going to have to come up with a story, and fast. He couldn't wait to see what lie she came up with next.

Without pause, just as he thought, Renee jumped up, grabbing for her cell phone. She hit the speed dial, and it began to dial while he just looked on, trying to listen in. While he could only hear her end of the conversation, he heard the relief in her voice when the person she was trying to reach answered. “I need you to get over here now,” he heard her say. “Tyree knows something. I don’t know how much, but he knows.”

Just waiting patiently, he heard her continue. “That’s beside the point. Get over here now. I’m alone.”

She hung up, sighing into the air, not knowing that Tyree was sitting outside the door listening in. He shook his head and eased toward the stairs and out the back door. Once in the car, Tyree replayed in his head the conversation with her and the one with Kyan, and he tightened his grip on the steering wheel. There was definitely something to Kyan’s uneasiness, and he knew for sure Renee was lying about something. Feeling stupid for ever trusting her, he sped off to the hospital, wishing he had never brought her into his son’s life. He was determined to get to the bottom of whatever she was hiding to make sure he hadn’t done all this in vain. He had given up the woman of his dreams to nail the lying bitch carrying his baby.

Chapter Twenty-six

Running her hand over the wedding band she kept on a necklace, Mia ripped it from her neck, sending it flying into the wall of her bedroom. She had come down to the old house to pack her and Kyan's things to get ready for her trip. Milan and Jackson were waiting up at the house with the kids, and she just needed time to clear her head while gathering what she needed. She had the radio playing, loudly, and she was singing along.

While she shuffled through what to leave and what to take, Mia was oblivious to the fact that she was being watched until a person cleared her throat. Jumping and dropping everything in her hands, she turned to find Milan standing behind her. Reaching over to turn the music down, Milan took a seat on the bed, picking up the fallen items and tossing them in a bag.

"Mia, are you okay?"

"Yeah, I'm sure I will be. I just need some time," she replied quietly.

"Well, this here won't help." She giggled. "You're doing this listening to depressing music thing again. You know this 'Un-Break My Heart,' 'Breathe Again,' 'Another Sad Love Song' madness is not the answer. You'll get even more depressed. I remember the last time I had to pry you out of this mood. Me and Asha were cursing Toni Braxton for life." She laughed, patting her hand.

"This time is different. Don't get me wrong, I'm hurt, but for different reasons. This time, he didn't turn only on me; he basically said he didn't care about ever seeing our son again."

"Yeah, after you yelled out that he was never going to see him. I'm sure he only said it to set you off. You know how you both hate to lose face."

"Whatever." She flipped her hand up in the air. "I just need to get away from him before I murder him and that dust witch he's engaged to."

"Dust witch?" Milan laughed.

"Yes, dry-faced whore. I just wanted to mutilate her."

Milan shook her head, looking amused by the serious expression on Mia's face. "You wouldn't. You might get mad enough to smack her around, but you wouldn't do anything to seriously hurt her."

Mia nodded in agreement. "Maybe not, but a girl can have dreams."

"You can think whatever you want as long as you don't act on it. I need you around, and so does your son. I just wanted to check on you and see where your head was and make sure you weren't going to do anything so drastic as move back to Paris. I know this place has its reminders, but it also holds all of our good times. I just don't want to go two years without seeing you again."

Mia dropped the items in her hand and sat down, laying her head on Milan's shoulder. "Honestly, I have nothing to go back to there. All I did was throw myself into work and since I don't have that anymore, what else is there?"

"What about Jake? I know you said he wasn't the one, but are you sure you couldn't be happy with him?"

Smiling subtly, Mia ran her hand through her hair. "With Jake, it's uncomplicated, easy, but I still don't see it working out. Right now, I need to focus on my son and finding what makes me happy. I can't focus on a man."

"Understandable," Milan agreed. "Well, should we get back up to the main house? Cassie wants to do a quick lunch before we get out of here."

"Yeah, let's go. I think I have all I need." Standing and looking back at her room, Mia let out a sigh, knowing she would never be able to stay there again without thinking about the times she shared with Tyree. Growling and slamming the door, she hissed into the air, "That bastard."

Walking into the main house was bittersweet for Mia. She had been so happy there the night before, only to wake up to the nightmare that Tyree was only using her. He had been so gentle in his touches the night before, and it was almost impossible to believe it was all a lie.

Tyree had given her false hope of happiness and a life together only to snatch it away. He said it was his intention, but she was finding it hard to believe he would be so cold, especially to her. They hadn't had the best few years, but he had always made it clear that the love was still there. Could he have been faking everything?

While she thought about all the broken promises Tyree had whispered to her in the heat of the moment, the frustrations building inside her started to win and, before she knew it, her arms swung out and connected with one of the flower vases in the foyer. Cassandra came running out to find Mia with a blank expression. She ran her hand over Mia's cheek and forced her to look her in the eyes. Mia just stared blankly until Cassandra's voice snapped her out of the trance.

"Mia, don't do this."

Mia felt bad for startling her beautiful sister-in-law.

"We can get through this. It's not over, and you know it."

Mia looked at her in confusion and shook her head, trying to think rationally. "He left me, Cassie. I don't know how you think we can get through this. I'm just tired. I'm tired of my heart hurting. I know I've made mistakes, but I can't keep paying for them this way."

"Sweet girl, I know that young man, and he loves you. This story isn't over for you two. It's just one fine mess you're in. You've been through worse."

"Never like this," she whispered with tears streaming down her face. "No matter what, there has never been the possibility of either of us having a child with someone else. That was always something special. He said he would never share that with anyone else."

"You can't dwell on this, darling. It was before you came back, and I'm sure it wasn't his intention. This all just screams setup to me. Tyree was conflicted before you got back here, which is why I called you. He was stuck somewhere between trying to move on and still holding on. He couldn't let go of you then, and I don't think he ever will."

"He let me go," she hissed angrily. "He let me go and humiliated me in front of my family. I felt so stupid. I just want to make him hurt like I do."

Cassandra scanned the room, looking at the broken glass, and let out a chuckle. "I hate that my decorations had to pay the price, but I understand."

"Oh, God," Mia gasped. "I'm sorry. I didn't mean to make a mess of things."

"Don't you worry. I'll have one of the staff clean this up."

Mia nodded and walked away with her hand latched on to Cassandra's. Just as they made it to the dining area, Mia's cell phone rang. She stopped, nodding for Cassandra to go ahead, and she took the call. As she listened to what was being said, her hand found its way to her chest, and she felt the wind leaving her. She was gasping for air and had to ease into one of the vacant chairs. She was trying to regain her senses as her mind was flooded with so much information, way too much to process.

Mia held the phone in her palm for a little while before hanging it up. She had been so quiet that Cassandra came back out to find her. Cassandra was talking, but Mia wasn't able to process any of the words. Everything was a blur until she jumped up and walked into the dining area. Taking her seat, Mia smiled at her family and ran her hand down to grab her son's. She could tell he was confused as he turned from Sydney, but he just gave her a squeeze for support. She knew he was wondering what was going on and why they were leaving when he had been promised they would be a family, but she couldn't speak the words, so she just sat there.

Her thoughts were broken by the sweetest words: the words of redemption, the words of acceptance, the words of love. "Mama, you're the best. I love you."

She looked down at his innocent face and smiled her first real smile all day. She knew he felt her tension and she cursed herself for letting it show. He didn't need this. He was the innocent one in it all. "I love you too."

She studied him as he looked away and went back to his playful banter with Sydney; and she made a decision, one that would shape their future. Now that her mind was made up, there was no turning back. She had to push forward no matter what the costs were.

Chapter Twenty-seven

Tyree walked into Miguel's hospital room with a heavy heart. He had seen him the previous night, but it was still weird seeing him with all the machines around. The hospital room was quiet and smelled of alcohol. Tyree laughed as he made his way farther into the room and a thought came to him. He always knew Miguel was a neat freak, and he probably demanded they douse his room with antiseptic. It was refreshing; it let him know that his brother was truly awake.

Reaching the side of the bed, he placed his hand on top of Miguel's and patted it slowly. Reacting to Tyree's touch, Miguel eased up in the bed.

"Quite a scare you gave us, little brother," Tyree said softly.

"You know me. I have to keep you on your toes."

"So, I guess I'll ask you the question of the year. Who did this to you?"

Miguel ran his hand over his face and plopped his head back on the pillow. "You know I wish I had that answer for you, but all I remember is packing my stuff up and leaving right after you. Everything else is a blur. I don't even know how I ended up back in my office. It's all weird for me."

"It's okay. I just wanted to see what you remembered. From what I saw on the footage, the person was covered everywhere. You couldn't make out a face. I couldn't even tell if it was a woman or man."

"Felt like a man." He pointed to his head. "If it wasn't this will be very embarrassing."

"So, my next question: did you wipe your own computer, or did they?"

"Everything is gone? All my work files? What about my laptop? I had all the plans for the next few months on there."

"It's all gone; everything."

"Damn." Miguel slammed his hand into the sheets. "Well, I guess we will have to rework it."

"Yeah," Tyree agreed.

"So, why are you here alone? Where are Mama Mia and little man? I would think my mini me would be here jumping at the chance to see his favorite uncle. You know, I really love having him here. I can't wait to spend more time together."

Tyree looked off and huffed.

Miguel sat up, watching him stall. "What's going on? Why are you looking that way?"

Tyree leaned forward and placed his hands on Miguel's lap. "Look, a lot has happened today and last night. I need you to know that whatever the thing was with Mia and me is over. I broke it off this morning."

"What?" Miguel asked loudly. "What are you saying to me? Why did you end it?"

"I had to make a decision, and I made it."

"It was the wrong decision. What about your son? You might as well have given her the green light to pack up and move him across the world again."

"If that's what she feels is best, then so be it. It's statements like those that made my decision easier."

"What decision? I'm lost here."

"Renee is pregnant."

Miguel rolled his eyes, slapping his hand to his forehead. "I thought you were careful with that girl. Aren't you just the least bit suspicious of the timing? Plus, how could you leave Mia for her? She has your child too."

Nodding, Tyree crossed his arms over his chest. "I know Mia does, but it's not the same. I trust Mia with Ky. As messed up as everything is right now, I never question her judgment when it comes to him. She has always been the one he could count on."

"When are you going to let the past go? It wasn't your fault. Stop blaming yourself for something you couldn't control."

"I could have, but that's not all it is. I know I'm to blame for a lot of what went wrong, but I just know she's better off without me. If I had come to her straight up, she wouldn't have listened."

Looking at the guilty expression on his face, Miguel almost flew off the bed. "What did you do?"

"I did what was necessary. She hates me, but at least she will be gone. I want her and Kyan away from me."

"Are you retarded? Why would you intentionally run off the only woman you ever truly loved?"

"I'm messed up. Only someone as messed up as me can relate, and that happens to be Renee."

"Bullshit," Miguel hissed. "It's a mistake you're making."

"It's for the best."

"What is?" Both brothers turned to find their father and mother walking in with cheerful expressions, and Karen walked over, taking Miguel's hand, rubbing it lovingly. "What were you guys discussing? What's for the best?" Karen asked.

Tyree looked at her, knowing what he was going to say was going to shatter her world, but he knew he should tell her before she found out some other way. Letting go of the breath he was holding, Tyree walked over, taking her hand in his. "You're not going to like this, but Mia and I are no longer together. We decided to end things for good."

While Karen looked horrified, Tyree studied the look on John's face and fought the urge to wrap his hands around his throat. He knew the old bastard would be happy, and it did nothing to lessen his rage. Breaking things off with Mia wasn't what he wanted, but he needed his parents to think it was.

John had never let his disdain for his and Mia's relationship remain a secret, but for him to stand there with such a gleeful expression struck a chord. "I know you're excited, but you don't have to look so damn happy." Tyree had never meant to let his anger flow so freely, but John had that effect on him. He always seemed to make everything worse.

Tyree was within arm's reach when Terence and Asha entered the room. They both saw the scene unfolding, and Terence interjected himself, cutting Tyree off. "I wasn't going to touch him," Tyree hissed. "I just wanted him to look me straight in the eye when I told him to go to hell. Me and Mia may be over, and I may have chosen to stay with Renee and raise our child together but, make no mistake, he is never going to come in here smiling about it."

Terence was holding him back, and although Tyree was speaking in a calm, even tone, he knew Terence could feel his rapid heartbeat. "I will never let you say one damn thing about our relationship when it's your fault she left in the first place."

John looked as if he had seen a ghost as Tyree's rants went on, and Tyree saw when Asha looked over to Miguel, who had his eyebrows raised in question.

"This is going to be golden." John chuckled. "How am I to blame for your wife leaving you, and for a private investigator, no less?"

Tyree pushed on Terence's arms with no luck in breaking free. "You and your demands. You always wanted too much from us! We are not your puppets. We are our own people. I had a life. She was my wife. I chose her."

"And you chose wrong," John snarled. "You chose her and ruined our relationship. You damn near ruined your life, and what did she do? She ran at the first sign of trouble. She ran because of finding out you received a trust fund you only had to use because of the shitty decision to marry her!"

"John." Karen raced across the room to slap his face. "I told you that you were done interfering, and here you are meddling again. It's enough, and I'm tired of it!"

John held his hand to his face and let out a sinister laugh that sent a chill through the room. "You baby them too much. That's why he's sitting here sneaking around with one woman and he has a baby on the way with another. He needs to understand at some point that you have to make sacrifices for the greater good."

"No," Karen snapped. "He should never have to sacrifice his happiness for any of this. What allowances have you ever had to make? You have everything you ever wanted, so why would you expect them to have any less? I always knew you valued the company above all else, but I never knew exactly how selfish you were until just now. I can't do this anymore."

"What are you saying, Karen?" John asked harshly.

"I'm saying until you figure out what's important in life, you will no longer be allowed in our house."

John reached out, pulling Karen to him roughly, grasping her wrists. "If you think you're kicking me out of our house, you have another think coming. You side with these kids if you want, but you will soon regret it. Now"—he tossed her back—"I'm leaving you here with them. You take some time to figure out what side you want to be on and let me know."

While John stomped out, Tyree walked over, pulling his mother into his arms. He could tell how upset she was but, surprisingly, she didn't seem shaken. It was like she was used to this type of behavior from John. He pulled her back to study her eyes. "Mom, I need to know, has he ever grabbed you like that before? Has he ever talked to you like this before now?"

Karen scanned the room, looking into the worried expressions from her children, and she ran her hand through her hair. Tyree could tell she wasn't sure exactly how much to reveal to them. After a moment's deliberation, she came up with a response. "Son, don't worry about me. Your father is all bark and no bite. I know how to deal with him. I'm dealing with him."

"Dealing?" Tyree questioned.

"Don't worry. I have this under control. I'll be fine, but I'm worried about you. What's this I hear about you breaking things off with Mia? Tell me it's a joke."

"Tyree, you didn't," Asha hissed, anger present on her face. "I thought we discussed this. You made this decision without us?"

Karen scanned the room, and Tyree knew she was trying to figure out what was going on with her children. As her head whipped back and forth, she let a tear fall. Asha rushed to her side and hugged her. Tyree followed suit and so did Terence, until Karen broke from the huddle. She looked like she had something on her mind and, before she could leave the room, Tyree pulled her arm.

"Mom?"

"I have to take care of something."

"Will you be back?"

"Later. What I want you to do is go over there and talk to Mia." Tyree opened his mouth to protest, and she slid her hand over his lips. "Don't argue with me. You know you will regret it if you let her go again. You have to think of you and what you need sometimes. Stop always trying to be her protector and let her protect you. You might not think so, but your heart is fragile. She is the only one who can take care of it the way you deserve."

With that, Karen spun out of the room, leaving it silent. Tyree was staring at Asha as she glared at him. He knew she was in a mood he couldn't pull her out of with words. She and Mia had always been close, and he knew she was thinking she was going to lose her again.

Before he could voice his apologies, Miguel broke the silence. He placed his hand to his forehead and shifted toward his brother. "Ty, how . . ." He was stuttering as tears flooded his eyes. "How did Dad know that Mia found out about the trust fund? You never told anyone that. You didn't even tell me." During the argument, Tyree hadn't caught it but, being a spectator, Miguel was able to catch everything. Shaking his head gently, Miguel began to ramble. "It was him. I couldn't believe it was true."

"What, Miguel? What do you remember?" Asha asked softly, taking his hand in hers.

"Rock," he stammered. "Get Rock in here now. I need to know—"

"Miguel," Asha pleaded, seeing his agitated state, "you need to calm down."

"You lied to me," he gasped. "You told me it was going to be okay. You lied," he snapped at her.

Tyree was confused for a second, but once everything clicked, he knew. Now, all he could do was rock himself back and forth, trying to rid himself of the sick feeling in his stomach. If he hadn't known before, he knew now that they were better without him, and he had to make sure that was set in stone. He had asked Miguel to get involved in this mess in the first place. Now, he had unearthed something that was supposed to have been buried with Janelle and Helen.

Reaching for his cell, he dialed the number. With shaky hands, he held his breath until he heard a voice.

"Did you do it?" he questioned anxiously.

"Yeah, we made it, but there was a problem."

"What kind of problem?" he barked, startling the room. "Where is my son? Is he safe?"

"Kyan is fine. He is right here."

Tyree's breath caught in his chest and then he exhaled before asking the next question. "Mia?"

"She's not with us. She was all set to come and then something happened. We tried."

Tyree knew his anger was wasted on Jackson. After all, he was doing a favor for people he had known only for less than a week. He felt horrible for his reaction and sighed. "Look, I'm sorry. Thank you for taking him. I can't understand why Mia would do this. I swear this woman is more stubborn than I thought."

"It's no problem. Just know your son will be safe with us. I'll look after him like he is my own, and Millie will spoil him."

"Thanks." Tyree hung the phone up. As he slid down in a seat, he thought back on the night before and dropped his head in his hands. His mind drifted back to the conversation they had the previous night that set everything in motion. It all began after Tyree, Asha, and Terence left the restaurant.

Tyree entered the hospital room with Asha and Terence trailing behind him. At first, they weren't sure what to expect. The phone call he received was so vague, and he was thrown off. When he walked closer to the bed, he saw Miguel lying there. His head was bandaged, and he had his eyes closed. Even with all the machines surrounding him, he looked peaceful. Tyree dropped to his knees when he reached the bedside, and Asha followed, stroking Miguel's warm skin.

"What happened to you, little brother?" Tyree asked quietly. "What did I get you into? What did I do to you?" Tyree held Miguel's hand as he felt it move. Startled, he dropped it and backed away slowly. "What the hell? He said you were . . . What's going on here?"

Miguel looked around the room and saw Rock enter. Once he had the door secured, Miguel sat up, putting his hand to his head. "I'm sorry. It was the only way to do this. I needed them to believe I was still out. I think they wanted me out of the picture, and I would have been if it weren't for Rock. He came in just as they were coming to finish me off."

"'They'? Who is 'they'?" Asha questioned.

"It's a long story, but I just needed you here because you have to protect yourselves." He turned to Tyree and shook his head sadly. "Ty, they're not safe here. You have to get them out of town as soon as you can. I think Richmond is trying to kill them all."

"That's silly," Asha piped in. "He's an asshole, but he wouldn't kill his own kids."

"Yes, he would," Miguel retorted. "He killed Janelle and Helen."

Tyree swallowed hard and locked eyes with Miguel again. "How do you know this?"

"Minutes before I was knocked out, I received a video. On the video, it showed Helen the night she died, in the study."

"Okay . . ."

"He was there. I heard his voice. He was in the room with her the night she died. They were arguing."

"About what?"

"Him being there; but there's more."

"What?" Tyree was shaking. He knew he didn't want to hear what was going to come next, but he still waited for it.

"Kyan was in the room. I only caught a glimpse of it, but he was definitely in the frame hiding in the closet. I don't think Richmond noticed him, but he had to have found out Kyan was there, and that's why he was kidnaped. Now this all makes sense. Your suspicions, Janelle's suspicions. She was helping you prove it was him and, now, she's dead. Kyan was in the room, and he got kidnaped shortly afterward, and Mia's accident . . ." Miguel looked at Asha and shut down when he saw the expression on Tyree's face.

"Accident, what accident? What happened to Mia?"

"She just went through a lot when you were gone. It was a tough time for all of us." Asha cut her eyes at Miguel.

"I don't buy that. You tell me what happened to her," he yelled loudly. He was bordering on hysteria when Rock stepped in, placing a hand on his shoulder. Tears were littering his cheeks when Rock pulled him into a rough embrace. "I just . . . I never knew they suffered so much while I was gone. I never knew what she went through."

"It wasn't your fault. It was Richmond. He set this all in motion, him and John."

"Dad?" they all snapped, looking at Rock anxiously.

"Your father, he isn't as innocent as he claims to be. He has a larger role in the downfall of all those companies. All of this is the result of their competition with one another and good old-fashioned greed."

Tyree's anger took over, and he toppled the tray holding Miguel's water pitcher before dropping to his knees. "All this over a damn company. Rock?" He looked over at him like a wounded puppy. "How do you know this?"

This time, Miguel spoke up. "Rock isn't just our security. He's with the FBI."

For some reason, it all clicked to Tyree. "That's why you were never around full time until now? Why are you here now?"

"I'm investigating your father, trying to bring him and Richmond down. I needed the information Miguel had, which was why I was coming by. I knew you were looking into Richmond. I've been watching you, helping you when I can. I wasn't supposed to tell you anything, just protect you, but you seem to have some source we haven't been able to reach. As much help as the information is, now I need all of you to back off. It's too dangerous. I already informed Miguel he needed to play along. It needs to appear that he hasn't been awake all this time. He needs to seem like he doesn't remember a

thing about any of this. That way, whoever is after him will think they got away with it; and now that we have the proof that Richmond was there for Helen's death, we can bring him up on charges. The only thing is—"

"What?" Tyree snapped.

"We have nothing on John that will hold up. For all we know he was in on the accidents that took Janelle and Helen down. He covered his tracks well."

"So, you're saying he could come after my son and my wife? Have you found Richmond? He shouldn't be hard to find seeing as how he has taken over the damn company." All he could think about was the danger they were in. "Who was in my house that night?"

Shaking his head, Rock crossed his arms over his chest. "I wish I could tell you I knew. Honestly, I'm not even sure who is sending the anonymous videos. I tried tracking the IP address, but it's blocked. I'm sorry I had to manipulate you guys, but it was the only way. Once your father finds out Miguel is here, this room will no longer be safe to talk freely. You have to make sure not to slip up and mention any of this to anyone. He has people everywhere. Always remember that.

This attack was meant to get you out of the way," Rock whispered, holding up a syringe. "You were meant to die in that office, Miguel."

Miguel's breath caught in his chest. "Did my father try to have me killed?"

Closing his eyes and exhaling, Rock stepped back. "It's a possibility."

"No. He wouldn't. He is my damn father. How in the hell could this company mean more than us?"

Asha crawled in the bed with him and pulled him close. "It's okay," she whispered against his temple.

Tyree just watched. He was at a loss for words. He didn't know what to say or think. He knew he always hated John, but to think that he would try to kill Miguel was too much. He couldn't process anything. He just knew what he needed to do. He needed to see Mia, spend one last night letting her know how much he loved her; and then he had to let her go. He knew making her stay was a huge mistake he would only live to regret. They were safer, better without him.

When he reached for the door, Terence stopped him, placing a hand on his shoulder. "Don't do it. I know what you're thinking, and it's not true. You can be with them. Stay with them."

"I can't. They wouldn't be here if I hadn't made her promise me. She needs to take him and get far away from here, far away from me."

"Tyree, no," Asha interjected. "You just leave with them. It was what you wanted before all this."

"Yeah, before I found out about Renee and the baby. I can't just allow her to raise my child alone. I don't trust her that much."

"Tyree, you can't worry about Renee. She is not who you think she is." Pausing, Asha crossed her arms over her chest. "What about Mia? She will be alone if you do this."

Not missing the obvious hesitation in his sister, Tyree decided not to push. He knew if Asha was holding something back, it was just because she didn't have it all figured out. "Mia is a wonderful mother. She doesn't need me. She takes better care of him than I ever could. I'm not saying I won't see them again, just not for right now; and I know, after this, we will never be together again. As for Renee, I guess this is my payback for all the things I've done wrong."

"We can figure it out," Terence pleaded.

"By the time we figure it out, they could be dead. I can't take that chance."

"So, you're giving up?"

"No. I'm saving her. I can live with being unhappy as long as they're safe."

"She will never forgive you if you do this."

"I know." He walked out the door.

After leaving that night, Tyree went back to the house, where he explained everything to Rick and made him promise to double security. He also explained things to Jackson and stressed the importance of getting out of town the next day and persuaded him to take Kyan and Mia with him. He told him that he had set something up on an island in Maui. He knew no one would find them there. He had planned for it to be their first stop on his extended vacation with them.

Tyree had given the plans to only one person besides Jackson so that it would remain undisclosed. He had it listed that they would be traveling back to Paris just for the books. That way, if anyone were to look for them, they would be at one hell of a disadvantage. He wanted to make sure he covered everything well. He needed them to be untraceable.

Once all the planning was done and everyone knew their roles, all Tyree had to do was carry out his part. It was going to be the hardest thing he ever had to do, but it was necessary. Letting her go a second time was going to crush him, but it was going to save her. He kept telling himself that ranked above all else. He also knew that if he left, he would never figure out Renee's secrets. Asha's slip-up earlier let him know that there was something there, so he decided to make a few calls. He knew one person who would know more than anyone else: her mother.

As Tyree's mind glided back into the present, he jumped to his feet, reaching for the door. His adrenalin was pumping. He needed to know why she hadn't gone on the trip. He knew this visit wasn't going to go over well, but he had to make her go by any means necessary. He was halfway out the door when he thought about something and flew back inside.

"Don't talk about anything here. As a matter of fact, don't talk about anything at the office."

They all nodded as he sprinted out of the room. He saw the handful of guards Rock allowed, and nodded, smiling at them subtly. He was sure they were fine, but he couldn't be too cautious. Rock had hand-picked the entire squad. The one person's judgment he trusted was Rock's. He knew he would never allow anything to happen to either his brother or sister. He was thankful for that. At least he knew they were safe. Mia, she was a different subject. He knew she had no idea, but her reckless attitude was endangering her well-being.

As he sped over to her house, he couldn't help the smile that tugged at his lips. As angry as he was that she wasn't somewhere on a beach, gazing at the moon, hopefully thinking of him, it was going to be good to see her. The last time he saw her, watching the tears fall from her eyes, he almost dropped his act and pulled her to him. He knew it would have defeated the purpose, but now that she was staying, he thought, why couldn't he hold her again? He knew it was selfish to think that way, but he wanted the warmth of her touch. He needed to feel her love once more.

Chapter Twenty-eight

"Everything is going to be okay, right?" Cassandra made her way into Rick's library. She scanned the walls, looking around at the freshly painted room. The shelves still had the new wood smell, and the floors sparkled like nothing ever happened there. It was almost like Helen's death hadn't happened. He still hadn't responded by the time she rounded the desk and took a seat in his lap. Brushing her hand down his cheek, she leaned in, placing her ear to his chest. She could hear his uneven breaths. "Honey, is it going to be okay?" She sat up to look at his vacant expression.

"I don't know," he replied quietly. She barely heard him until he grabbed her face and pulled her forehead to his. "You should go. Staying here isn't good for you. This place is cursed. There is nothing but horrible memories between these walls."

Cassandra allowed tears to cascade down her cheeks. “Don’t say that. We raised our daughter here. Your family was raised here, you and your sisters.”

“And they also died here or came damn close to it. No matter how many times we redecorate, this will always be a fortress of misery. I can’t stand being here. How can you?”

“Memories,” she whispered. “A lot of terrible things happened, but so many wonderful things have, too. You can’t blame this place. Places don’t kill, people do.”

“Yeah, we come from a family where husbands kill their wives and fathers kill their daughters. Goddammit! Why couldn’t I save them?” he screamed. “I had one thing to do, look after my family, and I couldn’t do it. Mia, Janelle, Mom, they all counted on me, and I let them down. I failed them.”

Grabbing his face and making him stare her down, Cassandra sighed. “You always protect everyone. You do it for me; you take care of Whitney, Kyan, and Mia. You shouldn’t beat yourself up for this. It won’t help anything.” She placed a light kiss on his lips. “Now, cheer up, handsome. I need you at your best with this most recent mess.”

"How can I just take it back? How can I just step back in like nothing has happened? I can't take this company that's laced with my mother's and sister's blood. They died for this."

"You take it and make them proud. Neither of them would want you struggling over this. Helen knew what Richmond was capable of, and Janelle wanted to stop him, obviously. They would be proud of you for going on with your life. You sitting here feeling guilty is the last thing they would want."

"I just . . . I don't know how."

"You will, and I'm here to help you," a voice sounded out behind them.

"What are you doing here?" Cassandra scowled. "You have to leave."

"Dang, Mom, I thought you would be happy to see me." Whitney dropped her bags to the floor.

"Sweetheart, I told you not to come. I needed you at school."

"You see, I'm not one to stand back while my family is in turmoil."

Cassandra wanted to rush her away, but she couldn't help admiring her beautiful daughter. Her appearance had changed since the last time she saw her. Her hair was in its natural ringlets, but it still draped past her shoulders. Her golden skin was glistening under the low lights of the office, her brown eyes sparkled with hope that couldn't be denied, and her smile brightened their gloomy moods.

"How did you know anything about this?"

"Word travels fast on the World Wide Web, Mom." She held out her cell for them to see. "This is everywhere."

Rick took her phone, reading the headline: TAINTED LEGACY, RICHMOND LIVINGSTON KILLS WIFE AND DAUGHTER IN ATTEMPT TO STAY AHEAD OF FELLOW ATLANTA MOGUL. Cursing and shoving the phone back in her hands, Rick retreated to his seat. "This is a circus. Who in the hell leaked this?"

"So it's true? Granddad killed Aunt Janelle and Gran?"

"This is way out of hand," Cassandra supplied, not offering an answer to the awkward question. "Whitney, sweetheart, your dad and I love seeing you, but now isn't a good time. I think you should go back."

"Mom, I can't. I'm no better off there than I am here. I didn't find out just by surfing the Web. I had swarms of reporters outside my dorm room. It seemed like as good a time as any to come home."

"Fuck," Rick snapped. "I'm sorry, princess. Let me send you somewhere remote. How about a vacation until things blow over?"

"Dad, I'm fine. You guys need me more than I need to be on some island. Plus, I haven't seen Aunt Mia in so long. I want to catch up with her."

"Your aunt won't be good company, I'm afraid. She isn't herself these days."

"Uncle Tyree?" Whitney questioned with a dreamy look. She was always quite fond of him. "What happened? The last time we talked everything was great."

"It's complicated. They just need to find common ground."

"They will." She smiled at her mother.

"I don't know this time," she said and looked away sadly. "There may be too much to come back from."

"Have faith, Mom. They are soul mates. They give me hope."

"Hope?" Rick questioned. "Is some little boy trying things on you?"

"Rick," Cassandra snapped. "She is a grown woman. If she wants male company, she can have male company."

"I'm glad you said that, Mom." She walked backward, grabbing a nervous young man from behind the door. He was tall, about six feet two, thin, but not frail. He had a muscular physique and light brown eyes that rested behind his dark-rimmed glasses. He was a milk chocolate–skinned, handsome boy. Cassandra was impressed and couldn't help but break into a smile while Rick was eying him skeptically.

"Who are you?" Rick's voice was slightly intimidating.

"Mom, Dad, meet my boyfriend, Jude. Jude is a second-year law student and comes from an impeccable family, not that it matters. Our family may be known around the world, but it is seriously damaged now that Granddad has ruined us."

"We're not ruined, darling, just rebuilding; and it's nice to meet you, Jude." Cassandra offered her hand for him to shake. When Rick just stood with his arms crossed, she nudged him, narrowing her eyes at him. "Say hello. Stop being rude."

Reaching his hand out, Rick grabbed Jude in a rough handshake. "Where are you staying?"

"Here, of course," Cassandra interjected, rolling her eyes at him. "I'm sorry we're meeting under these circumstances, but you will be safe here. We have security everywhere."

"I'm fine, ma'am. I just wanted to make sure Whitney would be safe. I fought our way out of the dorms and threw her on the first plane out of there. It's my fault she came here. I apologize."

"No need. You thought fast. It's admirable. Right, Rick?" She gave him the evil eye.

"Right," he hissed quietly.

Turning away from Rick, Cassandra plastered on a smile and looked at the two kids before her. "Whitney, take Jude upstairs and put him in one of the spare rooms."

"Preferably not one close to yours," Rick called out.

"Sure, Dad, I'll give him the one directly next door to me." She walked toward the stairs.

Once they were gone, Cassandra turned and smacked him on the shoulder.

"What was that for?"

"Being an ass. Our daughter never brings guys home, so she must be serious about this one, and you treat him like he has the plague. You're ridiculous."

"No, I'm not. If he's sleeping with my little girl, I hate him."

"She's twenty-two. She makes her own decisions, and she could do a lot worse. He has to be intelligent to have gotten into law school. Obviously, he has focus, and he got her out of there when she was being hassled. You owe that boy an apology, and you damn well better issue it as soon as they come back down those stairs."

"I will not. Not in my house."

"Unfortunately for you, it's my house too, and I say you will. You will do it, and you will mean it, or you're going to be servicing your own needs for a long time after this."

Rick huffed, and she knew she had him in a tough position. After several moments of deliberation, he nodded in agreement. "Fine, I'll do it, but I want a close eye kept on him. Dammit, this is not the time for company when we're in such a precarious state. Things are so messy right now."

"Things are always messy around here. This time just sticks out more than the others." She turned on her heels.

Watching as Cassandra disappeared upstairs, Rick flopped into his chair. He had picked up a few papers, and he was looking them over when his phone rang. He picked it up hastily, not really wanting to be bothered. When he heard the chilling voice on the other end, his anger rose.

"You have to be out of your mind calling here."

"You have to be out of your mind thinking I'm just going to let any of this stop me. I told you to stay your ass out of the business, and here you are knee-deep in it."

"You have no say, bastard. You lost all your rights when you killed my mother and sister. When they find you, you're going to burn in hell."

"They won't find me until I'm ready to be found. Until then, you better keep your sister and yourself away from Livingston, or you can start plot digging."

"You can't do shit. You step within a hundred feet of anyone in this family, and you'll be executed. If the feds don't do it, then I surely won't hesitate."

Rick heard Richmond's wicked laugh and shuddered. "I know you're probably trying to trace this call but, let me assure you, you never will. I'm smarter than you all, and I'll never let you turn me over. This is all done on my terms. Always remember that." He continued to laugh, and Rick fought the urge to slam the phone in his ear. "Oh and, by the way, tell your sister I said hello. It's been so long since I've seen my beautiful dove. You tell her Daddy will see her soon."

"You stay the fuck away from Mia." He jumped to his feet.

"Good-bye." He hung up, and Rick was left gasping for air. His head shot down to Mia's house, and he sighed in relief. He knew they had guards everywhere, and there was no way he could get to her, but he still wished she had gotten on the plane with Kyan. He didn't know what had changed. She was packed, she even seemed open to the idea of spending more time with

Milan, but as soon as they got to the jet something snapped in her. She refused to get on, and she gave Kyan a tearful good-bye before turning and hopping into a cab they never knew she had called. It was all strange, but he knew one thing for sure: Tyree was going to be livid. After all he had gone through to get her to leave, for her to just change her mind was going to send him off the deep end.

Chapter Twenty-nine

Mia stirred a little as she felt a pair of strong arms encase her. She was already in bed, fast asleep, even though it was only eight-thirty. She had said good-bye to her son for however long and, the more she thought about it, it was probably for the best. He didn't need to be around for the drama surrounding her life. She knew Milan and Jackson would take excellent care of him.

In a way, she envied them for the connection they shared; it was the same connection she thought she and Tyree had up until this morning. He really made an ass of himself and embarrassed her in the process. She wasn't sure if she could ever forgive him; but him slipping in now, holding her so closely, was clouding her brain. She wanted to be a person who could turn and kick him out, but she honestly needed him.

As she snuggled closer to him, he leaned in, nibbling her ear. It was odd; he was never one to nibble her ear in the past. Before, when he knew he was in trouble, he would have just leaned in, placing a sweet kiss on the spot on her neck that always made her cave. In all the years they had been together that was where he began his attack. He called it skipping straight to the point.

After a few minutes of the nibbling and silence, Mia was growing impatient. It wasn't that it didn't feel good; it just wasn't enough to make her forget the scene he caused. She was weak. She almost caved until her sense kicked in. He was going to explain himself before they went any further. Just as she was about to pull herself out of his embrace and voice her frustrations, the bedroom door flew open, and the light turned on. The shock was present in the angry eyes she was greeted by, and confusion clouded her brain.

"What? How are you . . . how are you there if . . ." Mia pulled the covers back to find Jake lying beside her, and a tear trickled down her face. Tyree looked like he wanted to kill them both, and he punched the wall beside him. When Mia jumped and threw the covers from her legs, he held a hand out to stop her from coming closer. She reached for him, and he slapped her hand away.

"Don't you dare touch me."

"Ty, baby, I don't—"

"Shut up," he yelled. "Just shut the hell up. I don't want to hear another lie come out of your mouth. This, us, we're done."

Mia was overcome with tears. She was completely caught off guard when he stormed in, and she almost forgot the argument they had earlier; almost. When everything registered in her mind, her arms crossed and her expression went from sad to irate. "Fuck you!" she snapped, undoubtedly jerking him out of his anger into surprise. He was looking at her with such heartbreak, it nearly made her stop short, but her anger was too great. "I gave you everything, and you tossed me aside for that bitch!"

He slammed his hand down hard on the entertainment center holding her TV. The TV toppled over, and Jake walked forward only to be stopped by Mia's outstretched arm. When Tyree saw him advancing, he moved closer, and Mia wedged herself between the two angry guys, knowing neither would swing as long as she was there. Tyree looked down at her pleading eyes and took a step back; she knew he was trying to calm himself down. "Get him out of here now! I want him out of our room and out of our house."

"I'm not leaving her here with you," Jake said, facing Mia. Then, turning to Tyree, he said, "From what I hear, she's not your business anymore."

"Shut up!" Tyree moved up again, and Mia planted her hands on his chest. "She was never your business. Your check-to-check ass could never hold down my woman. She needs more than you could ever offer. Get out of my house and back to your little nine to five."

Jake was unwavering and stood still until Mia turned with tear-filled eyes and nodded toward him. "Maybe you should go. I'll call you later. We have things to talk about."

"Mia," Jake said quietly, "he's not thinking clearly. He could hurt you."

She shook her head and held her ground. "As crazy as it may sound, Tyree would never hit me. He's not that type of guy." Wrapping herself around Tyree tightly to restrain him, Mia watched as Jake left the room, closing the door behind him. Once he was gone, she jumped back, feeling his stiffness. Trying to gauge his reaction, she took a seat on the bed still at a loss for words. She was brought back to reality when he dropped down in front of her on the floor.

"What was he doing here?"

"I . . . I don't know. I—"

"Why was he in my bed?" he cut her off, having heard enough of her stuttering. "I thought it was clear that I never wanted another man in the bed I share with you. What in the hell were you thinking?" His voice was low, but the anger was apparent.

"I swear, I thought he was you. I never thought he would just crawl into bed with me."

"You said I was the only one who made you feel like you were burning from the inside out when I touched you." He got on his knees, running his hands up her thighs. "You said when I kissed you here, it made you cum before I was even inside you." He ran his tongue down her neck before kissing the spot throbbing below his lips. "You said it was only me." He pushed her back on the bed, grabbing a handful of her hair and latching his lips on to hers. "You promised me."

"I did," she panted between the kisses that were weakening her senses. "You are."

As if flicking an invisible switch, he sat up, pulling away from her. "Then how in the hell could you think he was me?"

Flustered and caught off guard, Mia sat up, pushing her long locks from her face. "What is your problem? Are you just here to hurt me? If you don't mean any of it, just leave me alone. I know I hurt you, but I can't keep going through this pain because of you."

"You didn't hurt me; you broke me. I needed you, and you were here moving him into my house. I know what I did this morning but, damn, you let him creep in here already?"

"It wasn't like that. Not that you deserve any kind of loyalty from me. I didn't know it was him. Ty, I promise you, we never . . . Not here. After what happened, I just needed someone around who knew how I felt. We bonded over our past losses, that's it. It never became more until after we moved."

She saw his expression change, only to harden a few seconds later. "It doesn't matter anymore. I was just here to find out why you sent my son on a trip without his mother or father present. Where is he?"

"How did you know he was gone? What is going on with you?"

"Don't try to throw me off. Rick called me, but that's beside the point. Where is my son?"

"He's fine. He's spending time with his family. That's all you need to know."

Tyree slid off the bed and jumped to his feet. "Fine. You know what? I don't need this tonight. You do what you want. Fuck him if you want to, but it better not be in my house. If I catch him in here again, I'll burn this shit down with both of you in it."

Mia laughed sarcastically, and Tyree's head snapped back. "What? What's so funny to you?"

"You sound just like them."

"Who?"

"Richmond and John. I see the apple didn't fall far from the tree. I see keeping my son away from you needs to be a priority. I can't have you rubbing off on him."

"Do what you want. Honestly, I don't care anymore. All I know is you won't keep him from me. If I want, I will go and find him and bring him right back here."

"You wouldn't."

"Try me. You know I don't play those games. You get your ass to him, or I'll go and get him myself."

"I won't bring him back here."

"I don't want you to. I want you to follow his lead and get the hell out of here. I'm tired of looking at you."

Mia felt the tears rushing to her eyes, but she refused to let him see her this way. Instead, she crossed her arms and stood tall. "Get out."

"Oh, I'm leaving." He pulled the door open. "There's nothing left for me here."

After he was gone, she dropped to the bed in a puddle of her own tears. She sobbed quietly for a few minutes before pulling herself up and throwing on a fresh T-shirt and jeans. She knew she couldn't let herself get too emotional, not when she had other issues to deal with. Jake had to be handled. He had to know there was nothing left for them, even with Tyree out of the picture.

When she walked, sulking, down the stairs into the living room, she found Jake sitting up on the couch looking at the front door. He hadn't noticed her in the room until she sat down next to him. He reached for her hand, but she slid farther away, knowing the distance would help her drive her point home. Hurting Jake was the last thing she wanted to do, again, but she had to be honest. Her heart wasn't with him. It never was.

As if sensing her thoughts, he spoke. "I hid out in the kitchen until he was gone."

Pressing her hand to her temple, Mia looked to Jake and sighed. "Why did you come here? Why were you in my bed?"

"You needed me. He hurt you again."

"How could you possibly know that?"

"I came to see you this morning. You never saw me, but when the whole scene erupted in the foyer, I was outside watching. I saw him leave with her."

Mia smiled at his sincerity but shook her head gently. "You shouldn't have come. I know you thought it was a good idea, but you need to leave."

"Mia, I can't. Not until I know you will be okay. It's what we do; we save each other."

After holding her breath, she exhaled loudly, trying to steady her body, which was beginning to tremble. “Jake, you didn’t save me. You enabled me to mask my feelings, falling into false happiness. The truth is, I was never happy. There wasn’t one day when I didn’t think about being here with my family. With or without Tyree, I’m not leaving them again. I can’t go back to Paris with you.”

“We can stay here; we can be happy.”

Her frustrations took over, and she stood from the couch, moving farther away from him. “Jakc, we will never be happy because I don’t love you. I tried. I really tried to make myself love you, but I just can’t. I can’t replace her for you.”

Jake’s worried expression fell and was replaced with anger. Mia knew right after it left her mouth that she had crossed a line, bringing up Jake’s dead wife. When she met him, he told her all about how his wife committed suicide after suffering a major loss. He never told her what the loss was, but she always assumed it had to be big for her to kill herself.

“You don’t get to discuss her, ever! Not when . . .” He stopped his statement and jumped off the couch, walking toward the door. “You knew what she meant to me! You were never to bring her up in the same conversation as him.”

"Jake, I'm sorry." She reached out to touch him, but he snatched himself away.

"No. I'm leaving. You don't have to worry about me any longer. I'll leave and never see you again, but you remember one thing."

"What?"

He walked over and whispered in her ear, "I know what you did. I'm sure your golden boy would never look at you again if he knew." Placing a rough kiss on her cheek, he pushed her back and walked out, slamming the door.

Mia's eyes were wide with shock, and she slid down the wall to the floor, breaking out in a horrifyingly loud sob.

Chapter Thirty

"Renee," Tyree called out searching around the house. He wanted to check on Renee, knowing that Mia's decision to stay must have reached her. He just wanted to pacify her. She needed to feel like she had nothing to worry about, especially now. After the conversation with Kyan and the one with Asha, he started looking into what she had been up to and figured out she was lying about so many things. He needed to get to the bottom of it all, and to do so she had to trust him.

Tyree continued to call Renee's name and didn't hear anything from the upstairs. Heading down, he heard a small commotion in the kitchen and headed toward the noise. When he opened the door, he found Renee looking flustered, and he walked inside. When he reached her, he felt her shiver at his touch, and he turned her to face him. When he saw her tear-streaked cheeks, he smoothed the tears away and pulled her to him. "What's wrong? Why are you crying?"

"I was alone. I thought you were going to be gone all day. I just needed to vent about this. I didn't want you to see me like this."

"This is about Mia still being here?"

"I know we're happy, but I just feel unsure. I mean, she was the great love of your life. You've loved her since you were children. How does anyone compete with that?"

"It's not a competition. I'm with you, and you're here. I might have loved her since we were children, but it's a love you outgrow when you realize there's something more in store for you. The fact is, Mia left when I needed her the most. You were there for me. You loved me. You saved me."

"I know, but is that enough?"

"It's everything." He framed her face and leaned in to kiss her softly. "Don't worry about any of this."

"Are you sure? Because if there is a chance that you still love her, I'll give you the space you need to figure it out. No one wants to be second best."

"You're not second best. Right now, you're the only choice. My choice." Tyree kissed her and left the kitchen with a huge smile on his face, knowing he had fixed the problem temporarily.

***

Once Renee heard the outside door open, signaling that Tyree was gone, the pantry door flew open, revealing the true reason she was in the kitchen. When a large hand planted itself on her shoulder, she jumped and then relaxed, realizing who it was. “Nice speech.”

“Yeah, he almost convinced me too.” Renee sighed. “So, now that she’s still here, we have a serious problem.”

“I don’t see a problem, just an opportunity,” John said. “He may not want to let her go, but she will give him no choice. No matter what he does, she won’t forgive him. The pain runs too deep.”

“And what if she does, then what? All of this will be for nothing.”

“Actually, it won’t.” He leaned in, kissing her until she molded to him. “I don’t know if you got the news, but I finally did it.”

“Did what?”

“She kicked me out. Now, I have no reason not to file the papers and take everything. All I need now is the proof I require to get my fortune and hers.”

“And where is this proof?” She wrapped her arms around him, pulling his head back to hers.

“Being delivered soon,” he smirked, backing away toward the door.

Renee smiled deviously, and John disappeared out the back door, closing it behind him. She was pleased with herself, feeling like everything was falling into place, until she heard hands clapping. When she turned to find Rock standing behind her, she froze until she saw a smile appear on his face. He had always been an easy person to read, but now everything about him was a mystery. She couldn't tell if he was actually happy or about to blow her out of the water.

Renee sat quietly, looking ahead until he walked up, pulling her into a firm embrace. "I'm sorry to stop by unannounced, but I hadn't gotten the chance to get my congrats out."

Renee was thrown off, but she went with it. "Thank you." She stepped back, running her hand down to her stomach. "We're so excited."

"You should be." He grinned, running his hand down to Renee's stomach as well. "The only question I have is, whose excitement are you sharing? Tyree's or John's?"

"What?" she hissed.

"I know you've been helping John," Rock spat out. "You helped him make sure Tyree and Mia would stay apart. He placed you in Tyree's path and made sure that if you couldn't turn his head, you would take the fall for everything he had done."

"What?" Her eyes teared up as she questioned his accusations. "What do you mean take the fall?"

"Your name is all over his business papers. Every bad and crooked deal he made has you listed as the one at fault."

"But I didn't–"

"I know you didn't, but it looks like you did. For all the shit you helped him pull, you deserve to fry along with him, but we need your help."

"We?"

"Yes, we." Karen seethed as she spoke, walking into the back door. "You owe my family, and you're going to pay up." Karen reached out and slapped Renee so hard it sounded through the kitchen. "I know you helped him kidnap my grandson, bitch."

"I . . . I didn't."

"How would my son feel if he knew you were fucking him and his father? I would never do anything to hurt him, but you're going to stay here and play your role. You committed to this with John and, as far as he knows, you're going to see it through. You give him one inkling that we know what he's done and I'll kill you myself. You belong to me now."

"What am I supposed to do? He will kill me."

"Better him than me," Karen growled. "You give Tyree or John any clue what you're doing and you might as well off yourself."

Renee's face went blank at her statements, and she stepped back feeling faint. She felt as if the walls were closing in on her and she slid to the floor. When she heard Rock's light laughter, she began to shiver. She was on the floor, trying to think of a way out of this, but her brain was scrambled. Nothing was coming to her.

"You can't do this." Renee was in tears as she spoke. "How could you just leave me here knowing what you know?"

"Wait for our instructions," Karen ordered. "Tyree must not know until the time is right. He will go after John and ruin everything if he knew what we had planned."

Rock was leaning down beside Renee when she heard Tyree's voice calling for her. Panic rose in her chest when she realized Rock and Karen were probably about to blow her entire cover. She was blinking rapidly and drawing in deep breaths until Rock leaned to her ear and whispered, "I'm just here to make sure we're all on the same page. You need to make sure you remember why you're in this house." With that he stood, slipping out the back door with Karen following, moments before Tyree walked in to find her on the floor.

When he saw her, he rushed over. "What happened to you? Are you okay? Is it the baby?"

Looking around to make sure they were fully alone, she nodded, leaning into his shoulder. "Yeah, I'm fine, just a little dizziness."

Tyree pulled her up, wrapping her arms around his neck. "Which is why you should be in bed letting me feed you. Come on."

As he turned, heading to their room, Renee looked back, noticing that Rock was standing outside the door looking at them. When he saw he had her attention, he winked, causing a chill to run through her.

"What's wrong?" Tyree questioned when she stiffened in his arms.

"Nothing, just tired," she lied.

"Rest is what you need." He kissed her on the forehead.

"Yeah, rest. It's exactly what I need."

He carried her to the bed and laid her down in it and disappeared into the bathroom. While he was gone, her cell blinked, and she reached for it hesitantly. When she saw the message, she felt tears developing in her eyes.

I mean what I said, and you better not squeak one word of this to Tyree, or there will be consequences. We mean business.

Damn. When she was brought here, it was never supposed to get this complicated, and she was never supposed to get this involved. The truth was, after it was all played out, she wouldn't get either of the men she loved. As crazy as it sounded, she loved them both. John and Tyree each held a special place in her heart and, now, she wasn't going to end up with either. Just as she had done to Tyree, John had betrayed her.

Chapter Thirty-one

Three weeks had passed since the scene at Mia's, and Tyree still couldn't get the look on her face out of his mind. He knew he had done what he needed to, but seeing her expression almost made him pull her to him and tell her everything. It was the last thing that needed to be done; and, from what he had heard about the time he was away, he knew she was more fragile than he originally believed. He still had no clear answers on what happened, but he knew it had to be bad because everyone was so tight-lipped about it.

As much as he missed Mia, he knew he had to push it out of his mind. She had to be secondary to what he was doing right now. Although Rock had asked them all to step back, Miguel had continued to receive anonymous tips on Richmond every day after the attack. They had so much proof linking him to Janelle's and Helen's deaths, it wasn't funny. Miguel seemed to be the person deemed worthy of having the proof even the professionals couldn't find. It was confusing as hell. They turned everything they had over to Rock as it came in, and he assured them that they were getting closer to apprehending him. He had been doing a good job of keeping them in the loop, and he informed them that his team thought they had a location and would be making a move soon. Rock also informed them that he had a new ally John wouldn't see coming. Tyree already knew it was his mother. He had overheard them discussing ways to deal with John.

Tyree only hoped the plans panned out because he wanted to get back to the point where they didn't have to walk on eggshells, but that would only be half the problem. With John back at Johnston, Tyree felt more unsure than ever. John had been behaving himself, but Tyree still thought it was odd. He seemed almost gleeful, as if he knew something they didn't, even though he still hadn't been allowed to return home. Karen had really surprised them all by putting her foot down and actually meaning it. She had never gone this far before, and Tyree only knew his assumptions were dead on when it came to her plans.

Trying to focus on work was becoming an almost impossible task every day for the Johnston trio.

Miguel had returned with his “lapsed memory, ” and every time he was in the same room with John, Tyree could feel the tension. He had never seen his brother afraid of anything, but Miguel was definitely not his normal confident self, and Asha was no better.

Asha had been tiptoeing around them all like she had a secret of her own. Tyree almost thought she was going to tell him about it, but she clammed up every time she got close. The truth was, after everything they had been told, they weren’t sure where a safe place was to discuss anything. It was as if they were under constant surveillance, and Tyree didn’t feel like he could trust anyone but his siblings and mother.

Karen had never given him reason to doubt her, and he had been leaning on her for support through this whole ordeal. She didn’t know anything about the mess they were in, but she wasn’t stupid; she knew something was up. It was that very feeling, Tyree supposed, that had kept John out of the house. Tyree had a strong bond with his mother and knew she could sense his pain, but she never once asked him the question he knew was on her mind. He knew she wanted to know why he wasn’t with Mia.

After the blowup between him and her over Jake, he hadn't been by her house, and she hadn't come to see him. He would have been racked with grief if Rick and Cassandra hadn't been keeping him updated about how she was doing. They told him she refused to stay at the main house with them, but Whitney and Jude had been staying at the house keeping her company. He was relieved that she wasn't alone, even if he felt he was. He had been sharing a bed with Renee and, to keep her from getting too suspicious, he had been having sex with her.

To say the sex with Renee was unpleasant would be an understatement. It was like torture to him. He had grown so suspicious of her, and he had convinced himself she was hiding something. Kyan kept playing in his head; the things he said were what jumpstarted his suspicions.

Lying next to Renee every night was making him crazy. Every time she kissed him, he closed his eyes and thought about Mia and the last time he touched her soft lips. Even though they were angry kisses, he wanted them. He needed them at that moment. He had to show her that, no matter what happened with Jake, he was the one who owned her body and, for a brief moment in time, they were those two people who meant everything to one another.

Tyree's mind drifted to better times. He was really going through a lot to keep Mia safe, and she didn't even know it. Although his intentions were great, he couldn't help the voice in the back of his mind that told him it was for nothing. After all he had done, Mia was still in town, much to his dismay.

When Tyree saw Asha standing in the doorway watching him, he put down what he was doing and smiled. "Hey, baby girl. It's getting late. What are you still doing here?"

"I saw your light on and thought I'd say good night to you. I've just been a little uneasy leaving you two here after what happened to Miguel," she said honestly.

"You don't have to worry about me. I can take care of myself, and Miguel will be fine. I won't leave until he is out of the building. I promise."

"Why don't you just go now? You could go by and see—"

He held up his hand, cutting her off. "We've discussed this, and you know I won't be doing that. It's in the past, so let's move on. She made her choice on that matter long ago. I'm trying to build with Renee now, you know that." He shifted his head to the side slightly. Picking up on his double meaning, she nodded, and he looked down, grabbing his cell.

"Well, I guess we have to agree to disagree this time, but I'll see you tomorrow. I'm gonna go get dinner started for Terence and Meelah."

"Kiss my niece for me." He grinned before focusing back on his phone. Asha was in the hallway when her phone buzzed, and she retrieved it to look at the message.

I wish I could say that I miss her out loud. God, I miss her, and I miss my son. I wish I could hold her in my arms, but I know I can't. I feel like I'm suffocating without her. I have to put on this fake smile and act like I'm not dying inside when all I want is her.

Her response hit him like a knife in the chest because it was all he wanted to do but he knew he couldn't.

Call her. Tell her this. Tell her everything. She can take it, and once that girl has the baby, you sue for custody. You don't have to ruin your life to protect your child.

His response went out a minute later: I wish it were that easy. Thank you for letting me vent to you, baby girl. I love you. Be safe.

Shaking his head, he couldn't help the grin that appeared with her last message.

It is that easy. Think about what I said. You deserve to be happy. I love you too. You get out of that place before you go crazy.

Tyree gave a small laugh at her response, and he went back to what he was working on. They had several big deals set up in Europe that he had to oversee, and he wanted to make sure he had combed through every detail before he signed off on anything. He had to be sure at least that part of his life was going perfectly when everything else was in shambles.

While Tyree worked for a few more hours, he knew Miguel was down the hall doing the same. One of the traits he shared with both of his siblings was that they were all dedicated to the job. They always gave everything they had to it. They shared this with John, but his devotion outweighed theirs. It was almost like he was obsessed with the business, obsessed with being number one.

Just as Tyree was coming to a stopping point, he set his papers down and sighed. He knew Renee would be home waiting for him, and it made him sick to his stomach. He didn't want to be in the same room with her, let alone have her falling all over him like he knew she would. She was really starting to work his last nerve, and all the constant complaining about her pregnancy was pissing him off.

Mia had never been so unpleasant. She treated her pregnancy like it was the best time of her life. She was always reading to Kyan and telling him loving things in the womb. He really missed those times: those blissful moments when he would catch her standing near the window, gazing out, running her hand up and down her rounded belly. They were perfect. Tyree's smile widened on his face as he thought about Mia. He hadn't seen her in so long, and he wanted to. He wanted to hear her voice and see her beautiful smile. Closing his eyes, he tried to envision her and then he heard her sweet voice beginning to crowd his brain.

After a few minutes of his sinful delusions, he swore he felt her touch, smelled her scent. Not wanting to break from his daydream, he kept his eyes closed, mumbling her name. He kept mumbling until he heard his name spoken lightly and felt a hand run down his neck. Opening his eyes slowly, his smile deepened when he saw her. Her hair was draped over her shoulders, her makeup was flawless, and those eyes, the ones he used to see his future in, sparkled brightly. He hadn't seen her look this amazing in quite some time. She had a glow about her that left him speechless until she spoke again. His name rolled off her tongue, and he had to fight the urge to pull her into his lap.

"Kit . . . Mia, what are you doing here?" He wanted to kick himself for his lack of restraint.

"We haven't spoken since you were there last and I couldn't leave things like that between us. I know you hate me and you probably should, but I just needed you to know that he hasn't been back since then. I would never let him come into our bed. No matter what we go through I would never be that disrespectful."

Tyree just smiled at her rambling, and he reached over to give her hand a gentle squeeze. "I don't hate you, you know that, and I'm sorry I blew up the way I did. I had no right, and you don't have to explain things to me. We've been through so much, and we can't treat each other that way, no matter what. We have a beautiful son to think about, and I will always be grateful to you for the wonderful job you've done."

"Don't you mean what we've done? You're his father, and he loves you. He looks up to you so much."

"I know, but I haven't been there as much as I should have. I just don't want to make that mistake with this one. I can't have them grow up and end up hating me."

"You will do great, Ty." The look on her face said she was going to dread her next statement. "Just be there for her and give her the you I know, and you will be great. You really made me feel special. Like I was the most important thing to you."

"You are." He caught himself. "You were."

"You are too." She smiled and turned to leave.

"Mia," he called out.

"Yeah?"

"Why don't you just get out of here? I know being here has to be hard and me acting like an ass . . . You just deserve a break. Go join Ky, enjoy the beaches, and kick your feet in the sand."

"As much as I would like to do that, I can't. He's safe, and he's having so much fun, and I miss him, but I'm needed here. I can't leave until I know everything will be okay. I can't leave my family."

Tyree nodded and tried to force a smile. As much as he wanted her gone, he knew she needed to do this. She had to be thinking of Rick and Cassandra, trying to help them pick up the pieces of their broken family. At that moment, he loved her even more for putting them over the heartache he knew she was feeling because of him.

"I understand, but I wish you would go. I need you to. You take care of yourself and please . . ." He paused, trying to gather his emotions.

"Please, what?"

"Be safe. If you feel any inkling that something is wrong, you call me. I don't care what it is, I'll be there."

"What about—"

"Mia, I don't care," he cut her off. "You still mean something to me."

She smiled sadly and, for the first time, he saw the calm front she was trying to keep up waver. "Yeah, I'm something, just not enough to mean everything. Not anymore." Before he could say anything, she backed closer to the door and rushed out into the hallway.

He knew letting her leave was the best decision, but it was one he couldn't stand by. He needed to make sure she would be okay, considering that all the pain she was in was his fault.

When Tyree raced out of the office, he was running so fast, trying to catch her, he completely missed Miguel leaning his head out into the hallway trying to find the source of the commotion. Miguel sat watching Tyree search the hallway frantically before he found Mia leaning against the elevator door in tears. He watched as Tyree ran a hand down her arm and pulled her to him. He couldn't be sure what the argument was about, but he knew he was damn tired of seeing them this way. He knew his brother was going through hell without her, and she seemed to be doing the same.

Watching the way Tyree was with her sparked an idea in his mind and, as if sensing his thoughts,

Melvin, the building's head of security, stepped over doing his nightly rounds. Motioning for Melvin to join him, Miguel slipped into his office, shutting the door behind him. With a devious smirk, Miguel filled Melvin in on his plan and asked what they could do to make it happen. Melvin too caught the devious grin and walked out quietly, telling Miguel to follow closely behind him. The two men slipped down the stairs Melvin had just vacated, and they disappeared down the long halls.

Tyree was still tending to Mia, and Miguel and Melvin were gone, so no one noticed John peeking out, watching everything. He had been in the office the entire time, waiting to see what would happen with his son and the girl he had grown to despise more than anything. He saw her when she first arrived, and he figured she would come in and throw him off his game.

Sure enough, here Tyree was in the hallway, blubbering like an idiot trying to get her to calm down. He always thought Mia was bad news; now he only saw her as weak. A weak individual who needed to be handled once and for all if his son was going to be the man he needed him to be. While Tyree still hadn't looked up to see the old man brooding down the hall, John slipped back into his office with his wretched thoughts taking over his entire night.

Tyree ran his hands up and down Mia's back as he whispered in her ear. He could tell she was going through so much and was trying to keep it all bottled up. He was one of the few people who could always draw out her truths and make her feel at peace with whatever was haunting her. He wanted to be that again even though he knew he shouldn't.

"What's wrong? You can talk to me. I swear I'll just listen." He felt her shoulders move up and down with the tears and he felt like an ass. He was responsible for this. He was the reason for her pain. He knew his decisions had affected her, but he never wanted this. He felt responsible for breaking the one woman he loved more than his own life. Feeling the guilt rise in his chest, he pulled her back, running his hand down her wet cheek. "I know I was wrong and I hurt you so much, but you have to believe me, I'm sorry. I never wanted this for us. All I've ever wanted was to be with you. I wanted to be so much better than this."

Looking into his sorrowful gaze, Mia shook her head. "It's not just you. I've done and said things I never should have. If I had just followed my heart instead of listening to things being shoved in my face, we would still be together.

We would be with our son and probably have other children to love. You wouldn't be tied to that girl, and we would be happy."

Tyree put his forehead to hers, knowing that what she said was true, but he was still struggling with his role in it. "You deserve so much more than this." He looked up, hearing the ding of the elevator.

Slipping out of his arms, she found her way to the elevator and gave him a forced smile. "It's okay. Don't feel guilty. We both had a hand in this, and now I have to let you be free. I don't want you carrying around our mistakes on your shoulders. Forgive yourself, because I've forgiven you, and I'm sorry."

Tyree watched as the elevator door began to close. In his mind, it was symbolic. She said she forgave him, and now the door was closing on that chapter in his life, but he couldn't help the pain that shot through him with the realization. The elevator was almost closed when he kicked his foot in, forcing the door back open. He saw the surprised look on her face, and he rushed in, wrapping his hands around her face.

"No."

She looked stunned, confused, and unsure of what was going on. "What do you mean?"

"You're not leaving me, not like this." He knew he shouldn't be saying this so openly, but he was past the point of caring. Things were a mess, and if she refused to leave, all he could do was be there for her.

"But I thought you wanted . . . You asked me to go. You said you needed me to go."

"I know what I said, and it's what I need because being with me, around me, only complicates your life. Letting you go would be the most noble thing for me to do, but I'm selfish. I can't let go of you; you're the biggest part of my life besides my kids, and I can't let you go."

"You have to. You have to think of your child."

"I can't breathe without you. I'm drowning, kitten. I need you to go, but I want you to stay. God, I wish things could just work in our favor for once. I just wish we could catch a break."

"I love you so much. I can't imagine if I could never be with you again. It's something I can't allow myself to think about."

"Then don't." His hands, which had been framing her face, slipped down. One hand was on her neck and one on the small of her back, pulling her to him in a rough kiss. Her breathing became shallow, and her body began to tremble, feeling him pressing up against her. Just as he saw her begin to lose herself and let go of any inhibitions, the elevator jolted and came to a stop. Tyree pressed himself harder against her, turning his back and bracing his arms against the wall in a protective stance. "You okay?"

Nodding slowly, she pressed her chin into the back of his shoulder. "I think so. What was that?"

Grabbing her hand, he pressed a light kiss on it; and then he walked up to the buttons, pushing them and trying to figure out what caused the problem. He pressed several buttons and felt nothing happen. He was attempting to remain calm, but the more buttons he pushed, the more he came to realize they were stuck. Trying not to alarm her, he turned with a simple smile.

"I'm sure it's nothing. Don't freak out. I'll just call down to the security booth and see what's up. You just stay right there."

Tyree walked over, breaking into a light sweat, and pressed another button and waited for Melvin's response. He waited for a few seconds and felt relief wash over him when he heard Melvin's voice on the other end.

"Hey, man, what's going on with the elevator? We're stuck. Are you guys doing some kind of maintenance or something?"

His smile fell with Melvin's response. "Uh, actually, there is a problem. The elevator isn't working properly. They haven't been for a few hours. I've contacted some repairmen, and they should be here in a few hours. Until then, I'm afraid you're stuck."

Tyree didn't want to turn and look at Mia because he knew she was probably damn near hysterical by now. Getting trapped in that elevator had to be one of the worst things that could happen to a claustrophobic person. Mia was deathly afraid of tight spaces and had been since they were children. Turning slowly, he found Mia balled up in the corner, and he walked over, reaching for her hand. She didn't move; she wouldn't even look at him. He dropped down in front of her and sat back, pulling her into his lap.

"We're going to be fine, I promise you. I know you're scared, but I need you to think about something, anything other than this. Think about anything other than where we are now."

"Saint Lucia," she whispered, and a smile crossed his lips.

He knew it was an amazing week for them, the week of their honeymoon, the first week of being man and wife. "Yeah, that was great, huh? We barely left the bed, but when we did, that last night was amazing. The sunset was beautiful, and you looked so damn good in that white two-piece."

"When the waves hit the sand, it was the most refreshing feeling in the world; and when your arms wrapped around me, I felt safe." She was now smiling.

"Why wouldn't you feel safe? At the time, we had no problems, we had the world at our fingertips, and we were so in love."

"We're still in love. I never stopped, it never stops, but everything was so new. I was scared, afraid I wouldn't be able to be the wife you deserved."

"Why did you never tell me any of this?"

"Scared." She shrugged. "How do you tell your new husband you're not sure if you will be a good wife?"

"I wasn't just your husband; I was your best friend. I still am. I would have understood because I was feeling the same things, only compounded by the secrets I felt I had to keep. I didn't know how to tell you what was going on and how stressed I was, because I thought you were so happy."

"I was happy. Being with you made everything so much better. It made my life have meaning. With everything that was going on with my parents, being with you was the only thing that made sense."

"Being with you is the only thing that makes sense to me now. With all this confusion surrounding me, the only thing that is clear to me is you. I love you so much, and I know it's wrong to jerk you around like this, but I just need for you to be safe. I just feel like being here isn't where you can be safe. I wish I could just close my eyes and go back to that week where everything was new and we had the world at our fingertips."

"I get that you're worried, but I won't just walk away. I can't leave my family."

He hadn't caught it the first time, but now he knew what she meant back in the office. He was her family. He was the reason she wouldn't leave. Tyree tried to keep his feelings from affecting the decisions he made, but he couldn't hold back anymore. He lifted her chin and locked eyes with her. His lips found their way back to hers, and she placed her hands on his chest. He sank into the kiss until he thought about things and pulled back.

"Why? Why would you do this for me after the way I treated you?"

"Because you're my everything. I promised not to walk away, and I wasn't going to give up unless I knew you were okay. You hurt me; you hurt me so bad, but I figured it was how you felt when I left you. I never gave you a chance to win me back. I just ran like a coward." Laying her head on his chest, she took a deep breath, and he held her tighter for what seemed like forever. He was sure this wasn't what was best, but if his little act didn't force her out of town, there was nothing more he could do except cling to her and hope that things would work out; they had to.

Waking up with a smile on her face, Mia reached out, pulling Tyree's lips to hers. Standing up and pulling her with him, he ran his hands from her face to her neck and then moved in a slow manner all the way down her body. Goosebumps appeared with each new area he touched. His lips were on her neck, and his hands were doing the most amazing things. Her body was sensitized everywhere, and his skillful kisses were pushing her over the edge, and he wasn't even inside her.

She couldn't think straight, and when his fingers found their way under her skirt and past her panties, she felt herself sliding down the wall to push him farther inside her. She had to make herself ignore the fact that they were in an elevator with cameras probably watching them and she rolled her hips, pushing his fingers deeper, all the way to the knuckles. When he drew his fingers out and surged back in, she closed her eyes, trying to prolong her orgasm.

Tyree must have sensed her hesitation, and he pushed her farther up the wall, wrapping her legs around him; and then he tore at her shirt, ripping it into two pieces. She laughed at his impatience and then stopped when he reached behind her, undoing the clasp of her bra. She couldn't help but feel cheated when she realized she was half naked, and he still had on all his clothes.

Unwrapping her legs, she pushed him back and moved his shirt off his shoulders and tugged at his tie, tossing it across the elevator. While she was doing all this, he was kissing her neck again, weakening her senses. She felt her legs shaking forcibly, and when he let her unzip his pants and push them down along with his boxers, he slid down on his knees, slinging one of her legs over his shoulder.

His warm breath tickled her center, and she just knew he was about to begin, but instead, he just sat there. Her body was tingling, and sweat was on her brow, and he was just sitting there. When she looked down to gauge his reaction, he was smiling; the teasing bastard was smiling. Just as she was about to slide her leg down, he leaned in, flicking his tongue over her sensitive flesh. She wanted to scream at him for keeping her waiting so long, but the way he was working her took over every instinct. The only thing she could do was moan his name while rolling her hips forward with each flick of his tongue.

For the situation to be what it was—them trapped in an elevator and uncertain about their shared future—he took his time, giving her what only he could: complete ecstasy. His tongue was driving her into oblivion, and she clutched his head tighter as he delivered the final thrusts that made her leg tighten around his neck. She could feel his smile as he lapped up all her juices.

Moving her leg down lazily, she wanted to give him equal treatment before she allowed him to enter her, half because she wanted to please him, and half because she didn't feel like she had enough energy to perform at her normal level. He had literally sucked the life right out of her.

Before she could take her place on the floor, he grabbed her legs, pushing her back against the wall, and he pushed himself deep inside her. Her insides quivered, and he thrust deeper, taking her legs in his arms. Even though her body was exhausted, she found the strength to roll her hips forward, taking him farther inside her, and he let out an excited moan. Feeling his grip tighten on her thighs, she reached up to massage her breasts. Seeing her actions made him go crazy.

Knocking her hands away with his head, he leaned in, taking possession of her right nipple, licking at first and then gently nipping. Her moans got louder, and he pushed faster, gripping her tighter, increasing the suction on her breast before switching over to the other one. She didn't know where she was for a minute. She thought she was trapped somewhere between heaven and hell. Being with him was pure heaven, but when they were done, she would be back in hell, without him.

Tyree was still flicking his tongue over her breasts and thrusting into her, making her body overheat, and she whispered his name, drawing his attention back to her face. He planted his lips over hers, and she could taste herself on his mouth. His tongue greedily searched her mouth and mated with her tongue, taking her breath away before he pulled back to lock eyes with her. Her body tensed as she felt her orgasm approaching and then, without warning, he lowered her legs, withdrawing from her body.

Mia looked at him in confusion and closed her eyes, hoping he wasn't playing another cruel trick on her. When he grabbed her hips twirling her around, slapping her hands against the elevator wall, she gasped as he plunged back inside her. She could tell he felt her shock, and he leaned in, placing his head on her shoulder, kissing the one spot on her neck that made her crazy. Lacing his fingers with hers, he proceeded to take her over the edge. She was ready to let go until she felt her head being pulled back and he whispered exactly what she hoped he would say when this all began.

"Kitten, I love you. I want to be with you."

"I—"

"Shh, don't say anything. Just let me have this moment, and when we get out of here don't forget that. I have some things I need to do, and I know it's going to be hard, but just remember that it's you. I need you to be patient with me. I need you to love me because I love you so much. I know I haven't shown you anything that should make you believe me, but there is a reason for all this."

She knew there was a reason. She had been analyzing everything since the day he left her, and nothing added up. The night before he broke things off, he kept rambling about one last night, and he had her mind racing. She also kept replaying the way he looked when he saw Jake in her bed; his actions weren't those of a man who didn't care. They were the actions of a man in love, and she knew him better than he thought she did. She knew when he was hiding something. Whatever it was had to be explosive for him to have acted the way he did.

He never stopped pounding into her during the whole speech, and before she could voice a response, she felt herself gasping for air. Her lungs felt heavy, and her chest was heaving. She couldn't think rationally, and with his last thrust, she braced her hands against the wall and began to shake. Her body spasmed, and he wrapped a protective arm around her waist. When her walls clamped down on him, he released inside her, still holding her in place.

Looking around the elevator, Tyree sat back, pulling Mia down onto his lap and she laid her head against his neck. He ran his hand up and down her arm and, out of nowhere, she began to laugh. He looked at her questioningly, and she placed her head on his chest, listening to his heartbeat.

"What's so funny, babe?"

"You ripped my damn shirt. Now I have nothing to wear out of here, nothing but my bra."

Sitting her up and reaching over for his own shirt, he wrapped it around her and slid his hands down to button it up. She stood in front of him and twirled around. The shirt was two sizes too big and it swallowed her, but the way he was looking at her in it was adorable. Smiling at her, he reached his hand out, and she came willingly.

Once she was straddling him, he took the bottom of the shirt, tucking it inside her skirt. "Now, you look beautiful." Sweeping her hair to the side, he began to kiss her neck, and she slammed her hands down on his shoulders.

"Stop, baby. If you keep, uh, doing that, you might as well take this right back off." She tugged at the shirt, and he started to pull it out when they heard Melvin's voice on the speaker.

"You guys, the repairmen are here and, guess what, it was just a switch they needed to flip, and now we're back. The door should be opening in just a few minutes."

Tyree looked at Mia and lifted her off his lap and rushed to throw his boxers and pants back on. Mia stood in the corner laughing but, when the reality hit her, she stopped and looked at him. He was amazing, everything she ever wanted but, after this, she would lose him. He was no longer hers when they stepped off this elevator. She was standing back silently when the door opened, and he turned back reaching his hand out for her. "You coming, kitten?"

Mesmerized by his dazzling smile, she nodded and placed her hand in his. His lips instantly found a place on her forehead, and he tugged her out. He spun her around in his arms, and he pinned her against the wall, kissing her hard.

Her eyes fluttered, and he ran his hand down her cheek, leaning his forehead to hers. "Wait for me. Tonight, just head home, pack you a bag, and wait for me."

"Where are we—"

He kissed her again, stopping her question. "Just pack. I'll be there in an hour. I love you."

"I love you too." She walked back into the elevator.

"You sure about going back in there?"

"Yeah, I'm all right; and besides"—she nodded toward Miguel and Melvin standing behind them—"I'm starting to think we didn't really get stuck. Seems more like a setup to me."

As Mia stepped into the elevator, Tyree turned to look at his brother and Melvin, and she could hear him yelling before the door closed. "Repairmen my ass. You trapped us in there? Miguel, you know Mia is claustrophobic. She almost freaked out."

"I'm sure you found a way to calm her down. By the way, where's your shirt?"

"None of your damn business, but I need to talk to you. Meet me in the parking lot in ten minutes." As they joked around, she blew him a kiss as the doors closed. She knew things were still a mess, but at least now she knew he still wanted her. She wanted him too.

Mia walked out to her car on cloud nine. She had her cell phone out ready to call Whitney and let them know she was going to be gone for a while. She had just dialed the number and heard it begin to ring when a car pulled into the parking lot, and she almost walked in front of it. When she jumped back, she saw the door swing open, and she contemplated running until she saw a familiar face emerge. Her cell phone was quickly forgotten when she saw Rock step out.

She smiled in relief and walked over, chuckling gently. "You almost gave me a heart attack. What are you doing here?"

"The boss sent me. I have some business here."

"Well, Tyree and Miguel are upstairs with Melvin if you want to run up."

When Rock stepped forward and placed a hand on her shoulder, she felt a nervous feeling wash over her. At that point, she stuffed her cell phone in the waistband of her skirt without him noticing. She wasn't sure why she was so nervous, but she was. True, she had known Rock for a while, and he had never touched her in a way that made her feel threatened, but tonight was different. She felt like she was in danger and she tried to step back. When his grip tightened, she winced in pain, and he pulled her toward the door, pushing her inside. Every instinct in her said to scream, but her words were muted. She opened her mouth, but nothing came out.

After she was inside, Rock jumped in, slamming the door behind him. When Mia scanned the car, she saw who was inside and gasped loudly.

"Hello, Mia." He laughed sinisterly.

"John." She gripped her purse tighter.

Nodding, he told Rock to snatch the purse. "You won't need that where we're going. You should have just stayed away, young lady. I never wanted it to result in this, but you gave me no choice. Now, you have to be eliminated."

Mia looked out the window, taking one last glance as they sped off. She only wished she had seen her son one last time because something was telling her this was it. The look on John's face was not one of a person who was joking. He was going to kill her, and she couldn't understand why. She knew things were bad between them, but she never knew they were this bad. She studied his face and searched it for the right answers and, just like that, it clicked in her head.

"It was you. You turned him in. Only someone who was there would know all the details. You knew because you helped him. So, which one of you was it who killed Janelle? Did he make the call or was it you?"

"You think you have it all figured out, do you, little girl? Well, let me tell you, you have no clue what's going on here, and you have no clue what you've done. My son was going to be great. He was going to be the best before you came around, and now he can't think straight because of chasing you around the world. He needs to get back on track, and the only way he will do that is with you gone."

"You can't kill me. You won't get away with it," she hissed.

"I will because it won't be me. You will die today, but it won't be at my hands. You will have dear old Dad to thank for that."

Mia noticed his sinister expression and looked away defeated. She was afraid now, and with Rock sitting beside her she also felt betrayed. Rock was supposed to be someone she could trust, and now he was just the man leading her to her execution. She wished she could see Tyree one last time. She wished she had said the things he needed to know if this was the end. Now they really were over. She was going to die at his father's hands.

Chapter Thirty-two

Tyree tossed on a shirt he had in his office and rushed out, trying to meet Miguel in the parking lot. He had made up his mind that he was going to grab Mia and meet up with Jackson and Milan to get Kyan, and they were going to take the trip he had originally planned. He knew that, before he left, he needed to fill his brother in and then he needed to let Renee know he was leaving. He knew he should feel like an ass for leaving her pregnant, but he couldn't stay with her just because she was. He would try his best to be present for her appointments, they would talk and discuss custody after the baby was born, and he was prepared to support her financially, but he couldn't stay with her, not when his heart belonged to Mia.

Everything was going to be okay, he convinced himself. He already knew what his siblings' views were on the matter, and his mother would be thrilled. He hadn't seen her in a few days, but he knew she would be happy for him. She never liked Renee, and she loved Mia like her own.

The transition would be smooth, and he had already decided to let Renee keep the house they were living in for her and the baby until they could come up with a custody arrangement. He didn't want to toss her out because he knew she didn't have much, and he just knew it wasn't right. He only hoped she would give him custody and not put up too much of a fight. It was wishful thinking that, he knew, was never going to happen. He knew once Renee found out it was going to be like World War III.

Stepping out of his office, he saw Miguel coming out, and he nodded to the elevator, smiling while remembering his time in there.

"Why are you grinning?" Miguel asked.

"Nothing. How did you know to trap us in here? I mean, do you have ESP or something?"

"I saw you in the hallway and thought, what the hell, maybe a little alone time will fix things. So did it?"

"I'm good, if that's what you meant."

"Nope, I meant did you get some? You've been on edge like a man who hasn't had a good lay in a while. Only Mama Mia can put that kind of smile on your face. So how was it? Give me the details."

"Don't you have something else to think about other than my sex life with my wife?"

"Your wife, huh? Must have been damn good for you to be calling her that again. So, what's this talk you want to have?"

"She is still my wife no matter what a piece of paper says. I can't believe all the stupid shit I've done up until this point. I almost pushed that woman to the breaking point, but here she stands being my rock through it all. I thought when things got rough she might run, but she's with me. She still loves me. You don't know how good it felt to hear her say it; and, being with her, it was like I was home."

"That's great. I'm jealous."

Tyree's head shot up, and he looked at his brother in disbelief.

"No, really, I am. You're doing this, huh? You're going for it, taking your life into your own hands despite the old bastard and his games."

"He can't stop us. I won't let him interfere any longer. I won't let his selfishness keep me from her. I need that woman."

"Good. I know there is a lot of shit going down around here, but I don't want you to worry about us. I'll take care of Mom and Asha. You just focus on your family."

"I still feel bad leaving you here with him. What if he tries something?"

"If he does, at least we have backup now. Rock would never let anything happen to any of us."

"Yeah, Rock is a godsend."

Tyree and Miguel made it off the elevator just in time to see Asha's tearstained face rushing toward them. She was a mess, rambling and completely incoherent, until Tyree dropped his bags and grabbed her shoulders. She was shaking, and he held her in place.

"Baby girl, what's wrong? Why are you crying?"

"I didn't know, I swear I didn't. When I started looking into it, I thought . . . I thought he was just using her to break you and Mia up. I thought since you fixed it you would be okay, but I was wrong. He's a liar and I . . ." She was hyperventilating, and Tyree and Miguel were extremely confused.

"Ash, what is it? You're not making any sense," Miguel chimed in, and Tyree knew he was trying to make sense of it all.

"Renee! She's sleeping with Dad!"

Tyree's eyes bucked, and he and Miguel shared a brief look. "What makes you think this? Are you sure?"

Out of breath and still out of sorts, Asha held her cell phone up and displayed a picture of Renee sitting on John's lap without her shirt, and Miguel sighed. Tyree, on the other hand, began to laugh, throwing off both his brother and sister.

"That's great. Well, in that case, he can have her trifling ass. I was done anyways. I was on my way to end it with her. I was even going to let her keep my house. Wait, her baby, is it even mine? What the hell am I asking? Of course it's not. I was trying to figure out how she got pregnant when we always used condoms, and now I know why. At least I'm free. Now nothing is standing between Mia and me. Well, fuck going to the house now."

Tyree saw Asha and Miguel watching him to see if he was serious, and he made sure they knew he was. His smile never faltered, and Asha walked over, placing her hand on his shoulder.

"How are you not upset by this? Our father is sleeping with your fiancée who, until now, you thought was carrying your child. I know you love Mia, but you're allowed to be pissed about this. You gave Mia up for a child that probably isn't even yours."

"Mia came back to me. She still loves me. None of that other shit matters. The only thing that matters is that she loves me, and now I have no excuse not to be with her. In my mind, he did me a favor by sleeping with Renee. Now I don't have to feel guilty about leaving."

His siblings watched him as his smile fell and, just like a speeding bus, it all hit him. "Wait, you're right. I should strangle that bitch. I was an asshole to Mia. I put her through hell and made her feel like shit. I'm gonna get their asses, but it will have to wait until I see Mia again. She is more important than getting back at them right now."

Tyree turned away from Miguel and Asha and walked off to find his car. He was puzzled when he reached it and found Mia's car right next to his. She had been gone for quite a while now, and it was odd that her car was still there.

When he walked up to the car and saw no signs of her, he got a bad feeling in the pit of his stomach. Asha and Miguel walked over, sharing in his confusion. "Where is Mama Mia?" Miguel questioned.

"I don't know. She was supposed to be getting a bag packed for our trip, so it makes no sense for her car to still be here. She is obviously gone."

"Maybe she caught a ride. You know Whitney has been staying at the house with her. Maybe she picked her up," Asha offered, not sounding like she believed it herself.

Tyree wasn't buying one bit of it. Without hesitation, he pulled out his cell to call hers. It rang several times before going straight to voicemail, and he knew instantly that something was wrong.

Turning to look at Asha and Miguel, he yelled for them to call Rick while he headed over to the house to figure out what was going on. He wanted to kick himself for not walking her out and making sure she made it to her car. He should have known with all the drama to make sure she was safe. Here he was again, letting her fall into harm's way, and he only had himself to blame if anything happened to her.

Mia sat in the dark room wondering what she was doing in the office she hadn't set foot in for at least two years. She had no idea what they had planned for her, but she knew it was bad. She was just trying to figure out why she was at Livingston Enterprises and, furthermore, how John had access to the building. Things were getting more confusing by the minute.

Both Rock and John were nowhere to be found, and when her cell phone started vibrating, she tried her damnedest to reach for it. It was extremely hard, considering her hands were tied behind her back. She almost succeeded in her attempt until someone walked up behind her, snatching the cell phone from her grasp.

Hearing the wicked laugh, Mia realized there was another piece to the puzzle she hadn't figured out yet. There was someone else involved, a woman. When she heard the click of heels, she drew in a deep breath, waiting for the other participant to reveal herself. When the woman came around, standing in front of her, she hissed when she saw that it was Renee.

Before Mia could make a sound, Renee reached out, slapping her so hard her cheek stung. Mia wanted so badly to be able to get her back, but her arms were still restrained. Mia rolled her eyes, and Renee leaned over her, placing her hands on the arms of the chair.

"You know, I don't like you, bitch."

Mia huffed and stared her down. "Wow, how coincidental. I don't like you either. In fact, I hate you. So, let me guess: you're working with them, huh? You're a part of this plan to kill me?"

Renee laughed and flopped down in a vacant chair. "You don't get to ask questions. You will know what's going on soon enough and, soon after that, you will be too dead to cause me any more trouble."

While Renee and Mia were glaring at each other, Rock came in, signaling for Renee to follow him, and she jumped up, walking briskly over to him.

Mia could tell by the look on Renee's face that something was wrong, and she took this as a good sign for her and tried to relax. Maybe this meant there was a problem with their plan. She wondered who had called her. It was probably Tyree. She hoped he would find her car and know something was wrong, but she couldn't hold out hope that he would figure out where she was. It would be the last place he would look.

Tyree burst into the house, startling both Whitney and Jude. They were sitting on the floor with textbooks and looked to be studying. When Whitney saw that it was him, she jumped up, throwing her arms around him.

"Uncle Tyree! Oh, God, I meant to come and see you, but things have been so hectic. Dad won't let us off the grounds. I had to move down here to get any privacy. He is being an ass," she rambled, and the whole time he was scanning the house, looking for Mia.

"It's good to see you too, sweetheart, and I promise we will catch up. Where is your aunt?"

Whitney looked confused and tilted her head to the side. "She said she was coming to see you. I only assumed things went well because she was gone so long. Did you get into a fight?"

"No, things are great, but I need to find her. Has she tried to contact you in the past hour?"

Whitney's eyes drifted over to her phone on the couch, and she walked over, picking it up. "My phone is on vibrate. We were studying for our summer courses. I have a lot to catch up on, and the professors are letting me submit through e-mail because of what's going on. If she called, I'm sure I missed it."

Whitney unlocked her phone and scrolled through, showing him several missed calls, a few from friends, and one from Mia. "Yeah, she called like thirty minutes ago and left a voicemail."

Tyree felt relieved, thinking maybe she just caught a ride, and he sat down on the couch. "I wonder where she is." He sighed.

"Hold on, maybe she said something on the voicemail. I'm checking it now."

Whitney typed in her code and put the speaker phone on. At first, the sound was muffled, but a few seconds in, they could tell she just forgot to hang the phone up. They could hear a man's voice, and Whitney was just about to hang up when they began to hear the conversation clearly. Tyree snatched the phone away when he heard John's voice, and then the message ended.

"Oh, it's fine, Uncle Tyree. See? She's with Uncle John. I bet she will be here soon."

"Shit," Tyree screamed, jumping up with his keys in hand. "Whitney, you and Jude come on so I can drop you off at the main house. You have to stay there until your dad says it's safe."

Normally, Whitney would have opposed, but he knew she could tell by the look on his face that something was wrong. She got up willingly and nodded at Jude to follow. They grabbed their things quickly and raced out the door.

They reached the house, and Tyree had barely stopped the car when they jumped out and took off toward the door. "I'll let Dad know about Aunt Mia," she yelled with her back turned to him. Tyree nodded and was about to pull off when his passenger door flew open. Rick jumped in and buckled his seat belt, and Tyree hit the gas, speeding out of the gates.

"Where is she?" Rick questioned.

"I don't know, but I'm going to find her."

"Where do we begin?"

"My parents' house."

"Why would she be there?"

"She wouldn't, but he keeps everything in that damn safe, and I just happen to know the combination."

"Well, step on it. If he is in this as deep as Asha says, there is no telling what he will do."

"He better not touch her."

"You call Rock?"

"Yeah. He's not answering."

"I wonder what that's about."

"Me too."

While Tyree drove, his brain pounded, thinking of how scared Mia must be. He knew the majority of this was his fault for keeping her in the dark about everything he knew, but he was only trying to protect her and Kyan. If anything happened to her, it would be on his head, and he couldn't live with that. He had to get to her before it was too late. He had to save her from the nightmare he helped create.

Chapter Thirty-three

Mia tried to get her hands free while they all seemed to be occupied elsewhere. She was working on sliding her hands out of the ropes when Rock entered the room with a bottle of water. He was wearing a smile that threw her off. If he was sent in to kill her, then why did he look so reassuring?

"Here, drink this," he offered, pulling down the scarf Renee had tied around her mouth. When she just looked at him, he inched the bottle closer and offered her another warm smile. "I know you have to be thirsty. I promise there is nothing in here. It's just water."

She opened her mouth, and the cool water felt good rolling down her throat.

"See, I'm not the bad guy here. I promise you this will all be over soon."

For some reason, she believed him. He was gentle with her, unlike John and Renee had been, and he was trying to make her feel at ease.

Leaning in, he grabbed the scarf, pulling it back around her mouth, and whispered in her ear, "Just close your eyes and think about Maui."

Her eyes widened at the statement, and she figured out he knew where Kyan was. It should have made her nervous but, instead, she was calm. The way he said it almost made her believe he meant it for that effect.

He was watching her, almost looking sad that he had to be there, until John waltzed in with Renee on his heels. "How could you be so stupid?" He grabbed her by the shoulders. "It needs to look like he did it. He would never tie her up and shoot her. You saw what he did with the other two. He likes to make it look like they were accidents."

Mia knew then and there that they were trying to make it look like Richmond killed her.

"I had to restrain her. I don't know if you remember, but she did jump me one time. I wasn't about to let that happen again."

Rock started laughing, dropping the nice expression, going back to his sinister demeanor. "She didn't jump you; she whooped your ass. If Tyree hadn't stepped in, she would still be kicking your ass. Let's not downplay it."

Renee rolled her eyes and turned to John. "Tell me again why we need him."

"He is important. They trust him, and he can sway them to our side once the truth about us comes out."

"Yeah, maybe, but do we really have to kill her? Can't we just lock her up somewhere?"

John's head snapped back, and his eyes bored into her. "Of course we do. We need everyone to think it was Richmond and then we will be one step closer to getting Livingston. If we kill her and then get rid of Rick, we will own this damn town. Besides, we need to get her away from Tyree. He turns into a useless teenager around her. Fucking in elevators? That's not what I expect from my son."

Mia couldn't believe what she was hearing. She always knew John didn't like her, but she never thought he would go to these lengths. She was watching him with tears stinging her eyes when he looked over at her.

When their eyes locked, he let off a wicked laugh. "What? You thought only your daddy was capable of coming up with such a brilliant plan? He wished he could take all the credit for his success but, in truth, I built that company just as well as I built Johnston Incorporated. Your father was struggling when I met him, and it was my idea to bring in outside investors to build. I made him what he is."

Mia was confused. From what they had always been told, Richmond took John under his wing.

"Yeah, I found the companies and gave him the go-ahead to pull the trigger and take over. Some came willingly, but some, they were tricky. When that happened, they were taken care of by any means necessary." In the middle of his rant, he walked over and pulled the scarf down, taking a seat in front of her.

"Why are you telling me this? Why don't you just kill me and get it over with?"

"In due time," he snickered. "Before you die, I just want you to understand what my son could have been without you." She blinked rapidly when he stood and grabbed her chin, forcing her to look in his eyes. "You ruined him, you little bitch."

In the middle of his ranting, she saw Rock step back, placing a text; and then he stuffed his phone away quickly. He offered her a slight grin that threw her off, and her thoughts went hazy. She was so confused, and nothing made sense. All she knew was she was in trouble, and she closed her eyes, hoping Tyree would find her soon.

"Please find me," she whispered into the air and allowed a tear to drip down her face.

***

Tyree and Rick both burst into the house to find it dark and empty. Tyree had no clue where his mother was, but he didn't need her for what he was doing. He just needed to get to the library and pray that what he was looking for was in the safe.

Tyree knew John always put his most important documents in his safe, and he had been trying to find some way to access them. It wasn't easy getting the code to the safe, but he figured it out one night after trailing John to the house. He hid the entire time and watched as John opened it up and stuffed something inside. Rock had asked them to lie low and, for the most part, he had, but this was different. He just couldn't leave well enough alone, and he was glad he hadn't.

Once he got to the safe, Tyree began typing in the numbers, hoping he had seen the code correctly. When the machine just beeped, he started to get upset; and then the door opened. He sighed as he reached inside, pulling everything out. The contents were bundled up in separate envelopes, and Tyree was growing impatient as he shuffled them around.

"How in the hell am I supposed to get through all this in time? She could be . . . No," he snapped.

"I won't think like that. Nothing is going to happen to her. I promised her, and I will get there." He tossed a handful of envelopes over to Rick, and they both began ripping them open, searching for anything that could lead them to Mia.

Tyree had gone through three envelopes and found nothing of use, and Rick was on his fourth when Tyree's phone began to vibrate. He snatched it up quickly, hoping for some word on Mia, and when he saw the text, his heart stopped. It was a picture of her tied down to a chair. He had no idea who it came from. The number was blocked, but he knew without a doubt she was in real trouble.

"Rick." He dropped everything, letting the papers fall to the floor. "We have to go. We have to find her."

When Tyree waved the phone in Rick's face, he snatched it and sank to the floor. "My sister, I promised I would be there for her." He was beginning to hyperventilate until Tyree saw something click to him and he jumped up, looking at the phone again. "This picture, it was taken at Livingston. She's at Livingston!"

"Let's go!"

Tyree raced out behind Rick, who still had a stack of envelopes in his hand. They both jumped in the car not even bothering to lock up the house and sped off toward Livingston. Rick tried to settle himself by opening the remaining envelopes, and they both got the shock of their lives. "Ty, how long have you known Rock?"

Tyree took his eyes off the road for a second and looked at him. "For years now, why?"

"He's sleeping with your mother, and your father knows."

"That's crazy. Mom wouldn't do that. I mean, I hate the old bastard, but she wouldn't cheat on him."

"She is and has been for years now if this is correct," he said, holding up a few pictures.

"It would make sense, but why would she stay with him if that's the case? Why wouldn't she just go and be happy with Rock?"

Rick looked at the papers that were also with the pictures and then he sighed. "Because if he could prove she was cheating, he gets everything in the divorce. This says the company was never his to turn over. He was just placed in charge for a certain amount of time. Akio set it up to where, on Asha's twenty-fifth birthday, the company was turned over to the three of you, but if you hadn't come back to the company, everything would have gone to Karen. John would have nothing, but if he could prove infidelity on her part, he inherits all of her money. I'm assuming he was fine with that because he knew he could weasel in on the company. With you back, he still has a shot at getting back into the company, and we all know how obsessed he is with it. My guess is he was going to target Asha because she is the one who bends over backward for him."

"Bastard," Tyree growled. "So why didn't we know? How has he been getting away with this?"

"You see, this is the will he never meant for anyone to see. He must have given another copy to the lawyers."

"Why hold on to it? Why keep it if he would end up with nothing?"

"Insurance. If you hadn't come back, he would still have the leverage to take your mother's money."

"So this shit is all a game to him? So, tell me, why take Mia? What does she have to do with any of this?"

"He sees her as the obstacle between you two. We have known for a while how John feels about Mia. He knows she's the only one who could ever make you walk away from it all."

"And I gave him the ammunition, dammit!" He banged his hands against the steering wheel. "I sat there in that fucking dinner and told him I was leaving with her and Kyan! Fuck!" Rick looked like he wanted to say something to reassure him but, honestly, nothing would make Tyree feel any better. They were just going to have to wait and see how things played out.

Just as he was about to suggest calling the police, Tyree's phone rang, and he put it on speaker. They both sat there horrified as they heard what was on the other end.

"What have you done?" Mia gasped, taking in the sadistic look on John's face.

"First of all, let's not sit here and act like you're surprised by any of this. Your father has done way worse than I have. At least I didn't kill my wife and daughter to stay on top. Now that's cold," he laughed. "I did what was necessary to ensure my kids' futures. I always knew I wanted kids, but I couldn't have them with just any old woman, which is where Karen came in. She was perfect: worldly and well trained. Her parents made sure she had class, and she had connections none of those other women could have dreamed of, so I approached her. I knew all about her arranged marriage, but she didn't stand a chance against my charm. I made sure when I wooed her to plant my seed and secure our future."

"So, you never loved her? Why stay with her?"

"She served a purpose. She gave me my beautiful kids and got me into all the things I needed with her international connections. Akio all but gave me the keys to the kingdom once he saw Tyree and Miguel. I knew then and there my boys would be something special, and then Asha came. My little doll face made my life almost complete. I could have been happy with Karen if you hadn't come along."

"How did I affect your marriage?"

"When you started fucking my son," he growled. "He was smart and focused before you. When you started throwing your ass in his face, he lost his way. He was meant to be great, and you made him mediocre. I was fine with Karen until you made me realize what women like you and her do to men like us."

"He's nothing like you, him or Miguel. They're caring and two of the most decent men I've ever known. You would be lucky to be half as great as they are."

"Miguel? That's who you praise?" He laughed. "Tyree stood a chance before he met you, but Miguel lacked the motivation. He's a good boy, but he never would have achieved all Tyree could, and he was too nosy for his own good."

"So you tried to kill your own son for not being as great as you thought he should be? That's outrageous."

"No! You know nothing. He was never going to die. I just needed him out of the way. I needed him out of it. You know, all of this could have been avoided if you would have just died when you tried to off yourself two years ago. You're messing up all my kids' lives; you, and that damn spawn of yours."

Mia's breathing became shallow as the realization hit her. Now she knew why Kyan left so quietly and why there was never an attempt at a ransom. John had taken him. "You took my son?"

John didn't respond; he only laughed.

"How could you kidnap your own grandson?"

"He is nothing to me. You're lucky I didn't kill the little bastard like I planned. You're lucky my girl has a heart."

Mia's eyes shifted to Renee and then back to John. When Renee cast her eyes down, Mia knew something more was going on. "So, the information Jake had, where did he get it?"

"You know, it's easy to place things in plain sight and sit back and wait for the results. Your little lover boy picked up all the crumbs I left and reported back to you just like I assumed he would. When I saw how you reacted, I felt like it would be better for me to go a different route.

The rest was all on you. I couldn't have planned it better myself. You offering Tyree those divorce papers and skipping town was more than I could have ever hoped for, but then you had to bring your ass back."

Tears were streaming down Mia's face, and he grinned, looking pleased with himself. "Yeah, I might have manipulated it, but you made the final call. How does it feel to know he was willing to give up everything for you and you were such a selfish bitch?"

"I love him. If you had just let him be, he wouldn't hate you so much. What's wrong with you and Richmond? Why couldn't you just let us be happy?"

"Happiness just because of love is for the weak. I want my son to have happiness because he's untouchable. You could never help him accomplish that. It's not in your DNA. Your whole family is pathetic. That's what made it so easy to destroy your father."

"How?"

"Richmond was a gofer, a lackey. I found the companies. I made the calls. I just sent him in to do the dirty work. We built these companies together, and he wanted to try to fly solo after I made him what he is. That wasn't going to stand. I made damn sure of it."

"How?"

"I turned him in. His name was all over everything, and I got to play the innocent role. I always made sure to keep my name off everything."

"How could he take over anything without a name?"

"Oh, there was a name; it just wasn't mine." He laughed, standing up, turning his back to her. "It was nice chatting with you, but it's time for you to die. Say hello to Janelle and Helen for me."

He cocked the gun back and aimed at her. Mia felt the air leaving her lungs, and she was sweating bullets. She wasn't ready to die. She still had her son to think about, and she had Tyree. She couldn't say good-bye to him, not yet. Without thinking, she screamed out at them.

"Tell him I love him. Would you at least do that?"

"He will know nothing of this. Just shut up."

Mia closed her eyes and tried to do like Rock said and picture Maui; and then the lights flickered off, and gunshots rang out in the room. Mia felt herself being pushed to the floor and felt her arms being untied. When she let out the breath she had been holding, she felt a pair of lips on hers. It was pitch-black, but she knew Tyree's kiss anywhere. She felt him pull her toward what she assumed was the entrance and then she felt the fear shoot through her when she realized he was gone.

The gunshots had stopped by then, and when the lights flickered on, she saw John on the floor in a puddle of his own blood with Renee standing over him. Mia scanned the room further and found Rock, Rick, and Tyree in a huddle with a few task force officers. She was confused as to what was going on, and it was only heightened when Karen rounded the corner and placed a hand on her back. "Don't worry, sweetheart, you're fine now." She pulled her into a rough embrace, and Mia wrapped her arms around her waist.

"What the hell is going on around here?"

"Tyree will explain everything to you. Right now, let me go and make sure they're all okay."

Watching his mother cross the room, Tyree shivered when her hand hit his shoulder. Turning to face her, he held her tightly. "Dammit, Mom, why didn't you just tell me about all of this instead of giving me a heart attack? I was scared out of my mind."

"That's why I called you. I knew you would be, but I needed you to know we had it under control. If you had barged in here when you first arrived, she would have been shot. I knew Rock had this under control."

"Yeah, well, a warning would have been nice. Snatching her in the parking lot had us worried."

"It had to look authentic. If you had known, you would have never let us take her, and we needed her to actually be frightened, so it made it all seem real for him."

"And Renee? How is she involved?"

"She was in this with him, but Rock flipped her. Now she's working for us."

"Us? What is all this?"

John was on the floor gasping for air, and Renee pushed her foot down on his shoulder wound. "Shut up! You deserve everything you get, you sorry bastard."

"You little bitch," he snarled. "How could you betray me?"

"The same way you betrayed me! I guess you didn't think I figured out that all that shit was in my name. You had it switched over last year, so if anybody was going down for this, it was going to be me."

"You were just collateral damage. You were nothing to me!"

The other occupants of the room had stopped what they were doing and turned to look at the bickering couple. Tyree reacted to the craziness of it all with short bursts of nervous laughter, and he turned to look at Mia. She offered him a sad smile and then walked over to meet him. She stopped short when she heard the glass break. Tyree raced over, covering her with his body as they waited for the noise to cease. When he lifted himself from her, he turned to scan the room and see what happened and turned to find John with two more gunshot wounds. He was gasping for air, flailing his hands around, signaling for help, and Renee was lying beside him shaking. She had a gunshot wound to the chest.

Tyree raced over to Renee and tried to sit her up. He could tell she was trying to tell them something, but her breathing was so shallow, he could hardly make it out. He leaned his head closer, but all he could understand was, "Get Richmond." She was fading fast, and then he heard it again: "Get Richmond to . . ." He tried to hold pressure down on her wound, but she died right there in his arms.

Mia was next to him in an instant, taking his hands and removing them from Renee's body, dragging him away. "Come on, baby," she whispered, pulling him to her.

"I know I shouldn't care, but she saved you. She shot him to save you," he whispered into her hair.

"She shot him to save her own ass," Karen boomed behind them. "He was planning to kill her after Rick and Cassandra."

Upon hearing that, the situation seemed to really take hold in Mia's mind, and she buried her head into Tyree's shoulder, sobbing. He tried to soothe her, but he knew it was no use. It was just too much to take in for one day. While he held her, he looked over to see his mother on the move.

Karen went over to John, pulling him away from the open window, and she leaned down to whisper in his ear, "You got what you deserve. Burn in hell, you evil bastard."

Right after the words left her lips, Tyree watched John's body go limp in her arms. A few seconds later, the building was filled with agents taking statements. Tyree was giving his statement, but he couldn't help looking out the window. The officers had swept the roof of the other building and found no trace of the shooter, but he knew in his mind who pulled the trigger. He knew it was Richmond.

Chapter Thirty-four

The week had been a blur, and Tyree was still unable to wrap his mind around it all. After giving their statements that night and seeing his mother off, Tyree took Mia home and put her in the tub. He scrubbed her body and placed her in the bed. When he went in to take his shower, she screamed out and ended up running back into the bathroom with him. He finished his shower quickly and hurried to get back to the bedroom. Knowing she was still shaken up, he decided against what he really wanted. He wanted the answers only she would have about that night, but he didn't want to badger her after everything she had gone through.

He knew sleep wasn't coming to him, but still he lay back on the bed, trying to help her along. He felt her drifting off after a few minutes, and he tried to will himself to go, but couldn't. Instead, he ended up watching her sleep.

It was like this every night for a week. Tyree had tried in so many ways to get her to speak to him, but she had yet to say a word. Every day, he cooked, and she picked at her food, taking a few bites, and then she fell asleep. He had been in touch with Milan and Jackson, and they were returning to Los Angeles and wanted to know if keeping Kyan was an option, and he told them yes. Honestly, he didn't think bringing him home now was for the best. Mia wasn't herself, and he didn't want him seeing her that way.

He assumed this was what everyone had been telling him she was like when he was gone, and it broke his heart. His father had caused it both times, and there was no way to make it up to her. All he could do now was make sure she knew he wasn't going anywhere. After all, he wasn't leaving her side until she was better.

They had buried John a few days earlier and sent Renee's body to her mother, and he was still trying to make peace in his mind about it. His heart was conflicted. John was his father, but he had also hated him for almost half his life, and Renee was the woman he once wanted to marry who had turned his life upside down.

Even though Renee had changed her mind about everything, she was still the one who assisted in helping John create this nightmare in the first place. That fact alone made his blood boil when he thought about her. As much as he hated Renee, even she outranked John in his opinion.

He had grown to have no emotions when it came to John but, for some reason, he was sad. No matter what happened between them, he never wished him dead. He actually wished he had lived so he could at least get the closure he needed. He wanted to be able to tell him how much he hated him and be able to see the look in his eyes when he said it.

When they had arrived at Livingston that night, Tyree and Rick had heard the better part of the conversation, thanks to Karen. She was hiding out in the hallway, watching the whole scene unfold. She'd pulled him to the side and explained that this was all a part of some plan she cooked up with Rock and Renee to get John to admit to everything. They knew he would be stupid enough to give away everything if he had Mia in front of him. He hated her enough to let down his guard and gloat about all his past misdeeds.

Once Rock had his confession recorded, one of the undercover officers killed the lights, and the extra gunshots started because John fired off his weapon. It was all supposed to go off without anyone being shot or killed, but someone had other plans. They could never prove that it was Richmond who ordered the second attack, but everyone involved knew it was him. If it hadn't been apparent before, when Renee uttered his name with her dying breath it was made clear.

Rock and Karen had been by several times, checking on them, and also to fill in the gaps. Rock told them all how he had found out that Renee was involved with John by following Asha and taking what he learned then to dig deeper. He then explained to them how that night in the kitchen was his way of letting Renee know he was on to them. She met him a few days later, and he showed her the proof that John had been using her as well. After that, she readily agreed to help and even helped in convincing John that Rock was to be trusted and only interested in Karen's money.

Renee was the one to tell John that Rock had been playing up his attraction to Karen to get a payoff, which John matched if he promised to provide him with proof of their affair. Renee had been such a help to him, but he could tell she was still hiding something. Even after all the information she gave them about John, Rock knew there was more and, now, he knew what it was.

When Renee entered Tyree's life, John had put her there, but when she entered John's life, Richmond had brought her in. Rock searched her things and found a paper trail dating back to before she met John with large sums of money, money only someone with Richmond's connections could provide. He also figured out through her journals that her car breaking down that night was staged. She had been given John's itinerary, and she knew exactly where he would be headed that night.

Her journals shed light on everything she had helped John with from the kidnapping all the way to her pregnancy. She and John had planned the pregnancy just as a ruse to get Tyree away from Mia. In her journal, Renee revealed her thoughts on the pregnancy and how she didn't even want the child. John was the father, she admitted, and she was just going to pretend it was Tyree's and end up using the child to forever be a reminder of his past mistakes. They had gone to great lengths to keep Tyree away from Mia.

Now that they had it all figured out regarding Renee, they still had more questions. They knew all the things she had done with John, but they were nowhere near closer to figuring out who the source was behind all the blocked texts and videos. Miguel had been the primary recipient, but that night when everything happened, Tyree had gotten one. He was lost, and they still didn't know for sure that it was Renee in the house that night when Kyan woke up screaming; she never admitted to it in her journal.

Tyree wanted to believe it was her, but something in him said it wasn't, and that feeling alone made him uneasy. That meant there was still a threat to his family, but he knew that already. As long as Richmond was still on the loose, they would always have to look over their shoulders, and he felt helpless because of it.

In the midst of everything, Tyree had to know about the envelopes he found. He was still wondering what was going on between his mother and Rock. He didn't object if there was a relationship, but he needed to know what the deal was.

When he asked, she looked him straight in the eye and stressed that they were just friends. She explained that Rock had only been a source of support when he was around over the years and had helped her through some rough times. They both explained that the photos John had were just staged to make him think he had an angle to get to his ultimate goal.

Tyree couldn't help but wish there were some sort of attraction between them. After all, Rock had been more to him than his own father. Watching them together, he could tell they had gotten close over the years, and he wondered how. They explained that Karen was the one to call and get the FBI involved in investigating John. After she called, Rock was sent to her and, after the initial shock had worn off that her security guard was an actual agent, they began to work together, gathering what they could find on John.

She had come across some of his documents and figured out he was just as responsible for the downfall of the companies as Richmond, if not more, but none of them retained his name. He was smart. The thing that made her make the call was when she figured out that he had staged the kidnapping of his own grandson; but she had no solid proof, just a phone call she overheard a few years ago. John seemed to be bragging about splitting Tyree and Mia up by using their child to do it. There was only one thing that came to mind when she heard this, but she wasn't completely sure what context he meant it in. With the lack of solid evidence, they had to gather more to nail him for everything.

For the past few years, they had been working together to get whatever they could find on both Richmond and John, but John was very elusive until a few months ago. That was when Rock came to them permanently, and they started to close in on him. Karen was to pretend to act normal with him until they had what they needed, but she got frustrated with him after Miguel's attack, and they had to adjust their strategy. She said she couldn't stand being in the same house with the man who possibly tried to kill their son. It was too much.

Tyree had listened to their story and was finding it hard to keep his temper in check. He was upset that his mother felt like she couldn't come to him with this, but he understood their need to be discreet. She only wanted to protect them. He smiled when he thought about how alike they were. He was always trying to protect them, and here she was doing whatever it took to do the same. She was amazing.

After all the visits had begun to die down, Tyree was left with Mia, who still hadn't said a word. She had been there sitting through all the conversations but had yet to speak. He was about to give up all hope and call in a psychiatrist until the night before Janelle's birthday.

Rick and Cassandra had started a ritual where every year on her birthday, they would go to her grave and have lunch, and they got everyone involved. They would sit and talk to her headstone about what was going on in their lives, and they planned to do so this year. Tyree and his siblings had been accompanying them, but this year, he thought he should skip it to be there for Mia.

He had prepared their dinner, which she picked over like every other night, and when he was washing the dishes, he heard her speak. He turned around slowly, thinking he imagined the words, but then he saw the tears on her face, and he walked over, stooping down in front of her. He could feel her warm tears dripping down his arms, and he let her cry a little longer before pulling her head to rest on his shoulder.

"It's okay, kitten. You're going to be okay."

"How can you say that? It's all my fault. I'm the reason all this happened."

"Baby, come on." He pulled back to look in her eyes. "I don't blame you. Don't let anything he said affect you. He did this to himself, and he tried to make you feel like it was you, but it was all him. You and my son are the best things to ever happen to me, and I will never let you feel like you did anything wrong."

"But—"

He pulled her lips to his, getting lost in her taste. He hadn't kissed her since the night John died, and he never realized how much he craved her. She didn't kiss him back, but he kept going, hoping she would fall back into her normal self. When she still didn't kiss him back, he released her and sat down, laying his head on the table. "I don't know what I'm doing wrong." He hadn't wanted it to come to this, but he was finally at his breaking point, and he felt tears slipping down his cheeks. "I know I wasn't there; I let him take you. I was supposed to be there." Feeling a hand hit his shoulder, he looked up to see her standing over him.

When he looked up, she ran her hand down his cheek and put her forehead to his. She whispered against his lips that she loved him, and he leaned in, kissing her gently. She slid her hands down, grabbing his ears, pulling him closer, drastically deepening the kiss and they stayed that way until air became an issue.

Smiling against her lips, Tyree pulled her hands between them and placed a light kiss on them. "Welcome back, kitten."

"I love you, Ty. None of this was your fault."

"I love you too, baby. So much."

He stood, picking her up, wrapping her legs around his waist and he found that spot on her neck that drove her crazy, and he grinned as her moans tickled his ear. It was a sound he hadn't heard in a while, and he savored the feeling. It was nice to have her acting like her old self, and it made him want to push it to the extreme. She was getting into everything he was doing, and he felt her body quivering back to life. He was going to enjoy this night more than he originally anticipated.

Laying her down on the bed, hovering over her, never breaking eye contact, he ran his hands up her thighs. She was only wearing the short silk gown he dressed her in and a pair of black lace panties that showed off a generous portion of her supple body, and he had to fight the urge to cum right then and there. Before he could fully enjoy himself, he had to be sure she was ready.

"Are you sure?"

Nodding, she grabbed his hand and slid it between their heated bodies. When he reached her center, he felt the wetness through her panties and felt himself stiffening, and suddenly the shorts he was wearing felt tight. Standing, he pulled them off slowly and felt himself swelling by the second. She sat up on the bed offering him a sweet smile, and he made his way back, covering her body with his. Locking eyes with her once again, he made sure he knew she wanted this, and she never turned away. He could feel her breathing intensify and he leaned in to claim her mouth.

Her legs spread. He felt himself brush up against her and he ripped off her soaked panties. The feeling of her was indescribable because he knew she was just as far gone as he was and they hadn't even begun. Leaning in, kissing her neck again, he ran his hand down her legs as she arched her hips to meet his hand. He grazed her folds with his fingertips and felt himself losing control. He needed to touch her, to be inside her again.

When he finally dug his fingers inside her, he felt her body quake, and he knew it was only for him. He always had the magic touch when it came to her, and when she pushed herself up and brought her lips to his neck, he stroked her harder, feeling every tremor she displayed. He twirled his fingers around, trying to explore every crevice of her while she assaulted his neck with her warm breath.

She was kissing him, running her tongue over him, biting at his neck with such intensity he knew it was going to leave a mark, but he couldn't worry about that now. He wanted to feel her in every way before she came. He wanted to feel her cum while he was inside her. He needed to feel her slippery depths before he made her scream. Her mouth was weakening his control.

She was sucking on his neck when he laid her back, placing his hands on her parted knees, pushing them farther apart. He trailed his tongue down her body, stopping at her neck, pushing himself inside her, losing himself in the feeling. Her breath hitched in her throat, and he grabbed her leg, wrapping it around him as he pushed deeper. She felt so warm, so wet, so amazing as he dug his nails into her flesh, earning a loud exclamation.

Digging her nails into his back, she rolled her hips forward while he bit down on her neck gently. He gripped her leg tighter, raising it a little higher and she dug her nails deeper, breaking the skin. His back was on fire from the sting of the sweat hitting the scratches, but he ignored it, still pushing deeper. He was pounding her so hard she was sliding backward, and the smile on her face let him know she was enjoying every second of it.

His breathing was shaky, and his hands trembled as he dug his fingers into her. Spreading her legs wider, he pushed deeper, grinning at the moan that tore from her throat. He couldn't think straight; he couldn't form a single thought that didn't revolve around her. Everything he was at that moment was poured into her.

Holding her to him, he whispered in her ear, "Tell me you love this."

Her eyes were dark with passion, and her response came out as a whisper that turned into a loud exclamation. "I love, uh . . . Shit! I love this."

It was the little things she did that made being with her so much better than anyone else. The way she rolled her body into his, making them one, always made him lose control. The way she whispered in his ear always made him want to push harder, and the way she looked at him always made his heart skip beats. It was as if he could see into her soul every time they connected. She always gave him that feeling.

When he leaned down, catching her earlobe between his teeth, he knew he took her by surprise. It wasn't something he did, but he could tell it felt damn good to her. He did a gentle nip and then sucked a little, and her body reacted by shooting up on the bed. He placed his palm on her chest and tried to calm her down with no luck. He could feel the pulsations in her chest and between her legs increasing, making him feel like she could explode at any moment.

Her body was jerking. He could feel the orgasm approaching, and he loved the sensation it gave him. Being inside her was more than he ever dreamed. It was a feeling he never thought he would experience again when he left her in the foyer of the main house weeks ago. He couldn't help the tingling that shot through his body, and before he knew it, he burst inside her and then felt her clenching around him. His last movement sent her into spasm, and he felt every ounce of his arousal covered in her.

He didn't want to move. He felt his body shut down while her body drank up every bit of him. He tried to catch his breath and was unsuccessful. When she reached up, running her hand over his lips, he kissed her fingertips and rolled off of her, pulling her to rest on his chest. His heartbeat had slowed, but he still felt it fluttering. He knew it was because she was so close. After all that had happened, he didn't think they would get this back: the intimacy they shared only with each other.

He was tracing patterns on her back with his fingers when he felt her head shift to look up at him. For a second, he just stared at her, looking into her eyes, finding what he thought he lost: their future together. She opened her mouth and then closed it with a silly giggle following.

"What is it, baby? What were you going to say to me?"

"It's nothing. I think it might be too soon. Just forget I was going to say anything."

He slid back, propping himself against the headboard, pulling her with him. "What is it? If it's something you want, something you need, I'll make it happen. You just have to tell me what it is."

Mia looked at him and sighed, leaning her head back to his chest. "Well, tomorrow is Janelle's birthday, and I kind of wanted to go to the graveside and join Cassie and Rick. I haven't been, and I feel guilty about it. I also thought I could go visit Mom. I mean, I know it's silly because Janelle's body isn't there, but having something there gives me something to hold on to. I just need to talk to her; both of them."

Tyree gave her a grin and kissed her forehead. "Sure, baby. I'll go with you. I usually go anyways. I was going to sit out at first because I didn't think you were up to it."

"I'm up to it." She smiled. "I never knew you went with them. It will be good to have you there. I just didn't want to be insensitive to everything that's going on. I know you say you're over it but—"

"We didn't have a funeral for him because none of us wanted to. Mom was over it, Asha and Terence wanted nothing to do with it, and Miguel has washed his hands of the whole situation. He tried to kill him, for God's sake. How can we mourn a man like that?"

"Because he's your father. He messed up so bad, he almost ruined us, but we're here. We have a long road ahead, but we're together. I'd like to blame it all on him, but I have to live with the choices I made, and we have to get over them. Holding hate in your heart for him will only make you bitter, and I don't like bitter you. I like the caring person you are when your mind is free. So, I had a thought."

He watched as her signature grin appeared and he pushed the hair back from her face. "Yeah?"

"You should go to his grave. Say all the things you would have said if he had lived, and then walk away. Leave the baggage behind, leave the regret, and leave the guilt because none of this was your fault."

Tyree was stunned that the woman in front of him was the same woman who was mute a few hours ago. She had amazed him yet again. She had her own demons but, when she saw him breaking down, she snapped out of it and stepped up for him. He owed her so much, and he was going to spend forever giving it to her.

"Baby." He slid his hand up, lacing his fingers in her hair. "Why, after everything I said and did, why didn't you leave me? I thought it was the only way, so I was an ass, but you wouldn't leave. Why?"

"If I tell you something, you promise you won't overreact?"

Sighing and nodding, he waited for her answer.

"That day, before I left the main house, after you acted like an ass in front of everybody, Asha called. I was packed and ready to get the hell away from you, but she told me that you were afraid for us. She wouldn't tell me why, but she said that I shouldn't take anything you said seriously. She told me you were going to do something stupid, but she had no clue you already had. I was so hurt at first, but when she called, I felt relieved. I knew you wouldn't have made love to me and made me all those promises just to break my heart."

"You knew the whole time? You looked so hurt the next time I saw you. Why didn't you say anything? Why didn't you just go?"

"On some level, I knew I deserved it. We had talked about everything, but I knew you needed to vent to me. Jake being here didn't help, either.

We needed to share those feelings to get closure on them for good."

"I didn't mean the shit I said to you."

"You meant the hurt you felt." She sniffled. "I caused that hurt, but I never will again. I love you so much for trying to save me. I owed it to you to be here for whatever."

"He could have killed you. John." Tyree breathed in her air. "And Richmond—"

"I'm not afraid of him. I used to be, but now I'm not. I knew our son shouldn't be here, but I wasn't leaving you. As pigheaded as you are, you needed me as much as I needed you."

He wanted to be angry with Asha but, he knew, without her he would have lost Mia for good. He couldn't help the smile that broke out on his face, and he began to massage her scalp with his fingertips in a soothing manner he knew she loved. She relaxed, and he lay back, getting comfortable.

"I did things when you were gone, things I'm not proud of, Ty."

"Shh." He held his finger to his lips. "That, I don't need to know. We both did things; mine were much more recent and probably a lot more painful. I should have trusted you more."

"You're not mad?"

"You're a stubborn ass, you always have to be right, you never listen to anything I say, and my sister is a meddling menace."

"Uh, okay," she said and giggled.

"I hate you."

"I hate you too." She grinned.

"Get some sleep."

She slid her body closer to his, and she closed her eyes once her head found a comfortable position on his chest. He rubbed her back for a few minutes before feeling her fall asleep, and he lay awake, thinking and listening to her breathe. He would never forget the gentle moments like these; they were what had sustained them over the cold, lonely years.

Chapter Thirty-five

The sun was bright, and a cool breeze swept through, offering a nice reprieve from the hot summer day. They were approaching the graveyard when Mia and Tyree looked up and saw the group of people huddled at the gate. As they approached, Tyree's grip tightened on Mia's hand. All of his siblings, his mother and Rock, and her family were waiting to go in, and it made things somewhat easier. They all shared glances, and Rick grabbed Cassandra's hand, pulling her with him. Whitney and Jude followed, but Tyree was stuck. He couldn't seem to make himself move.

Mia tugged at his hand, but he just stood there. When Asha saw what was happening, she and Miguel walked over, pulling him into an embrace, and Terence followed. Mia just stood back watching, rubbing his back soothingly. When Asha finally pulled him back to look in his eyes, he let a tear fall.

"I can't do this."

"You can," she whispered. "You can say your good-byes and never look back."

"I want to kick his ass. I want to spit in his face. I wish I could punch him out. He took my son; he tried to kill the woman I love. He deserves to be here to see us happy; he deserves my rage. Death was too easy for him."

"He tried to kill me to keep his secrets hidden. I wish I could see the look on his face when he figured out I knew. I wish I could see his face when he figured out I knew he was ready to toss me aside like trash for a damn company," Miguel spoke up.

Asha nodded and commanded the attention of both brothers. "I get that, and I understand you both, but you need to say your piece. Go over there, yell at him, kick his headstone, spit on it if it makes you feel better, but get it all out. We need this. We need to say good-bye."

"I just hate him so much. I try to figure it out in my mind how someone could be so evil, how they could have such little regard for life, but I can't." Miguel sighed.

"I don't understand how a man who seemed so loving and caring toward us could be so evil inside," added Asha, looking ahead.

They all linked hands and Mia joined Tyree, lacing her fingers through his, and they proceeded. Tyree was the first to take his place in front of the headstone. There were flowers there, and he all but lost it getting rid of them.

"Who brought these?"

"The groundskeeper does this once a month," Karen supplied, and Tyree went ballistic.

"He doesn't deserve shit!" He picked the flowers up, slinging them over the headstone. The petals were flying everywhere, and soon there were only stems left, but he kept swinging. "You bastard. How dare you make someone feel sorry for you? You tried to ruin us; you took our choices. I hope you burn in hell."

Tyree kept swinging until Miguel came over and pulled him back. Miguel stood there for a second and then pulled a picture and threw it on the ground in front of the headstone. "It's us," he sighed. "This picture was taken when we were younger on Christmas Day. I was so happy with my gifts, I ran to you, you swung me in the air, and Tyree and Asha hugged you around your legs. Mom took this picture, and I've had it at my house for years." He took out a lighter and set it on fire. "It was a happy day. We were all so young and looked at you like a savior. I would have never guessed in a million years that man would grow to be the evil bastard you were. I don't want your memories anymore. Now, I just want to forget you."

Terence pushed Asha, but she stood and shook her head. "I have nothing. I don't have a speech or a memory to burn. He didn't try to kill me, he didn't take my daughter, he left me alone, but I hate him as if he did. My brothers are broken; he broke them. I know they wish he was here to hear their rants, but I'm glad he's dead. I wish he would have died years ago to save us the pain."

Tyree looked at the vacant expression on her face and felt a chill. He had never seen her like this; she was never so unfeeling. "He was your dad, Ash. It's okay to feel something."

"I feel nothing for him!" she snapped. "He's dead; it serves him right. I wish . . . I wish . . ." She fell against him with tears streaming down her face. "How could he do this? I loved that man. I made excuses for him when everyone else said he was wrong. I let him become this by always upholding his bullshit."

Tyree just held her, rubbing her back and kissing her head. He was waiting for her to crack.

She hadn't cried one time since it happened, and he was relieved that she finally broke down. He was beginning to worry about her, but now he knew she would be okay.

"He was grown. He made his own decisions, and all you did was be a good daughter and love your dad. He did this, not you."

"They why do I feel so guilty?"

"I think you feel guilty because you did love him. It's okay to love him."

"I don't want to. I want to hate him. I want to be able to forget all the good things, but I can't."

"Then, don't." Tyree held her tighter in his arms. "You don't have to forget what he was to you just because Miguel and I have our issues."

"He tried to destroy you two. How can I love that?"

"Just remember the man in that picture. Remember the man who picked you up when you fell. Remember the one who walked you down the aisle at your wedding. We won't hate you for that. We won't hate you for remembering your good moments." Asha buried her head in his chest, and he held her tighter. "You know, this is what I needed. I'm glad I came."

Miguel joined them, and they shared a hug. There were a few minutes of silence, and they all walked off one by one: Miguel first, Asha and Terence next; and then Karen walked off as well. Tyree was the last to go. He and Mia stood there for a few moments longer, and then he grabbed her hand, placing a kiss on it, and she smiled.

"You're amazing."

He offered her a light smile and pulled her ahead.

Running her hands over his neck, she kissed him gently before beginning again. "Do you feel better?"

"Yes. Honestly, I didn't know if I ever would, but seeing them and their strength, I know we're going to be okay. They give me hope. You guys really are my life. You, Ky, and them give me what I need to push forward."

"I'm glad." She grinned, wrapping her arms around his neck. "Because we need you. You keep your family together and ours. Me and Ky would be lost without you."

"I'll never be like him. You know that, right? I'll never hurt you like that."

"I know." She pulled his hand to head over to Janelle's grave. Just as they approached, a long black Town Car pulled up on the street in front of the graveyard and Tyree had a strange feeling about it. Something about it rang so familiar to him, and when Mia leaned in to kiss his cheek, he shrugged calmly.

"I wonder who that is."

Mia took a seat next to Cassandra, ran her hand over Janelle's headstone, and smiled. "It took me a minute to get here, but here I am, baby sis. God, I miss you. Sometimes I laugh at the silly things we used to do, and I look back to see if you are laughing too, and I realize you aren't there. It's been so hard."

Tyree joined Mia on the ground and linked her hand with his. Cassandra had brought the lunch out before they all arrived, and the others took their seats, and Whitney passed plates around. They all fell into a comfortable silence until Rick spoke up.

"I know some people think we're strange for doing this, but it's become our thing. We come here every year on her birthday and, every year, I feel closer to her. I can feel her spirit." He looked over to the black car and nodded. "That car, it's here every year when we're here, and they sit here for a little while before leaving. I've never seen who it was or figured out if they were here because of her, but somehow I feel like they are. It gives me peace, feeling like someone else misses her as much as we do."

They all smiled, and Mia looked back at the headstone and then back at the people sitting around her. They had all lost something, they had all had heartache, but here they were together. She couldn't help the smile that broke out across her face. Tyree looked at her, and they held a gaze until she looked behind him and displayed a huge grin. When he turned to see what she was looking at, she saw his smile develop as he saw Kyan, running toward them.

Tyree and Mia stood, and Kyan ran into her arms. "Mama, I missed you."

He hugged her like it had been years since they last spoke and Tyree cleared his throat. "Dang, little man. I know you miss your mama, but don't you miss me too?"

"Hey, Daddy. Yes, I missed you, but are you done acting like an ass?" he asked, causing laughter to ripple through the group.

Mia knew Tyree wanted to scold him, but when she looked back, she saw him laughing. He pulled Kyan from Mia's arms and shook his head. "Yes, I'm done acting like an ass."

"Aunt Milan said you were just acting like an ass, but she was sure you would get over it. So, are we getting our new house like Uncle Jackson said?"

When Mia looked to Tyree, he held his hands up, chuckling. "Yeah, I'm buying you and Mama a new house."

"You're going to live there too, right?"

"Yes," he laughed. "As long as she wants me there."

"He'll be there." Mia leaned in to place a kiss on his cheek. "Now enough of the third degree." She motioned for Milan and Jackson to sit down with Sydney. "Let's eat and then you can tell us all about your vacation."

"Yes, Mama! Uncle Jackson and Aunt Milan let me swim with the fishes."

Mia smiled at the animation in her son's voice and mouthed a thank-you to both Milan and Jackson. Kyan was telling them everything he did, and she listened, soaking it all up. In the middle of it all, she turned looking at Janelle's headstone and smiled. "We did good."

Kyan went on with his story, and the others added their questions, and he was glad to answer, but Mia sat, smiling mindlessly at how perfect this all was. She looked at Tyree, and they shared a brief moment before she turned back to look at her son. He held her attention for a moment longer and then she found herself staring at the black car.

This had been her first time at the graveside with her family, but she couldn't shake a vaguely familiar feeling about that car. It wasn't the car itself, just a feeling she got when she looked at it. She stared at it for a few more seconds and then saw a man emerge. He was quite a distance away, but something about him held her attention.

The man seemed to be looking right at her, and she never broke eye contact. It wasn't until the sirens and flashing lights began that she turned away. She looked back at Tyree who had his arm around her and saw Rock rushing toward the cars and then it all became clear what was going on. Rick was next to rush in the direction of all the commotion, and all she could hear was, "They got him."

There was a battalion of officers surrounding the man as he dropped to his knees with his hands behind his head. Mia stood and felt her legs taking her in their direction, and she was stopped suddenly when Tyree's hand met her shoulder. "Babe, stay away from him. It's over; they caught him."

She looked at him with watery eyes and shook her head. "No. It's never over." While Tyree looked on confused, Mia's mind drifted to the last conversation she and Richmond had right after they kicked him out of Livingston.

"It's over, Dad. You've lost. Now you have nothing. No company, no family, and no leverage. Just for shits and giggles, I hope you enjoy that two percent you fought for and clawed to keep."

"I'm glad you think that way, my beautiful dove. Yes, you and your brother and sister have outsmarted me, and I must bow to you for your bold moves. I didn't think you had it in you."

"Yeah, well, I didn't think you had it in you to drive Mom to drugs, but hey, I guess we learn something new every day."

"You mustn't blame me for your mother's problems. Those problems were present long before me. Have you met your grandfather?" He laughed, looking pleased with his wisecrack, but Mia never cracked a smile.

"I guess you're satisfied with yourself. Well, I hope you know what your greed cost you. My son, you'll never be a part of his life, and Rick and Janelle are done. Now that you've been caught, we have nothing more to give you. No more love, no more time, and no more thought."

She turned to leave, but he grabbed her wrist and held her in place. "You may think you have all the pieces to the puzzle, but just know one thing: if I got caught, it wasn't an accident. Everything I do is always on my terms. Everything has a purpose."

Mia's mind focused back in on the present as she looked at Tyree's baffled expression. She was replaying his words in her mind and was silent, trying to figure out what it all meant. Tyree was watching her intently and then she felt his grip loosen on her shoulder.

"Just go over there. I know you want to."

"No. I just don't get it. Why now; why today?"

"This is what Rock was talking about when he said they were figuring out a location. Rick said he has seen this car here every year, but no one ever got out. Maybe, he's tired of running. Now that Dad is dead, maybe he can finally come to terms with what he's done."

Mia wished she could believe that was it, but she knew better. Her father would never come out in the open without something up his sleeve. She wanted the answers, but she didn't want to get close to him. He had caused them so much pain, and all she wanted to see was him being hauled off in cuffs. Instead of making a move immediately, she waited until they had him in the car and locked away before she advanced. Everyone's attention was so focused on Richmond and his arrest, they seemed to miss the black car, speeding off; everyone except Mia.

Instead of walking closer to where the officers held Richmond, Mia walked toward the spot the car vacated. She realized Richmond had left that spot for a reason. He seemed to be concealing someone in the car, but who could it be? He intentionally walked away from the car to give it time to speed away. He used himself as bait, she realized.

In the speeding car, a woman sat with a little girl sleeping in her lap. She kissed the little girl's head and smoothed the hair back from her face. As tears descended the woman's cheeks, she pulled out a cell phone, looking at the messages.

She had been the one to send the picture of Mia strapped to the chair but was still wondering where the pictures Miguel received came from. She was also the one in the house that night. If Richmond had known what she did, he would have killed her.

As much as she knew she needed to stay away, she had to go. She had to see what life was like on the other side. She wanted to know what it was like to be happy. Seeing the sleeping child that night, resting peacefully without a care in the world, was something she wanted for her daughter but feared she would never have. She just needed to feel what it was like to imagine it. She didn't know who was watching her, but she knew whoever it was would be a major problem for her plan.

Rubbing her daughter's soft curls, she placed a light kiss on her forehead, much like she did with Kyan that night. "I'm going to make this better for you. Now that he's gone, I promise you things will be better for you." The little girl never stirred, and she just sat, looking down at her, wishing for a better life.

Everything was becoming so confusing in Mia's head when she reached the spot where the tread marks from the tires were still fresh. She stood there for a while before looking down to notice a small picture on the ground. Mia picked it up, smiling at the beautiful little face that greeted her. It was a little girl. She couldn't be more than two years old, and she had a dimpled smile, much like her own. She looked at it a second longer, and Tyree, who was standing quietly behind her, took the picture, admiring it before flipping it over. Watching him, she noticed when his smile fell after looking at the back of the picture.

"Kitten, do you know this little girl?"

"No, why?"

"Look at the name."

"Yeah." She took the picture, reading it aloud. "Jenna Ann Livingston." Her breath hitched in her chest as a feeling came crashing through her. "What . . . who . . . why would he do this?"

"Babe, calm down."

"No, dammit! He had another child," she huffed, "and had the nerve to name her after my dead mother, the mother he killed. How could he give her Mom's middle name?"

Mia's mind was racing, and Tyree tried to offer his support, but she was still in a fit. She was shaking, and when the car that held Richmond drove by them, they both locked eyes with him and saw a devious smirk on his face. Mia felt a chill shoot straight through her, and her body tensed. She was quiet for a moment, and then he spoke, drawing her out of her silence.

"It's over. You never have to see him again."

"No, Ty. With him, it is never over. Him getting caught wasn't an accident. Everything he does is on his terms."

***

Two weeks later, while Mia was making dinner for Kyan and Tyree, she received a text from Rick that confirmed her worst fears. Placing a hand over her mouth, she looked up to see Tyree watching her with a questioning look on his face. Reading the text out loud, she felt a chill creep down her spine: "'Mia, Dad is on the loose. He escaped during transport. Be safe, sweetheart. He will be coming for us soon.'"